Reasons to be Cheerful

By the same author

FICTION

Man at the Helm

Paradise Lodge

NON-FICTION

Love, Nina

An Almost Perfect Christmas

Reasons to be Cheerful

NINA STIBBE

VIKING
an imprint of
PENGUIN BOOKS

VIKING

UK | USA | Canada | Ireland | Australia
India | New Zealand | South Africa

Viking is part of the Penguin Random House group of companies
whose addresses can be found at global.penguinrandomhouse.com.

First published 2019
003

Copyright © Nina Stibbe, 2019

The moral right of the author has been asserted

Grateful acknowledgement is made for permission to quote from
the following: on p. vii, 'Teeth' by Spike Milligan from *Silly Verse for Kids*,
by kind permission of Norma Farnes.

Set in 11/13 pt Bembo Book MT Std
Typeset by Jouve (UK), Milton Keynes
Printed and bound in Great Britain by Clays Ltd, Elcograf S.p.A.

A CIP catalogue record for this book is available from the British Library

ISBN: 978-0-241-24052-6

www.greenpenguin.co.uk

For Elspeth Sheila Allison
(formerly Stibbe, née Barlow)

English Teeth, English Teeth!
Shining in the sun
A part of British heritage
Aye, each and every one.

English Teeth, Happy Teeth!
Always having fun
Clamping down on bits of fish
And sausages half done.

English Teeth! HEROES' Teeth!
Hear them click! and clack!
Let's sing a song of praise to them –
Three Cheers for the Brown Grey and Black.

Spike Milligan, 'Teeth'

Prologue

It was quite normal for dentists to self-treat back in 1980, especially lone practitioners, but an intolerance to lignocaine meant that JP Wintergreen, dental surgeon, was unable to perform anything but the briefest procedures on himself – for only minutes after being administered a local anaesthetic he'd experience numbness in his synovial joints and therefore lose the ability to grip anything in his hands.

He could do the basics – scaling and the odd filling towards the front on the lower jaw – but, for anything further back, more complex or painful, he had to call his old pal Bill Turner from a practice five minutes up the road. It was a reciprocal arrangement.

Late one afternoon I noticed that JP had pulled the Medi Light 400S right over to the desk side of the surgery and was up at the wall mirror, licking his front teeth and picking at them with a probe. I was in a hurry to leave and my heart sank. I had to collect my baby brother from Curious Minds nursery by half past five – and it was already five to.

JP skimmed his dental record across the desk at me. 'Extract upper left and upper right one . . . fit partial denture, immediate restoration,' he said, meaning for me to write it up.

I glanced at the clock.

'Don't worry, nurse,' he said, 'I shan't take more than a couple of minutes.'

Marking up the chart, I recalled the sorry state of the teeth in question – receding gums, blackened dentine, transparency, stained ridges – and it occurred to me that I'd never have to see them again, grinning at his own joke, coated in coffee-skin, or sinking into the icing on a bun. Also, I reasoned, the post-treatment care usually associated with an extraction – that could take up to fifteen minutes – wouldn't be necessary, the patient in this case being a dental surgeon, and therefore I needn't panic about getting to Danny in time.

'. . . and fill out an FP 17 for the denture.'

He rifled among the instruments cooling on the draining board, eventually settling on a pair of straight anteriors, and, after tossing them from hand to hand like a hot potato, ran them under the cold tap and put them in his breast pocket beside a pack of Gauloises.

Back at the mirror, he loaded a syringe, lifted his upper lip and injected himself somewhere above the right incisor. This first jab was easy, although painful, and his tongue waggled from side to side like a snake's. The second jab, into the palate, was slower and required considerable force. His thumb wobbled on the plunger, the lids on his half-closed eyes fluttered, and a slight grunt escaped him. I looked away out of decency. When he'd done, he dismantled the syringe, jabbed the sharp end into the rubber of the cartridge and flung the whole thing into the sink for me to clear up later.

He tapped one tooth and then the other with the heavy end of the probe before inspecting a little denture he'd had made. It was rather smart with a cobalt palate that looked like liquid silver, and handsome clasping.

'Will you want me to assist chair-side?' I asked. I'd already folded the chair up for the night, pulled the treatment table in, and turned off the spittoon.

'No, thank you, nurse.' He worked his mouth. 'I shan't need to sit down.'

I'd learned during my months at the Wintergreen practice that teeth aren't pulled out, as such. 'Pull' is the wrong word. There is no need for leverage or brute force like in the old cartoons, no boot on the wall. Teeth are removed in the same way a gardener might take a radish from the ground – that is, with a push, a rock and a twist to break it free of its bindings. There's actually very little pulling involved, even with a turnip (our code for a very large, or difficult, multi-rooted tooth).

Numb now, JP tapped again and exhaled in short puffs. He

started with the upper left – a very compromised tooth with many restorations including an ancient buccal inlay and a mesial silicate filling. In other words, the crown was weak, there wasn't much actual tooth left and he'd need to be careful. (Imagine using a rusty, over-cut Yale key in a stiff lock.)

'All righty.' He curled his lip up and, breathing noisily through his nostrils, began a gentle but brisk revving. Then he stopped, leaned over and flobbed the inlay into the basin, where it would be caught in the amalgam trap. I stood quickly and turned on the spittoon.

More twisting, a loud groan and the rest of the tooth, minus its root, was there in the forceps, having snapped off at the gum line. Gah! How had he let that happen?

I glanced at the clock. I had less than twenty minutes now to get up to Curious Minds.

JP abandoned the upper left and switched to the upper right. This time he jammed the beaks up hard between the periodontal membrane and the alveolar bone and with two jolting twists brought the tooth out cleanly, root and all, clanging it into the dish with great drama. He spat into the basin leaving a fine bloody spray across everything for a yard around him. I slipped the plastic bib round his neck and handed him some napkins. When he spat into the sink again, a bloody string looped down from the rim to the skirt of his brand-new Latimer tunic. He was no better than a patient now; anxious, dribbly, high-maintenance.

Biting on a gauze wad, he looked up at the clock, mumbling, flexing and unflexing his fingers. Then, back at the mirror, he began digging around the ragged gum line and before you could say 'spoon excavator' the instrument fell from his hand and bounced off his plastic clog.

'Dammit.' He spat, coughed and then turned to me. 'Telephone Bill Turner, nurse. Tell him I need him to pop down and get this root out for me.'

I looked at the clock. I hadn't got time to wait for Bill.

'Sit down,' I said, pulling the Medi Light across.

PART ONE

1.   Dentally Particular

I'd been happy in my previous job as an auxiliary nurse at Paradise Lodge old people's home but after my mother reported the owner for tax evasion, I felt it best to move on and took a position at the largest garden centre in the Midlands, which had just opened on the outskirts of our village. I was put in charge of the newly planted display rockery (also the largest in the Midlands) and I'd have settled there and become a horticulturalist – but it was a temporary post and I was needed only until an expert arrived, who'd studied at Kew and would put their alpines on the map.

I spent dinner breaks drinking soup from my flask and scouring the classified advertisements in the *Leicester Mercury* looking for permanent work. I was old-fashioned in this regard, everyone else having gone on to instant ('just add hot water') soups by then but I wasn't convinced the pieces of dried veg ever fully rehydrated in the cup and would therefore have to do so in my stomach.

Getting a good job was a challenge unless you had O levels or a friend in charge somewhere, which I didn't. But this was late 1979 and the world was such that if you could demonstrate a bright attitude via a well-crafted letter, you might secure an interview, and with that, the chance to snatch the position from a more suitably qualified candidate. As with so many things back then, it was all about your choice of words, and luckily for me words had been abundant throughout my childhood and the imaginative use of them highly praised – written, sung, dramatized, televised, read and spoken. When my sister got herself into trouble at school for muttering, 'Oh, go and imbibe nightshade,' my mother had described it as 'Shakespeare coming through' and laughed so much she could hardly light her cigarette.

I had words in my head and at my disposal and now, for the first

7

time in my life, I could appreciate it. For instance, when the Wintergreen Dental Practice in Leicester was seeking a 'mature lady with previous experience' to be their new dental surgery assistant, though I was just eighteen and had no surgical experience whatsoever, I was able to put in a confident, creative application with a letter that included the following:

> While my own dental history has been uneventful, I have seen the effects of periodontal gum disease, acid saliva and unchecked dental caries at close quarters. In my previous position and the one before that, I maintained a large Alpine show rockery and over twenty sets of dentures, respectively – which in some ways were strikingly similar! I have been a patient at four different dental practices in the city of Leicester, treated by six dental surgeons (listed below) on the NHS and privately.

Any candidate might have used similar words, but they might not have written 'strikingly'. Strikingly being one of those words, like extraordinary, that mark a person out, in writing. You write it, and it somehow describes you. Which is why it's best to avoid negative words, like doubt, accident or presume.

An interview off the back of a cleverly worded letter brings with it certain pressures, though – if you've written of your ability to do a headstand on a trotting horse, then you must be able to demonstrate it if called upon to do so. Ditto, if you claim to possess 'a wide-ranging knowledge of all things dental'.

I arrived for my interview at the Wintergreen Dental Practice – as prepared as I could be under the circumstances – ten minutes late, it being my mother's fervent belief that on-time arrival is never desired by the host. A thoughtful visitor, she said, should aim to be fifteen minutes late and slightly drunk.

I was weak, medically speaking – but thanks to my stepfather, Mr Holt, having a good grasp of British social policy and a collection of reference books, I knew what percentage of the population had no natural teeth, the basics of the arguments for and against fluoridizing the water supply, and that the patron saint of teeth was St Apollonia. I also had a photograph of myself doing a head-stand on horseback.

My outfit consisted of a prairie skirt in cheerful pinks and light yellows teamed with a handwash-only bolero in bubblegum. The ensemble (unusual for me, a jeans-and-jumper type) gave off a whole-some pioneering aura and it was a stroke of luck that my interviewer that Monday was practice manager Tammy Gammon (apricot hair and matching lipstick) whose soft-fruits palette toned well with mine. The moment we met she made a tiny nod of approval and rec-ognition, and when she saw the book I held, she mouthed the title and said, 'Oh, golly!' in a happy, satisfied, slightly American way.

We took a flight of stairs to the staffroom where Tammy pointed to important features, like the window, kettle and fridge. I gazed at the view while she made three small cups of tea, and then we sat on low spongy chairs, opened our notebooks, and the interview began. She smiled at me for a long time, which I took to mean she wanted me to speak, so I did.

'Even as a child,' I began, 'I was dentally particular – I wouldn't dream of letting anyone use my toothbrush, especially not on an animal.'

' "Den-tally par-tic-ul-ar",' said Tammy Gammon, scribbling in her notebook, ' "not-on-an-an-i-mal".'

'And if by accident I ever left for school without brushing my teeth,' I continued, slowly, giving her time to write, 'I'd suck a Polo fruit at the first possible opportunity or brush them with my finger in the toilets, like a cavewoman.'

' "Cavewoman", gosh,' she said, writing.

Minutes flew by and I think I convinced Tammy that teeth were absolutely central to my life. She certainly smiled a lot, and nod-ded her orange head as she took notes. While the interview was under way, a separate but consecutive part of my brain tried to fathom her. Was she as nice as she seemed? Did she like me? How old was she? Thirty? Forty? Fifty? Why did she keep writing the wrong things in her notebook? Was she actually American, or just polite? And why had she made three cups of tea?

She reminded me of a diluted Dolly Parton in her sweet

womanliness, and though she was vague on dental matters, per se, she was profoundly interested in toothpastes and powders. She'd used more than thirty different brands in her life.

'I used to love Punch and Judy strawberry flavoured,' I said, 'and progressing on to Signal felt like a rite of passage.'

Tammy cocked her head, unsure. 'What's that?'

'It's an anthropological term for moments that mark a significant change in status.'

'But I don't remember any strawberry toothpaste.'

'Punch and Judy, it's for children.'

Tammy winced. 'Aha, that explains it,' she said. 'I was in the States for a bunch of years.'

' "The States for a bunch of years",' I wrote in my notebook.

'What do you use now?' she asked.

'I like Close-up.'

'Hmmm, not minty enough,' she said. 'I used to like Crest and Colgate but, overall, I guess I prefer Macleans nowadays.'

'Macleans!' I was impressed. 'But it's so strong.'

'Yeah, I know, not everyone can handle it to begin with, but you get used to it. It's the best if you want fresh breath, better than SR, in my opinion – but don't say I said so.'

Tammy told me that whoever got this job would never have to buy toothpaste or any dental product again. 'You live on the samples from the suppliers. Toothpaste, brushes, floss, Interdens, mouthwash, tongue scrapers, Sterodent – you name it.'

'Don't remind me of Sterodent!' I said, and told her about the mistake I'd made involving Sterodent cleansing tablets, which had her clapping her hands with glee.

She reciprocated with the time she'd written 'Left' instead of 'Right' on a dental card and a patient had had the wrong tooth extracted. 'Boy, that took some explaining!' she shuddered, thinking about it, and forced a little laugh. 'It didn't kill her though, and it could have been worse.'

After that, I felt it only fair to tell her about our bogus dental checks.

'Wait! Bogus dental checks?' she shouted, excited, alarmed, scribbling.

'Well,' I said, simplifying it for her, 'don't write this down, but my mother was in the middle of a mental breakdown and couldn't get out of bed to drive us to the dental surgery and, to make matters worse, she'd just had a disastrous affair with the dentist and he was by then trying to patch things up with his wife.'

'Yikes!'

'The thing was, though, my sister and I wanted a check-up.'

'You *wanted* one?'

'Yes, we did, so my mother asked her therapist to give us fake check-ups to put a stop to our nagging.'

'She should have refused.' said Tammy, indignant.

'I know, but this therapist put our mother's mental health before our dental health and so she poked around with a cocktail stick and a torch, and declared us dentally fit.'

' "Cocktail stick"!' Tammy, scandalized, turned to a new page in her notepad.

'Yes, but the point is . . . don't write this down,' I reminded her, wanting to get back on track, 'it was no substitute for an inspection by a qualified dental surgeon so we demanded that she get up and take us to see the proper dentist.'

'And did she?'

'She had to. My sister threatened to tell our grandmother if she didn't and she'd have called her names on the phone.'

'Names?'

'You know, "bad mother", "neglectful", "drunken menace" and so forth.'

'Oh, my heckedy!' said Tammy, with her hands in the air. 'This is exactly why I've never wanted children.'

I had pangs, sharing all this with a woman I hardly knew but, without an O level to my name, demonstrating my potential as an entertaining colleague was imperative. It was all I had and I was certain my mother wouldn't mind in the long run, and in any case, Tammy seemed delighted by her.

She told me that JP Wintergreen was a sole practitioner for the time being. And that he might or might not get a partner who would use the empty upstairs surgery.

'May I ask why the practice needs a new dental nurse if there's only one dentist?'

'Well, I shouldn't really tell you,' she whispered, 'but JP – the dentist – and I have got together and I'm going part-time.' She touched her hair and tried not to grin.

'What, like boyfriend and girlfriend?' I said.

'Yes, I've moved into his house on Blackberry Lane – you know, near the golf course. But I shouldn't really have said anything.'

'Congratulations,' I said. 'But I suppose you can't offer me the job now you've told me the secret.'

'Oh, no,' she said, putting her fingers to her lips, 'I can tell I can trust you.'

'I won't say anything,' I assured her, and at that precise moment a man burst in, asking where the hell the tea had got to.

'This is JP Wintergreen, senior dental surgeon,' said Tammy, biting her lip. I won't describe him in full detail now – just that he had surprisingly bad teeth (for a dentist), smelled strongly of vinegar and tobacco smoke, and the European way of arranging his trousers (hoist high, with everything all down one leg), none of which I held against him. He picked up a teacup and drank the contents down in two gulps.

'You won't say anything about what?' he asked, looking at me.

'About Tammy preferring Macleans,' I said.

JP didn't ask me anything about dentistry or teeth – only whether my father was a Freemason, or a Lion or a Flea. This was an unexpected line of enquiry. I paused momentarily to consider it and was about to say, 'No, he's in the Ecology Party,' but Tammy seemed to want me to say yes (frantic wide eyes and nodding) so I said, 'Yes, I believe he is.' JP then told me about a flat above us on the second floor that would be available to the successful candidate at a very reasonable rent.

'It'll work out cheaper than your bus fares,' said Tammy.

When we parted at the front door, I confirmed that I was available for an immediate start, and on the bus home I re-ran the interview in my head. I wanted the job. I liked Tammy Gammon and I could sense that JP would be manageable. I felt confident that Tammy would telephone later with good news. The flat sounded nice; washing machine and tumble dryer, and, with its two dustbin collections per week and the sitting room getting the evening sun, it would be tantamount to living in Australia. But it worried me. I didn't want it. I had no desire to live on my own, two floors up, my sister right over the other side of town, and everyone else miles away in a village. I decided I wouldn't even mention the flat to my mother. How would she cope without me? How would she get her novel finished or the baby fed? I wouldn't even bring it up. I wouldn't worry her.

At home my mother was excitable. Tammy *had* phoned and the two of them had had a long chat. 'They'd like to offer you the job,' she said, 'and it's all above board, salary, tax, national insurance and holiday pay and so forth.'

Apparently, my love of rabbits had nudged me ahead of a keen thirty-year-old who ran a Sketchley's but wanted a break from the fumes. I couldn't recall any talk of rabbits, but I began to tell my mother about Tammy favouring Macleans toothpaste for freshness.

'Yes, I know,' she said, 'I heard it all from Tammy on the phone – I know everything.'

'I bet she didn't mention JP Wintergreen's curly hair, or that he dresses like a rich Spaniard or that his leather shoes slip off his bare heels as he walks and dangle off his foot when he sits with a leg crossed. Or that the hairs on his legs stop abruptly at his ankle, like trouser legs, or a brown rooster. Or that Tammy herself has veins in her cleavage that look like the diagram of a lung.'

'No,' my mother conceded, 'but she did tell me about the accommodation above the surgery – sounds perfect.'

'Don't worry,' I said, 'I shan't take the flat.'

'What?' she cried. 'Of course you will – the flat is basically the pay.'

'But I'm not sure I'll like living on my own,' I said, 'in the city.'

'Christ almighty, Lizzie, are you mad? You can't turn down a flat of your own, you'd have to be crazy. Think of Cait and Baba moving to Dublin and dyeing their underwear black!'

'Yes, but Cait and Baba had each other. I'd be alone.'

'But you can write a novel or learn the mandolin in a flat.'

'I don't want to write a novel or learn the mandolin.'

'You'll have two extra hours in bed every morning.' Which, to be fair, was only a slight exaggeration.

And so, without my mother forbidding it, I had no reason to turn it down.

2. The Flying Pea

I'm not proud that my mother was still so important to me – I was eighteen years old and should have given her up by then, but to be truthful, she was like a character I'd come to know and love from a comic or a sitcom and, although I could often predict what might unfold with her antics, I enjoyed watching and I loved her and still do. It was as though all the other women in the world had decided to go along with everything, and to behave with decorum and sto-icism whereas my mother had taken it upon herself to wave things away and call them nonsense. She was there to announce that long hair didn't suit everyone, that dogs were preferable to children – if you had the courage to admit it – and that anyone who didn't make life an adventure might as well be dead. And that if she ever had to commit suicide, she'd break into an undertaker's at night and do it on a table there under a sheet with poison, to spare anyone having to find her poor dead body – except the undertaker, who was accustomed to dead people, and would take it in his or her stride.

People have tried to stop me writing about her – various rela-tives, envious of her popularity, and, on occasion, the woman herself – but she was as central to my life as dental matters, if not more so, and so here she still is. For at least half of my childhood she had battled drink and prescription drugs and needed a degree of looking-after, but now she only allowed herself a glass or two of wine per day or, in emergencies, sherry and a Valium, and was rarely what you might call drunk.

Career-wise, she was bored to tears, having been promoted from van driver to Customer Service Representative for the Snowdrop Laundry after a career break, during which she'd had a baby and tried to start up a pine-stripping business and almost fumed us all to death with Nitromors fluid. You might think the new job – which only entailed calling on the best customers to check on satisfaction – would be preferable to dashing around delivering laundry from a van and changing roller towels in filthy toilets, but you'd be wrong. She had loved being a van driver: the hard work, the laughter, the banter with van boys, pub landlords, shop women, factory workers and traffic wardens. Racing other vans up the A46 and bursting into the gents shouting, 'Lady with towels – coming in,' as the men hurriedly folded their penises back into their flies.

The problem with this new job was that it required her to listen to customers – who only ever seemed to complain and had no incentive to do otherwise. And this was problematic because my mother was temperamentally unsuited to that sort of thing. She despised any kind of moaning except when it occurred in a poem of heartbreak or injustice, and found it almost impossible to hide her annoyance. It was a miracle that she wasn't sacked for recommending that the manager of the Old Lion public house 'stop complaining for five minutes and listen to some Chopin'. Far from reporting her, he listened to some Chopin and gave her assorted salted snacks on the house the next time she called.

If it hadn't been for the platonic friendship that had developed between her and Abe, grown-up son of a garage-owning customer, Abraham's Motors in Highfields, she might have resigned after a few months. Abe certainly wasn't a moaner. He praised the boiler suits (roomy but stylish) and the towels (super absorbent) and was a genius with my mother's troublesome but much-loved car, the Flying Pea. It was actually Abe who'd spray-painted it green and christened it 'the Pea' in the first place. Mr Abraham senior had invested in a vehicle-spraying device and sought out vibrant car paints from India and Africa where life was brighter and people simply didn't want black or grey cars. He had single-handedly started the rage for painted cars, because of which they were one of the richest families in the city. They owned four garages, two homes and an aeroplane. Put it this way, if you saw a brightly coloured car in the Midlands in the 1970s or '80s I can pretty much guarantee it would have been sprayed by Abraham's Motors. Abe's own car was a Jaguar – in Parma violet.

My mother was a keen driver. She loved to talk about cars and their engines, and enjoyed nothing better than changing a tyre in full view of the traffic on grass verges with people driving past honking or even stopping to admire her or offering to help, and her being able to stand up, oily hands on hips, fag in mouth, and say, 'Do I look as though I need help?'

Abe used to say he wished my mother was one of their mechanics but never went as far as offering her a job because of a hunch that she'd be more trouble than she was worth. But he did like having her around, sitting on the workbench, stirring the oily sawdust with her bare toes, because he was training to become a counsellor and hypnotist specializing in shame and she was au fait with the jargon – and didn't mind being analysed by a novice.

In case you're wondering, my stepfather, Mr Holt, was most tolerant about this friendship but though happy with the free counselling, he drew the line at trampolining or yoga in case one thing led to another, which it might have. (Abe resembled the young V. S. Naipaul, but taller.) I recall Mr Holt one time asking how Mrs Abe might feel about it all.

'Don't worry, there'll never be a Mrs Abe,' my mother had said, and Mr Holt had said, 'Oh, I see,' and had been satisfied with that.

When people in the village heard I was about to start working in the city, they tried to unsettle me with tales of woe. I'd soon regret it, they said. The journey into Leicester was so long and winding and went all round the houses, I'd spend half my life on the bus and half my wages on the fares. When I explained I'd be living there too, they told me I needn't think city folk would smile at me or say hello because they wouldn't. And if I accidentally dropped my library card, they wouldn't run up the street to hand it back – they'd use it to borrow books like *The Tudor Appetite* and *The Betsy* and never return them and it would be on my record for ever that I liked porn.

The city was full to bursting with prostitutes, they said, and Asians, and people trying to sell you things you didn't need but would soon be addicted to – like feather boas, foreign cigarettes and ready-made sandwiches. The sun, blotted out by the tall buildings, couldn't shine and the rain was poisoned by the toxic fumes that poured from the sock factories. My skin would be covered in pimples from the hell of it all, and I'd develop sinusitis. My mother told me this scaremongering was a complex mixture of jealousy and abandonment, and took the opposite view, highlighting the cultural opportunities and the permissiveness.

'You're free to express yourself in the city any way you like,' she said. But she had to agree about the sinusitis.

Mr Holt moved me in the Snowdrop van the Friday before I was to start work on the Monday. We made a seven a.m. departure, in heavy rain, to beat the traffic but my mother, who'd planned to come along, appeared at five to in a nightshirt, and sifted through my belongings in the hall – looking for things I might have stolen. After an argument and the retrieval of a spoon and a *Godspell* cassette, she wished me good luck and took a chamomile tea back to bed.

Although Mr Holt and I had succeeded in beating the rush hour, all of nature seemed out to thwart us. First a small flood around the villages meant a tricky three-point turn, and then the vigorous testing of brakes (that I mistook for him having some kind of heart attack at the wheel) meant twenty minutes lost, and then a tree down, and two metal bins in the road with contents strewn, meant mounting a kerb to get by.

Mr Holt didn't say anything but I knew he was dubious about this move. He'd had years alone in rental accommodation before my mother had trapped him into a long-term relationship by deliberately getting pregnant with a baby no father could leave – my brother Danny, who you'll hear about in due course. So he knew a thing or two about town living.

I should explain that my stepfather was never called by his first name by me or my siblings. The reason for this being that he had been the foreman at the Snowdrop Laundry, and we'd known him as our mother's eagle-eyed stickler of a boss for many months before she managed to lure him home for sex and to fix our television. He'd been Mr Holt ever since.

'Just don't go around smiling at people,' he warned now.

We stopped at traffic lights on the brow of the hill approaching Leicester. Mr Holt yanked the handbrake and commented cheerfully that on a clear day you could see Old John from here, rising in the distance on the northern edge of the county, the beginnings of Charnwood Forest. I knew it well. My biological father and his new family lived that way and took Sunday walks together across the brackeny hills with their new dog, Mr Bingo (named after a terrible clown), and a picnic of hard-boiled eggs and mini-rolls. I knew this because on one of those walks, the yolk from my egg had fallen and Mr Bingo, who'd lain hopefully at my feet, had caught it in his mouth, swallowed it whole, and looked up for more. In the silence afterwards, just long enough to let the metaphor settle, I'd looked up to catch my father's eye but the noise had begun again.

'Naughty Mr Bingo ate Lizzie's egg,' chorused my half-siblings.

'Only the yolk,' I said.

But, as you know, the morning of the move was grey and rainy and we couldn't see that far. I gazed at my new city – out over the vast built-up hollow, the soot-coated bricks and endless streets with an oily sheen, and the chimneys and towers poking up into the yellowish sky. I was going to spend my life with a parent on either side of the county and me in the dip – at the bottom, like a piece of barley in a dish of soup, I realized, or a leftover cornflake – developing sinusitis from the pressure.

My best friend, Melody, was miles away, training to be a nurse at Luton and Dunstable Hospital. And my sister was the other side of Leicester (an awkward two-bus journey away), training to be a different kind of nurse. Occasionally I'd see the two of them together and they'd join forces to say just what a rewarding career it was. Especially when painful trapped wind turned into an unexpected baby, a lemon-sized lump turned out to be an actual lemon, or the female tramp with senile dementia turned out to be the Queen's second cousin and only dehydrated after a fall.

The cars behind us began to beep. A small van in the next lane crept forward even though the lights were still red. Cars behind egged us on. Someone shouted, 'Move on, mate, the bleeding lights are out!'

Mr Holt hated to jump a light but this wasn't jumping – the lights in all directions were stuck on red. If we obeyed, we'd none of us move and the lines of cars and vans would stretch back to Flatstone; no shops would open and not a single feather boa, or foreign cigarette, or ready-made sandwich would be sold. We edged forward and wove through a tangle of small vehicles and soon we were at the bottom of the hill, pulling into a mini lay-by which had been a tram stop in years gone by, right outside the surgery.

'This is it,' I said, surprised.

'I know,' he said, 'I had a practice run last night, so I'd know the way today.'

And though it was illegal, Mr Holt left the van there while we unloaded my things and made two trips each up the stairs.

I was proud to point out the staircarpet – brand new Axminster. It wouldn't matter how much horseplay went on, I told him, nor how many times I went thundering up and down because JP Wintergreen had paid for an extra few inches for each flight and therefore Harris's (of Granby Corner) could be called upon any time to lift the whole strip and shift the worn areas along the flight – with no need for re-tufting or patching. JP had told me this at the interview and Mr Holt was impressed.

'He's a forward thinker, then,' he said, tapping the nosing gently with his toecap, marvelling at the quality. 'Very good.'

Mr Holt had one last thing to do and that was to hand over the gift my mother had sent to celebrate the start of my proper career (as opposed to a cash-in-hand job). I wasn't feeling particularly warm towards her after our argument over the spoon etc. and her going back to bed instead of coming to settle me in, so I opened it grumpily.

It was a good-quality journal, with a beautiful marbled cover, sewn-in pages and narrow lines. She had taken the liberty of writing *Dentistry for Beginners by Lizzie Vogel – 1980* on the title page, and a letter had been inserted.

Dearest Lizzie,

Please write this journal as you learn the ropes. Things learned each day (or week, depending how dull or disgusting it all is), the tips and tricks, the rumours, the gossip, and funny vignettes about the patients – and your associated feelings and musings.

Later you might publish it to great acclaim. People are all for 'hearing it from the maid' these days. But remember, they are not sympathetic toward dentists and will not want to read much about teeth, especially rotten or broken ones. Skirt around as much as possible to make it readable.

I shan't miss you since I plan to visit you often.

Your loving mother,

Elizabeth Vogel-Benson-Holt

PS Please look out for a letter addressed to me.

At that time my mother most often signed her name 'Elizabeth Benson-Holt', but sometimes she included Vogel too, either to remind her children that they were bound together, in recognition of the long and winding road they'd been on, or perhaps just out of habit, a slip of the pen. The order of the names varied; it depended how she was feeling.

I read the note twice. I had no special desire to publish a book, especially not one on dentistry.

'Tell her I'd have preferred that spoon,' I said.

And it was on that sulky note that Mr Holt left and I was alone in my new flat. I put the journal on the shelf under the coffee table, picked up a copy of *Woman's Own* and read a perceptive short story by Penelope Lively about a schoolboy.

I had a wander about downstairs where I found piles of magazines stacked up in the utility room – more copies of *Woman's Own*, *Woman*, *Titbits* and others – and took a few upstairs with me. I was pleasantly surprised by these over the next few days and really took to them, even going as far as to imagine how nice it must be to write for a magazine like that. I wondered where you might learn all the womanly knowledge necessary to fill it week after week. It occurred to me that the best journalists must go about looking for women, to share their wisdom and anecdotes and use a tiny cassette to record them. I laughed at the idea of coming across one like my mother who might talk of her love of trampolining in her younger days, before her pelvic muscles had given out – the strange elation of airborne propulsion and the knowledge that one foot wrong and you could lose a front tooth or land in a heap of humiliation. In other words, it was a sex substitute – like having beauty treatments and doing macramé. Or they might phone Buckingham Palace and ask a royal receptionist how the Queen keeps her figure, and the receptionist might simply say that she counts calories, jogs on the spot, and spits out the walnuts off her Walnut Whips. A clever journalist would ask leading questions on the subject of dietary fibre and later tip off a colleague in the adverts department who might ring up Kellogg's and ask them to take out an advert for All Bran.

The surgery was closed that day but later Tammy Gammon came in to show me how the storage heaters worked, and how to light the grill on the cooker. 'If you forget to hold the red button down, you'll gas yourself, like I almost did when I lived up here,' she said, 'and we'll find you dead in the morning.'

She showed me the Hoover Aristocrat washer and dryer, and told me not to have them going at the same time because of overloading the adapter, and then she warned me that having one's own washing machine and tumble dryer was a mixed blessing. On the one hand you have your own facilities, but on the other, you end up with a constant stream of friends and neighbours appearing with bags of laundry expecting to put a wash through, in which case, you have to be firm and say something like, 'If you're just coming round here to use my washer and dryer then do me a favour and go to the launderette on Sparkenhoe Street.' Which she'd had to do with Rhona, Bill Turner's nurse from up the road, who'd kept appearing with a load of dirty laundry pretending she wanted to be pals.

She also reminded me that as a tenant I'd be permanently

on-call to go down into the cellar to switch off the generator – should it ever accidentally be left on after practice hours, which was the main reason for the cheapness of the rent.

'Also, JP will need to use your toilet in the mornings,' she said, with a tiny grimace.

'What? Why?'

'He often gets the urge after his mid-morning coffee, and he obviously can't use the general toilet on the first floor.'

'Why not?'

'He just can't – a patient might see him coming out and a dentist needs total privacy. He's fastidious cleanliness-wise, if that's your beef – and I should know, it used to be my toilet, remember?'

'I wish I'd known this before,' I muttered.

Tammy ignored this and told me I was welcome to the cactus on the ledge and then showed me a tiny under-stairs cupboard that should by rights come with the flat but if I didn't mind she'd like to keep it.

'For personal bits and bobs and things I don't want His Nibs to see – you know,' she said. 'Got to maintain the feminine mystique.'

After Tammy had gone, I strolled down into town and looked around the shops where I bought a curl-encourager hairbrush, some lemons (for show) and a coat. I hadn't set out for a coat but let me tell you briefly here about it. It was in the January sales and was only still in stock because it had been returned with a slight mark on one lapel. That dab of lipstick was of no interest to me. If it had been food or blood, I might have been put off, but lipstick was fine. The coat was a floppy tweedy material, wool but thin and very supple; the shoulders were slouchy and there was a seam running along each and right down the sleeve. All perfect, but the main thing was the herringbone pattern in the weave. Herringbone was like music and art to me, and science actually, and it felt so strong and so soothing. It was floors and bricks and teeth and bones. I can't state strongly enough how much I loved this pattern – more than a pattern, it was a system, a scheme.

Also, the colours, a gingery brown and a greyish cream, made the colour neutral. As for the lining, you won't believe it but it was bronze silk with tiny yellow dots that would flash whenever the coat opened, which would be often since I never buttoned coats, ever, unless I was in Alaska, and I never was. And anyway, it had no buttons, only a great belt with no buckle. And though it was a designated size (eight as it happens) it would fit anyone with narrow shoulders who wasn't unusually tall or incredibly broad. This was a coat that anyone would want, but it was available to me now because some woman had worn it at least once and smudged red lipstick on it, and had then rejected it (because of the smudge?) and returned it for an exchange – maybe a smart mac for the forecast wet spring, or a coat with buttons as not everyone would countenance a buttonless coat.

Or maybe she'd just got the money back, and not had another coat but the cash alternative. Perhaps she would have loved the coat but needed the money. I knew of this, the time my granny Benson bought me a swingy jersey skirt and matching bat-wing top in petrol blue and black stripes that made me look like Kiki Dee, but I saw on the tag that it had cost £25 for the two pieces and felt I needed the money more than I needed to look like Kiki Dee. So I returned it and got a credit voucher which I sold to my mother for £20 and she got some cowboy jeans so low on the hips you could almost see her pants.

The original cost of the coat had been immense. You could read the price on the tag before the two reductions. Now it was £7.50, which was cheap even by my standards and it was worth so much more. I thought it was going to change my life.

I took it to the cashier who folded it in an expert way, wrapped it in tissue and was about to slide it into a carrier bag so ridiculously, embarrassingly big that I said, 'Actually, I'll just carry it.'

3. The First Impressions

My first day as a dental nurse was patient-free training. I didn't even have to change into my white dress, which was a disappointment. I was greeted again by Tammy Gammon. This time her apricot hair was fixed by assorted slides and clips into a tight, headache-inducing ponytail. I noticed she had the same low, untidy hairline as Elizabeth Taylor. And a fine blonde moustache.

The surgery and waiting room were quite plainly decorated. All the better to show off Tammy's Christmas cactuses which were crammed in dustily by a console and trailed over the deep sill of a square casement window. They were in abundant flower then, it being midwinter, and the cascading flowers (fuchsia pink) hung from crocodile-like stems. Tammy frowned seriously as she explained the watering technique. 'Always rainwater, never tap,' she said, pausing to check I was taking it in. 'Always room temperature, never cold.' And finally, 'Always drip, drip, never gush, gush.'

I nodded gravely and reminded her that I was fresh from managing the largest show rockery in the UK and if anyone was going to remember how to handle the *Schlumbergera* (I used their official name), it was me. Her stiff little shoulders relaxed and she smiled.

'Don't worry,' I said, 'I'm very green-fingered.'

'Oh, yes,' she said, and then muttered, '*Schlumbergera.*'

'Glebe Gardens stock a wide range of succulents,' I said.

'By the way, children sometimes climb up into the windowsill for fun, and the parents turn a blind eye, but if I catch them, I drag them out –' Tammy looked stern – 'by the leg.'

'Right.'

The walls featured a map of the mouth, a small Dr Seuss poster which read, '*Only brush the teeth you want to keep,*' and a portrait of Henry D. Cogswell, an American dentist from the gold-rush years, a philanthropist and temperance man who donated cold-water fountains to the townsfolk to prevent them drinking alcohol. Apparently a distant relative of Tammy's.

A central table with liquorice-twist legs displayed yet more piles of *Woman's Own* magazine and some thin, stapled booklets that Tammy had produced, entitled *Dalrymple, McWilliam & Wintergreen*, containing out-of-date information about the practice and a few illustrations.

Next, Tammy introduced me to the appointments system, kept in a smart-looking book with a reusable leatherette cover in maroon. It displayed one week to two pages, with each weekday column divided into quarter-hours, and the months printed in gold. Tammy emphasized the crucial importance of booking patients in for their next six-monthly appointment.

'You've got to understand, Lizzie, people don't want to come here. It's something I've had to come to terms with. It really doesn't matter how nice I am as a person, how pretty the waiting room, how glorious the cactus – people would rather be anywhere but here.'

'Yes,' I said. 'I understand.'

'And when we see them, we're seeing them at their worst – weak, nervy, angry, in pain,' she said. 'So we have to be welcoming but firm.'

'Right.'

'If they say something like, "Can you tell Dr Wintergreen I'm really nervous?" you should say, "Dentists aren't called Dr – it's *Mr* Wintergreen," and that can take their mind off it.'

'OK,' I said, 'and what if they ask me about fluoridation of the drinking water or the toxicity of mercury?'

'Just fudge it and tell JP before you bring them through. He'll take them down a peg or two – he can't abide a know-it-all.' Tammy laughed.

'And if you don't book them in straight away for their next six-monthly appointment,' she continued, 'they might leave it ten months or even a year before they remember they're due for an inspection and that's the equivalent of taking JP's money and throwing it down the toilet.'

'OK,' I said, 'I'll be rigorous about rebooking.'

Apparently, I'd see life fly by now that I was working with six-monthly advance appointments.

'You're saying goodbye to a family of four one minute and, in the blink of an eye, they're trooping back in for their next check-up – with a squawking new baby and a change of address, and you've done nothing.' Tammy chuckled. 'And then, the next thing you know, the dad's gone under a bus, the mother's remarried and the baby's clambering around knocking the blossoms off the cactuses.'

'Yes, I see.'

'Names should only ever be written softly in the book, in pencil, so that if a patient phones to change their appointment, we can erase them easily without spoiling the page.'

We continued with a whistle-stop tour of the surgery, which was an incredibly crowded room. The 'treatment island', including two dental drill arms, a tiny white porcelain spittoon and a round marble tray on an extending arm, took up most of the space. Tammy demonstrated how to adjust the lumpy headrest on the fat leatherette chair, and affix the dribble bib correctly, without constricting a patient's throat. The treatment island sat on a disc of maroon rubber (the exact same colour as the appointments book) that tapered down to meet the grey carpet tiles; it reminded me of the grim black pond, in a horror film, which contained all the answers.

I noticed a dark patch where, I presumed, the spittoon must drip – or possibly droplets of mouthwash were slopped by shaky-handed patients. And a faded area, on the opposite side, where JP Wintergreen's Mediclogs must shuffle about, hour after hour, as he looked into people's mouths.

To the side, on a square metal trolley, sat the ultrasonic scaler. This was new, Tammy told me, and JP's pride and joy. It had revolutionized the cleaning of his patients' teeth and was also perfect for descaling the kettle and removing nail varnish.

In the corner, assorted in-trays, pen pots and papers sat on a desk. A calendar for 1980 featuring *Cacti in the Wild* hung on a pin to the side. January's being *The Original Prickly Pear of Kansas*.

We took a break and Tammy made some coffee in a jug with hot milk and granules. She popped a sugar lump into her mouth and pressed a buzzer by the door. Soon JP Wintergreen appeared, and after a few sips, which left a great piece of milk-skin across his lips, he took a pack of cigarettes and a chunky lighter from his pocket and offered them to Tammy. She took one, lit it, and then instead of smoking it herself, held it to JP's lips and fed him a puff. We drank our coffee and Tammy chattered, holding the cigarette and flicking it into a little glass ashtray, just as a smoker would, but never took a puff herself, only held it to JP's lips every now and again. If she left it too long between puffs, he would stick his lips forward and make a kissing noise.

'Are you a smoker, Lizzie?' she asked.

I'd just around then decided to smoke only when I really, really wanted to, which turned out to be hardly ever. So I replied, 'Not during the daytime,' which sounded aloof so, to make up for it, I described my smoke rings, including my trademark ring-within-a-ring and the perfect smoke square I'd once blown but had never managed to recreate. Tammy was captivated.

'Ooh, ooh, try now,' she said, and thrust JP's cigarette at me.

I had no choice but to take a drag and noticed that JP had wet the end. People do wet the end sometimes, I knew it happened, but this was sodden and seeing it (feeling it) I knew that nothing JP ever did in the future could make up for it. It was one of those things.

I tried to blow a smoke square but the unfavourable conditions (draught from the ill-fitting sash window), plus the pressure of being scrutinized by a new boss, meant I produced nothing more than an untidy puff.

'Sorry, that was rubbish,' I said.

'Try again.' Tammy popped another sugar lump.

I prepared for my second attempt by telling myself to 'buck up or fuck up', a thing my mother always shouted at herself in times of stress. I took another drag and blew out two perfect, quivering rings that hung in the air before dissipating, like a Hanna-Barbera tycoon's cigar smoke. Tammy clapped and I tried for a square – but to no avail.

'You shouldn't have clapped,' JP said to Tammy. 'You disturbed the air. Try again, nurse.'

'I can only really do squares in the mirror,' I said. 'I need to get my mouth right.'

JP and Tammy seemed let down.

'Do you have any other tricks?' asked JP.

And that was when I did my impression of Prince Charles. I had to hand the cigarette back because I needed both hands to push my ears forward. Tammy laughed so hard she fell sideways off her chair. It was hard to tell how impressed JP was because he had to help her up.

'Oh, my goodness, that is amazing,' she said breathlessly. 'Do it again.'

JP left us then and Tammy ran the cigarette under the tap, still laughing and saying, 'Oh, Lord.' She scrubbed at her fingers with some Sqezy and a potato brush, and gabbled on about nothing in particular, presumably to distract me from the fact that JP had gone upstairs to use my bathroom.

I hoped I should never be called upon to feed JP his cigarette and wondered how the ritual had started.

'We had complaints from patients about his fingers smelling of tobacco,' said Tammy, reading my thoughts.

'But he has no patients today.'

'I know, but he enjoys being fed now, like a baby with his bottle. It's soothing.'

'Right,' I said.

We went back down to the surgery. Tammy had suggested I listen in on any incoming phone calls, to get the hang of things, but the phone hadn't rung all morning except when my mother called to ask if I'd moved her car keys and Tammy had had to remind her I'd left home four days ago. After the coffee break, though, there was a bona-fide call. I felt quite relieved; the real world was still out there, and this wasn't some elaborate game.

Tammy answered and gestured for me to listen in. There followed an awkward conversation.

Caller: 'I'd like to make an appointment to see the dentist for a check-up, please.'

Tammy: 'Are you registered here?'

Caller: 'No.'

Tammy: 'Are you registered anywhere?'

'Not locally, I've just moved to the area.'

'Are you on social security benefits?'

'No.'

'OK, what name is it, please?'

'Mr Kapoor.'

'Oh, right, erm, I'm sorry, Mr Kapoor, but we're not taking any patients at the moment. You can come in for an emergency appointment but it will not be on the National Health, and you will have to wait until the dentist can squeeze you in, and you will have to pay in advance for any treatment and, I repeat, no National Health.'

'But, OK, I—'

'Sorry about that, Mr Kapoor, goodbye.'

Tammy hung up, cleared her throat and fiddled with her pendant.

'All right,' she said, looking at me, 'did you follow all that?'

'Not really.'

'So, we don't take NHS casuals unless they pay up front.'

'What is a casual?'

'Someone with toothache but no dentist.'

'But he didn't say he had toothache . . .'

'Yes, but he probably did though – he was tricking us.'

'How could you tell?'

'The name,' said Tammy, twisting the pendant. 'And JP isn't very good at handling them.'

'Who?'

'Indians.'

'So what will happen to Mr Kapoor?' I asked.

'He'll have to go and queue for the emergency NHS clinic on

Sunday,' she said, 'unless he manages to find a dentist before that – it's up to him, I don't know, it's not our problem.'

I went up to my flat at the end of that day feeling quite melancholy – I didn't like the idea of watching my life disappear patient by patient, appointment by appointment, page by page. I'd already wasted half my life worrying about my mother, various dogs and my siblings. I'd failed at the smoke square and had to resort to my Prince Charles. But mostly, I couldn't stop thinking about that phone call from Mr Kapoor.

One of the patients in my early days was Mrs Woodward. I found her waiting at the door when I opened up after lunch one day. She didn't have an appointment but had broken her partial upper denture, which she presented to me. It looked as if it had been run over by a car.

Mrs Woodward had been a patient of Mr McWilliam's so I had to look for her card in the old filing cabinets in the hall. Tammy helped and eventually found it in the wrong place. She apologized for having taken so long.

'The thing is, Mrs Woodward, your dental record says you died in July 1978,' she said.

'That's when I remarried.'

Tammy laughed. 'That will have been me then, filing you away in the deads. I'm always mixing up death and marriage.'

As it happened, Mrs Woodward's newish husband, Reverend Woodward, was the vicar of my granny's village parish and I had a clear recollection of her referring to him as a 'people pleaser' because of his comparing Jesus to Jimmy Young in a modern sermon.

I told Mrs Woodward to relax with a magazine and we'd do our best to fit her in as soon as possible.

'Hullo, hullo, Miss Wood,' JP boomed, some while later. 'Come in, come in, take a seat.'

'It's Mrs Woodward,' she corrected him, before describing how she'd only popped the denture out to remove a jam pip that had got underneath and, somehow, it had slipped from her hand on to the driveway where her husband – a novice driver – had let the car kangaroo forward over it. 'It was awful.'

She was currently wearing her spare, she told him, which didn't fit very well. She had stored it in moist tissues as per instructions, but they must have dried out over time.

'Well, it's a shame that you didn't store it correctly, Mrs Wood,' said JP, and, before she could protest, he lifted two sides of her upper lip and stared into her mouth, as if he were estimating the age of a horse at the fair.

'Uh huh, uh huh, uh huh,' he said. Then, 'Bite,' he ordered, and hooked his little finger under the palate to whip out the ill-fitting spare, which he ran violently under the tap, turning it over and over in his hands and gazing at it.

'Show me the damaged one,' he said.

Mrs Woodward rummaged about in the handbag in her lap and handed over the mangled pink plastic.

JP joked that her husband must have run it over deliberately, to stop her yacking. Mrs Woodward didn't dignify the comment with a response but instead told him she remembered giving his son driving lessons some years previously.

JP clicked the spare back into her mouth. 'So you did,' he said, 'and I seem to recall very slow progress – open again, please – no offence – and close again – open, please, bite – and now he's a maxillofacial consultant at the Royal Infirmary.'

Unable to respond verbally, Mrs Woodward opened her eyes wide in congratulation.

'Rinse out,' he instructed.

She did so vigorously and then asked, 'Any grandkiddies?'

JP stopped and stood slightly back. 'No, since you ask, and not likely to – he's just had a vasectomy.' His head wobbled slightly, a sort of defiant sadness.

'Good grief,' said Mrs Woodward, 'that's a bit drastic. He can't be more than thirty.'

'Thirty-two, and my only child.'

'What on earth has he done that for?' Mrs Woodward was shocked but somehow more confident now.

'His girlfriend's got three of her own and doesn't want any more, apparently.' JP blinked.

'Well, but . . .'

'I know. It's causing me something of an existential crisis.'

'I bet it is.'

Tammy chipped in from the admin desk, 'Are you still at the vicarage, Mrs Woodward?'

But the patient was preoccupied. 'You've got the girlfriend's kiddies, so all's not lost,' she said.

'They're no relation to me whatsoever, Mrs Wood. They barely speak any English.'

She tried to reply but he shoved his thumb into her mouth.

'I can't go teaching them how to make a reed-whistle or tearing them off a strip for busting a window, can I?'

'Give it time. Keep an open heart.'

'OK, we're going to have to make you a new upper denture. Can't have you walking around like a hag.'

Tammy telephoned Mercurial Dental Lab for a late pick-up while JP got on with making the impressions – first loading a palate-shaped plastic tray with alginate and then shoving it into Mrs Woodward's mouth, pushing it up into the roof with such force that she began to gag on the inevitable displacement of the pink goo. Oblivious to her discomfort, JP held the tray up with two fingers and gazed around the room, visibly thinking.

The extra inches of staircarpet that had once put him in such an admirable light sprang to mind now; they seemed to belong to a world of JP's imagination, populated with children running up and down the stairs, none of whom were his or related to him, and none of whom even looked like him; they did not speak his language or want his teachings. He would be irrelevant. Dead and gone.

'If it were up to me, I'd sue the surgeon,' JP said wistfully. 'He's ended my bloodline.' Then he looked at Mrs Woodward, without seeming to notice that she was on the point of suffocation. He eventually fished the impression tray out of her mouth and rinsed the slime off under the tap. Mrs Woodward sat forward, gasped, coughed and spluttered and, taking the tissue I held out, dabbed at her eyes.

'Yes, he castrated my only son.'

JP began the process again for the lower jaw, which was considerably less stressful, since Mrs Woodward had no lower teeth to displace the alginate. Afterwards she was sent to the waiting room to recover her composure, reapply her lipstick and do the paperwork, which I watched and learned from. And then, with perfect timing, the young man from Mercurial Lab appeared to collect the impressions.

It was our first official meeting. I'd seen him briefly a few times, delivering appliances – crowns and so on – and I always liked the way he narrowed his eyes when JP pontificated.

'Ah,' said JP now, noting his arrival, 'we've got some impressions for this replacement partial upper denture – now, just wait one second while I fill out a purchase order.'

While he scribbled, Tammy introduced us. 'This is Andy from the Mercurial Dental Laboratory,' she said, and turning to me, 'and this is Lizzie, our new girl.'

'Hello,' said the young man, 'I think we've met before.' I squinted at him. 'Andy Nicolello,' he said. 'I live near Kilmington.' I didn't speak. I couldn't quite believe my eyes. Andy Nicolello was a laboratory technician. It was like seeing Stig of the Dump all cleaned up in a suit.

He inspected the impressions and he wasn't happy. 'I'm afraid these have dragged a bit,' he said calmly.

'Let me see,' said JP, snapping his fingers. 'There's nothing wrong with them.'

'Is the patient still here?' asked Andy. 'We need better impressions than these, really.'

Mrs Woodward was called back in and to JP's annoyance she and Andy also knew each other – they exchanged a few friendly words about their mutual village and its exciting new bus shelter.

'Sit down, please, Mrs – would you, please,' said JP crisply. And then, 'Mix me another alginate, nurse.'

Tammy began measuring powder and water, while Andy watched from the door. JP loaded a new impression tray and was about to insert it when Andy interrupted.

'Actually, sorry, would you mind if I did it?'

JP threw his arms up. 'What? Oh, go on then, hurry up before it sets.' And then to Mrs Woodward, 'Sorry, Mrs Wood, the lab boy wants a turn.'

Andy brought Mrs Woodward forward in the chair so that she wasn't lying back, and put the filled tray into her mouth, angling and thumbing it into the upper palate with gentle precision.

'Is that OK?' he asked. Mrs Woodward nodded. While he waited for the alginate to set, Andy further irritated JP by giving a short talk on the best way to take dental impressions. 'Alginate mixed with cold water can be uncomfortable, especially for those with amalgam restorations. I'd suggest mixing with lukewarm water – it's a much better experience for the patient.'

JP ignored him and looked out of the window, bridging his fingers and humming 'Bright Eyes'.

'Breathe steadily through your nose,' Andy told Mrs Woodward, tapping the rubbery material under her lip. 'Not long now.'

Mrs Woodward nodded. It was clearly much less of an ordeal this time – none of the frantic gagging of the previous session. All was calm when JP suddenly said, 'I say, nurse, do your Prince Charles impression.'

I shook my head. 'No, I can't.'

'I think it would be entertaining for Mrs Wood,' he said. 'Take her mind off it.'

I did a diluted version and Mrs Woodward opened her eyes wide to indicate her appreciation. Andy Nicolello smiled politely and, after telling Mrs Woodward to rinse out her mouth, inspected the impression. 'This looks fine,' he said, wrapping it in wet paper. 'Right, let's get a wax bite, and we're done.'

After Andy and Mrs Woodward had gone, JP complained about his attitude. 'I'll give him "lukewarm water and a wax bite" – arrogant little B.' JP never liked saying the word but often wanted to call people bastards. 'I wish Mercurial would stop sending him. Whatever happened to old Mr Burridge?'

JP and Tammy left for the weekend in unexpected drizzle, both in grumpy moods. I tidied the surgery and thought about Andy Nicolello. The last time I'd seen him he was helping his brother dismantle a shed in my grandmother's garden and the two of them had carried the timber, bit by bit, across the fields to the shack where they lived. She'd given them an unwanted coffee table and a toy garage. I remembered being quite frightened of them. Neither spoke; they only grunted at each other.

I phoned my friend Melody at the nurses' quarters in Luton and Dunstable Hospital.

'Do you remember Andy Nicolello?' I asked her.

'Yes.'

'He works for a dental laboratory now and calls in at the surgery almost daily.'

'He can't do,' she said. 'He lives in a bus at the Midland Red depot – eats scraps from the Golden Egg and dresses like a tramp.'

'Well, his life must've taken a turn for the better, because he's now a respected technician who dines on shop-bought sandwiches and wears a Fred Perry.'

'Do you speak to him?'

'Yes, I spoke to him today and he's completely polite and normal,' I said, which he was – considering he came from a family that made mine look like the Leadbetters.

4. The Nuclear Bunker

The next morning a letter came addressed to my mother. I was a bit puzzled by its arrival at my flat but also excited to have a bona-fide excuse to call her. I loved speaking to my mother on the phone – it felt luxurious and adult.

'A letter has come here for you,' I said.

She was still cross about the spoon, I could tell.

'Oh, well,' she said, 'you'd better open it.'

So I did.

'It's from Curious Minds Day Nursery in Victoria Park.'

'And . . . ?'

' "Dear Mrs Vogel-Benson-Holt," ' I began.

'Yes,' said my mother, impatient.

' "We are delighted to inform you that in view of your recent move to the area, we are delighted to offer your son Daniel John Henry Holt a place in the day nursery, starting immediately." '

'Gosh, was that two "delighted"s?' said my mother.

'Oh, yes, they are delighted to be delighted.'

'Well, that's wonderful news,' she said.

Curious Minds was a fifteen-minute walk up the hill from the surgery and stood opposite the park very near the traffic lights which had stuck on red the morning Mr Holt moved me into town. It was much sought-after and my mother had jumped the queue due to having a local address.

'I hope you don't mind my telling a white lie,' she said. 'It's just that it's the best nursery for miles.'

'Of course I don't mind, but what's so good about it?'

'Well, for a start, it shares a nuclear bunker with the accountant next door.'

'Jacobs the accountant?'

'Yes, Jacobs, that's it – but it's not just the nuclear bunker,' said my mother, 'it's a great nursery. Danny will have number-knowledge and high self-esteem before he starts proper school.'

My mother wondered if I might consider collecting Danny once or twice a week to give her a bit of breathing space. I jumped at it.

'Oh, yes, I'd love to,' I said. 'I'm going a bit mad here on my own, I'm so lonely.'

'You should read some novels or write a play.'

'I'm reading *Woman's Own* back issues. We get it for the waiting room – it's marvellous.'

She groaned.

It was hard for her to hear this. I had been an avid reader; a bookworm, bookaholic, librarian – call it what you will – as much as the next brainy young person, having been exposed, no, subjected, to the classics, the southern gothicists, the modernists, the post-modernists, the angry young men and more. But there I was at eighteen, an ordinary young working woman; I had life to live, *real* life. I had no use for men harpooning whales to death, pouring leperous distilments into other people's ears, or Marge Piercy. The words that truly met my needs were to be found in the magazines in the waiting room. The world depicted therein, scattered with personal itching, erratic hair and special offers, was not only instructive, but unexpectedly soothing. I'd been unaware of it up to then – my mother being too intellectual to concern herself with the sort of things that went on inside those pages. Oh, but my goodness, how she'd missed out! How much nicer her life would have been if instead of punishing us all with Herman Melville, James Joyce and all that terrible Shakespeare, she'd known that sometimes people missed their own weddings or turned up at the wrong church (but saw the funny side afterwards), and that half a lemon dispelled fridge odours.

The practice had both *Woman* and *Woman's Own* delivered for the waiting room. The two were quite similar: *Woman*, 'the world's greatest weekly for women', cost 15p, while *Woman's Own*, Britain's 'top-selling magazine for women', was a snip at just 14p.

These facts were printed at the top of each. The former's claim to be the greatest irritated slightly, whereas I found the latter's more tangible 'top-selling' claim both impressive and reassuring.

Woman's Own encouraged me to change my flat from a boring wheat-coloured box of convenience into a vibrant French bistro – on a shoestring. It exposed me to special shampoo for brunettes, high-roughage breakfast cereals, clothing catalogues and the lesser royals. And, to borrow a phrase from the magazine itself, I was pleased as punch.

The writers knew that life could be tricky and lonely and painful. They knew you didn't earn a king's ransom, and that popping a sensible shirt dress over a colourful bikini turned office wear into beach wear.

I did wish there was more humour, though, more of the tone that you found in the readers' letters, which although sometimes judgemental, self-congratulatory or pathetic, were often at the same time quite funny.

I tried to explain the appeal to my mother on the phone but she thought it nonsense and then remembered with a jolt that she'd been told about Jacobs the accountant's nuclear bunker in strictest confidence. I mustn't gossip about it, she said, because Jacobs didn't want all and sundry arriving on his doorstep in the event of a nuclear warning, and barging past little kids to get to safety.

'OK, I'll keep it to myself.'

'Also, Lizzie,' she said, 'never admit to being lonely.'

The days went by and I learned the ropes quickly, and apart from the odd bumping accident or spillage on to the maroon rubber disc caused by the over-crowdedness of the surgery, all went well. There was an awkward pause when Tammy started to experiment with housewifery and came in only for odd half-days here and there, and we started to compete. We'd race to greet the patients as they arrived. We'd try to get the bib on or take it off, to mix amalgam, hold the aspirator, or perform surgical tasks – before the other had a chance. Don't ask me why we started doing this, it just evolved. It was quite inelegant, and sometimes dangerous. There was a terrifying incident in which JP tripped over one of us while holding the hand-piece (drill). He was supposed to take his foot off the pedal if things like that happened, but he'd gone into a catatonic state because we'd got the heater on. And another, when Tammy and I tried to slam beakers of mouthwash into the cup holder at the same time and it had been as brutal and desperate as opposing players in a rounders match racing to touch base. JP had had to shout at us, 'Nurses, please!'

It came to a head when I inadvertently used a blue ink biro to write a name (*Mrs Lydia Marshall – Insp.*) in the appointment book and Tammy asked me, tearfully, what I was planning to do if Mrs Lydia Marshall rang up to cancel.

'You won't be able to erase the name,' she said.

'Well,' I replied, 'then I'll resign.'

But this didn't go on for long. Tammy apologized for her mood swings. 'I'm sorry I'm being so snippy,' she said. 'It's the upheaval of trying to settle into this new life with JP – it's affecting my mental balance.'

I sympathized. We'd read the same article about how moving house was upsetting – like jet lag, only worse – and that even the driest hair could go greasy overnight and vice versa. 'Don't worry,' I said, 'my mother used to suffer with her moods.'

Moods notwithstanding, I preferred it when Tammy was in the surgery. There were certain jobs I disliked – wiping the cactuses down, waking JP from his naps, cleaning his spectacles and, worst of all, I hated break times with him – talking to him and feeding him his cigarettes – all of which I had to do when I was in sole charge. One break time when it had been just the two of us and I was feeding him a Hamlet while we had our coffee, he returned to the subject of his son's vasectomy.

'I know you must be thinking, "It's Junior's life," and up to him whether or not he procreates,' he said, 'but it has hit me hard, nurse. I don't think you could possibly understand.'

'Do you think it's because you want a grandchild?' I said.

'A grandchild, yes, of course, but it's more complicated than that, nurse. It's the sudden realization that my line – my bloodline – will die out.'

He sucked the Hamlet like an orphaned calf on a bottle and almost had it out of my fingers.

'Your quest for immortality has been thwarted,' I said, having recently read that this was essentially what drove the species forward.

'Yes, that's about it.' When he spoke, I could see the blue veins on the underside of his tongue as he rolled it – like a ham horn on a plate of mixed hors d'oeuvres – and exhaled through it.

'If you know that, why can't you just have another baby yourself?' I asked. 'With Tammy.'

'Tammy hates children – surely you've noticed?'

'Other people's, yes,' I said, 'but she might like her own.'

'She's a bit long in the tooth for all that, anyway.'

'My mother is the same age and she had a baby recently,' I said. 'Or you could go for a test-tube one, like Louise Brown.'

'Hmm?' he said, puffing away. 'Thank you, nurse.'

He took a few more puffs and left me in the staffroom holding the panatella. I heard him trot upstairs humming Bach's 'Air on the G String' or, as my mother would want me to point out, not Bach's – as such – but Wilhelm's arrangement of the second movement in the Orchestral Suite Number 3.

I was tempted to take a puff on the little cigar myself – it was most pleasant-smelling – but the end was the usual soggy mess. I stubbed it out, lit myself an ordinary cigarette and gazed out of the window, and I was just imagining a test-tube baby when I heard the door go and the call, 'Mercurial!' It was Andy Nicolello. I cantered downstairs as fast as I could.

'Hello,' I said, 'you're early.'

'I've got Mrs Woodward's partial upper.'

Before we could have our usual daily smile Mrs Woodward herself stumbled in. Tammy then came marching in too and announced for all to hear that she'd come back to work because she was sick and tired of throwing toys for the cat and answering the door to gypsies. Andy passed me the dental delivery and left. I watched through the window as he strode to the company moped, pulled on his helmet, flipped the visor down and disappeared into the traffic on Station Road.

Mrs Woodward had brought a leaflet for JP, which she'd obviously got from her vicar husband, entitled *Finding Acceptance through God*, and as soon as she had slumped into the chair, she handed it to him. He stared at it for a moment, and put it aside without making any comment.

'Right, let's try this new denture, shall we,' he said, and he angled it into her mouth.

I always felt it slightly intrusive watching a patient as they explored the altered landscape of their mouth after the fitting of a new denture, crown or filling. Rootling around with their tongue, concerned, blinking, assessing, nervous. It seemed so personal, so intimate, like watching someone eating a yoghurt.

Mrs Woodward's new denture fitted like a glove and she declared the breakage of the old one a blessing in disguise. 'I hadn't known a denture could feel this comfortable,' she said, sounding just like an advert, and with a new confidence she leaned forward, took up the leaflet and waved it in JP's direction. 'If ever you feel you'd like to talk things through, my husband would be more than happy—'

JP waved it aside, snatched Mrs Woodward's chin and pushed her back into the chair. 'That won't be necessary, Mrs Wood. I'd like you to be the first to know,' he said, 'my partner and I have decided to try for a baby of our own.'

Mrs Woodward's mouth fell open and her eyes strained to look at Tammy who stood up too quickly, steadied herself on the desk and sat back down again.

'Now, close your mouth, please.'

I didn't see Tammy for a while after the announcement of the baby; she had a few days at home 'taking cactus cuttings'. But when she returned all seemed well.

'So, you're trying for a baby,' I said.

'Yah, absolutely,' said Tammy. 'JP's got me on a fertility programme – I can't eat seeds or legumes or liver sausage, I can't go near caged birds, sheep, or people with diseases –' she listed them on her fingers – 'and I have to put my feet up.'

'Are you partial to liver sausage?' I asked.

'Are you kidding?' she shrieked. 'The only reason we went to the Ardèche last year was for the andouillette.'

'Bad luck,' I said.

'Good news though, JP's agreed we should get married.'

'Well, congratulations! Let me know if there's anything I can do,' I said, as if there'd been a death in the family.

5.   The Hoover Aristocrat

I had long telephone conversations with Melody who had access to a pay phone in the nurses' home at Luton and Dunstable that never asked for any money after the first coin. She loved Luton, she told me, especially the nightlife, and said the men there were streets ahead of Leicester men sexually – but though I loved to hear this, I never asked for details. She was particularly looking for a Virgo because they were good with money and people but avoiding a Libra because they were greedy and bad with people. I also spoke to my mother on the phone regularly because she was frivolous in that regard and would ring up to ask whether I'd borrowed her copy of *Roget's Thesaurus*, because Jack needed it for his essays, etc. I often took these calls in the surgery because the flex was so long and the chair so comfortable. I made the miraculous discovery that if someone rang me I could answer on the upstairs extension, hang up, run downstairs, pick up the receiver in the surgery and they'd still be there on the line.

These calls became important to me because I had surprisingly few visitors to the flat in the early days – my sister never seemed to fancy the two-bus journey – and no invitations out except from Tammy, and even they'd dried up once she was on the fertility programme. And whatever my mother might say about never admitting it, I was lonely. Adulthood had come upon me like the creeping darkness of night and I felt lost. As a child I'd have wandered about until I found someone to play with, whether their parents liked it or not, or a building site to run around, or an injured bird to nurse back to health, and that would have been me happy.

I wished I could go for a dog walk, because I was lonely not only for people but for dogs, and the sight of horses and cows, the early spring hedgerows alive with young sparrows and buds and new green leaves. Now all I saw were the khaki limbs and hairy, dust-covered leaves of Tammy's violets and cactuses, and the occasional, window-bound geranium or fake rose – whose petals folded back like the ears of an angry mule – and all I had to look forward to were potted daisies on dark steps and sunless streets, with velvety middles that were threadbare like old cushions. And the occasional sweet William, whose foliage would slowly rot in the water of the cut-glass vase.

And now all I had to do was trail around the shops looking at money-wasting, time-wasting, life-wasting rubbish, or issue vague invitations to busy people who only wanted to get drunk somehow, somewhere.

I offered the use of the Hoover Aristocrat to my sister. She thanked me but declined, claiming to enjoy going to the launderette where, apparently, fellow nurses and trainee doctors played 'Who Am I?' and '20 Questions' while their washes went through, and then helped each other with the folding. It was a student ritual I wouldn't understand.

Even my mother – who seemed like a frequent visitor – was actually most interested in the quiet solitude of my empty flat while I was downstairs, and used it to work on her novel in peace before collecting baby Danny from Curious Minds.

Andy Nicolello called at the surgery most afternoons to deliver or collect dental items, riding an old-fashioned moped with a huge box on the back featuring Mercurial's winged-feet emblem, and L-plates. One day I looked up to smile 'hello/goodbye' and to my astonishment he blew me a kiss. I caught it in my hands and then, realizing how silly it was, had to turn away, shy. It was as though he had dragged me into a silent movie with him. And then he was gone and the door clanged me back to my senses.

Tammy had noticed and though she smiled, she told me later that JP would hate it if I started going out with him. 'Oh, my gosh, please do not start dating Andy from Mercurial,' was how she put it. 'He really isn't suitable.'

She told me Andy was a radical. He'd protested outside the

Swan Hotel because the BDA hadn't invited the technicians to the annual winter dinner dance. 'The dentists and their wives arrived in their finery and there he was, with a placard.'

'Oh.'

'And JP literally can't stand him.'

'Hmm, I think it's mutual,' I said. 'I mean, Andy probably feels the same.'

'I know what mutual means, thank you,' said Tammy, which surprised me.

That blown kiss plus JP's theoretical disapproval plus general boredom/loneliness plus hormones urging me to procreate plus my athlete's foot had turned me into an idiot and soon I was brushing my hair and applying lipgloss after tea break in preparation for the thirty-second encounter I might have with Andy Nicolello. And, if there was no collection or delivery, or old Mr Burridge called instead, I'd be devastated and would will his old ailment to flare up and prevent him from making the next one.

'How's your phlebitis, Mr Burridge?' I'd ask, as if reminding him of it might bring it on. And finally one afternoon, when Andy appeared for a late pick-up, I found myself boasting of my plan to paint some shelves in the flat.

'Cherry red,' I said.

'What, you live upstairs, here?' he said.

'Yes.'

'On your own?'

'Yes. Come up and have a look.'

Andy very much liked my vision for the flat (French bistro). He liked everything – television, bathroom, views – but most of all he liked the Hoover Aristocrat and he squatted beside it as if it were a vintage car or a poorly alien we'd found in the cellar. And even though it was far, far too soon, I heard myself say, 'Bring a load of laundry over any time,' and he laughed.

'No,' he said, 'I couldn't.'

But after we'd had a cup of coffee and just before he left, he asked if I were serious about the laundry.

'Yes,' I said, 'deadly.'

I could never go out with Andy, I reminded myself, as through the window I watched him straddle the Mercurial moped and zoom off into the traffic. I couldn't care less what Tammy thought, or JP, but however handsome, likeable and normal he seemed nowadays, I could only befriend him privately. I couldn't go out with him publicly. I needed someone normal and so did he – God, he really did. I would never do. I'd never cope.

I must impress upon you that Andy was from the most famously eccentric family in the whole of the county if not the Midlands. I mean, there were probably worse families, but his was known about; celebrated, even. The worst of the rumours held it that his parents had entered into a suicide pact involving gas or cyanide and that one of them had tried to swerve it at the last moment only to die slowly and in agony. The two of us going out would be like when two really flamboyant people get together, or two extremely shy people, two clowns, two punks, two long-distance runners, two jailbirds, two space freaks, two artists – all the people around nudging each other and saying, 'Pity the children,' and that kind of thing. And apart from that, I couldn't see what we had in common.

I tried to picture us side by side, walking to the Princess Charlotte or the Arts Café, where the tables were in the shape of artists' palettes and the chipped mugs all had star signs and the customers were arty and unusual, but still all I could imagine was people shaking their heads and grimacing. I wondered if we might become close enough for me to put Abe from Abraham's Motors on to him, who was apparently becoming a dab hand at shame-counselling and dragging people out of the shadows of family madness, via positive chit-chat.

As luck would have it, Andy Nicolello's first laundry visit coincided with an impromptu visit from my mother and Abe. A mixed-coloureds load had just finished and he'd held his shirts up to the window, impressed, like a woman in an advert, and was hanging them over the rack when they appeared. I made the introductions. Abe, this is Andy; Andy, this is my mother; Mum, this is Andy; Andy, this is Abe.

There was high excitement because Abe's porcelain-bonded jacket crown (upper left two) had pinged out that morning while he'd been flossing. I must say, I admired Abe for flossing so thoroughly, when most men seemed to think it unnecessary.

The problem, and the reason they'd come to me, was that Abe's dentist, Dr Chandra, was based at the Government Dental College of Bangalore and Abe had no plans to go there in the foreseeable future.

'I wonder,' my mother said, 'do you think you might have a go at sticking it back in, rather than him having to fly all the way to Bangalore, or go on bended knee to some hideous old dentist?'

'If the crown and post are still intact, it's just a case of mixing a bit of cement,' I said.

And after some coffee, we wandered down to the surgery, switched the lights on and got Abe comfy in the chair. I turned the crown over in my hands. It was in perfect condition, as was the tooth post. I passed it to Andy who picked about inside the crown with a probe to remove the old cement. I mixed some new and gently, exaggeratedly carefully, stuck it back in. I held it in place for two full minutes and stared around the room, just the way JP did. I mentioned the weather and studied the skin around Abe's handsome eyes. I checked the bite with articulating paper and all was well. Abe took this in his stride. My mother seemed proud.

'Isn't she wonderful, Abe?' she said.

'Yes, she is,' he agreed.

Back upstairs, Andy adjusted his laundry on the rack while I made more coffee.

'How long until you qualify?' Abe asked, inspecting his smile in the mirror. 'Maybe I will finally leave Dr Chandra.'

'Oh, no, I'll never qualify – I'm just a dental assistant,' I said. 'I will only ever assist.'

'Lizzie's the type to paddle along with the tide for years and then suddenly win a dog-photography competition or some-thing,' my mother chipped in.

'Oh, you're a photographer?' said Abe.

'No,' I replied, 'she just means I'm not qualified at anything.'

My mother chose this moment to heap praise on my younger brother, Jack, who had been offered a place at the University College London and wouldn't have to paddle along waiting for a dog-photography competition.

'UCL,' she emphasized, 'where they display the preserved head of Jeremy Bentham in a special box,' as if this made the place even more prestigious. 'Jeremy Bentham the philosopher.'

'How's your training going?' I asked Abe.

'It's going very well, thank you,' he said, in a most considered manner.

'He's a marvel,' said my mother. 'He's cured my shoplifting.'

My cheeks flushed, I turned in panic to Andy to indicate that she was talking in jest, but he was nodding.

'That's good news,' he said, 'well done.'

And so I didn't have to apologize or try to pass it off as a joke. I was able to say how pleased I was too.

'I know,' she said. 'God almighty, we've had some scrapes.'

And we had. Not a month previously we'd been in Woolco and an assistant had followed us out of the store, calling, 'Excuse me, madam, excuse me.' And we'd both run full pelt into the car park with shopping bags containing two bottles of stolen Scotch and a block of Red Leicester cheese. When the assistant caught up with us at the exit it turned out my mother had left her cheque book in the store.

'Whew,' he said, 'I thought I'd never catch you.'

We had thanked him and laughed and said something about being in a hurry to get home.

'How have you cured her?' I asked Abe.

'I contacted her subconscious and found the reason she was shoplifting,' he said.

'And why was she?'

'I can't discuss my client.'

'Shops have got cameras, Lizzie,' said my mother. 'Hidden cameras.'

This really was very good news, not least because it meant I could go shopping with her and not have to constantly check my bag, pockets or hood.

Abe tried to give me some money to thank me for cementing his crown but my mother refused on my behalf – for legal reasons – so he insisted on taking us all around the corner to the Raj Restaurant for a lunch of spicy potato pastries, which was very nice. Abe kept pretending the crown had fallen out, which was funny the first few times, but my mother died laughing every time even though she'd had hardly anything to drink. Finally, they got up to leave.

'Remember to write this up in your journal, darling,' she told me, 'under G for guerrilla dentistry.'

6.   The Missing Premolars

One Sunday around then, my sister came and I served her a trad-
itional roast with all the trimmings, albeit no meat. She'd heard on
the grapevine that our father was planning to spend a year in the
USA, teaching at a management college in Massachusetts. His
wife had announced this possibility to the parents of a friend of
someone who knew my sister. So she now knew too, and though
my father and his wife didn't know that she knew, she was seriously thinking she might go with them.

This didn't interest me much but she was keen to examine the
subject.

'I quite fancy a year in America,' she said.

I only wanted to talk about Andy. I asked her what she recalled
of the Nicolello family, and of him. I was beginning to wonder
whether his good looks in adulthood might offset the weirdness of
his upbringing. That kind of thing.

'Andy Nicolello,' I said, 'do you remember him?'

'Rings a bell.'

'He was one of the Nicolellos who lived near the soap factory.'

'The Flintstones!' she said. 'Oh my God, I'd forgotten about them.'

'What about them?' I asked.

'Well, they were odd – didn't they live like cavemen?'

'They didn't have a telly, that was all.'

'No, it was more than that. They were bizarre.'

'In what way?' I pressed. 'What did they do?'

'Oh my God, the parents, the mum and dad,' she said excitedly,
then whispered, 'and oh my God, Lizzie – weren't they the suicide-
pact couple?'

'Yes, but the story is probably exaggerated. Anyway, he's really
good-looking now,' I said, 'and has a great job and loves telly.'

'You're not going out with him, are you?'

'Not as such. Why? Do you think it's a bad idea?'

'Yes, I do. How old is he?'

'Twenty-two, twenty-three.'

'Look – you're weird, he's weird, together you'll be a million times weirder. Your mutual weirdness will reflect for ever – like mirrors that face each other.' That was the way my sister thought and spoke.

I was a bit taken aback by this, to be quite honest. Sure, I was a secret non-drinker, disliked chips, didn't like eating in public, and didn't follow fashion quite as closely as other girls my age – but who didn't have a few quirks? And anyway, how did my sister become so normal that she could judge me? I changed the subject by reminding her that she was six years overdue for a dental check-up. She knew it.

'Is Wintergreen any good?' she asked.

'He's OK. Shall I book you in?'

'I suppose so.'

I was anxious when a week or so later my sister came in to see JP. Early experiences had turned her into a dentist-hater, plus she had a fear of throwing her head back and having things put in her mouth.

'Would you like to come through now, Miss Vogel,' I said, upbeat but secretly on high alert. She straightened the magazines and came through, unsmiling, then slid into the chair. After I'd put the bib loosely around her neck, she drummed the armrests and looked from side to side.

JP entered. 'Hullo, hullo,' he boomed, looking over his specs at her dental card. I'd written *Lizzie Vogel's sister* at the top.

'So, you're Lizzie Vogel's sister and we're going to take a little look at you, are we?'

Annoyed at being addressed in this manner and from behind, she twisted around in the chair.

'Are you speaking to me?' she said.

JP and I exchanged a look.

I'd filled out the card before she arrived and had found writing her details, which I knew so well, unexpectedly moving. I knew everything about this girl. I could mark up the tooth chart in the most exacting detail. I knew for instance that she had a tiny, slightly discoloured, distal silicate filling in her upper right two, that JP might suggest replacing.

I knew that, some years ago at aged thirteen and a half, she'd had both upper fours removed in preparation for orthodontic treatment she'd never completed.

My sister's name is Thomasin, after Thomasin Yeobright from Thomas Hardy's *The Return of the Native*. It's pronounced Tamsin, but she shortens it to Tina because when we were small someone struggling to recall her name landed on 'Tina' by accident and from then on that's what she's been. My mother only ever planned for it to be shortened to Tommie. Writing her birth date – which was and still is the most important day of the year, it being her birthday and the gateway to the autumn – I'd recalled the party games she loved, which were always taken seriously: picking up dried peas with a straw, hiding and seeking, pinning tails on donkeys, musical chairs, that kind of thing. She was an accomplished apple-bobber, knowing to go into the water hard, breathing out robustly, forcing the apple to the bottom of the receptacle so that she could sink both upper and lower teeth into it, and come up with it properly impaled. It's no good mouthing at the apple, trying to get hold of it as it floats. Only a shark could achieve that, or some kind of water snake. I'd never known her beaten, and yet, here she was now – two missing teeth, an uncorrected class two occlusion and, most poignantly of all, a nervous patient.

I'd marked her card *NP* which was our secret code for *Nervous Patient* and this I pointed out to JP. He shrugged and opened his hands – he'd forgotten the meaning. So I scrawled *Nervous Patient* across the top. I didn't want him assuming she'd have the same impressive pain threshold and cooperative attitude as I had – just because we were blood relatives.

'She's a nervous patient,' I said, annoyed with both of them.

JP moved to the treatment table and looked down at her. 'Is that right, Thomasin – you're a nervous patient?'

'She goes by Tina,' I said. I had written *Tina* in brackets on the card but that was too much for JP to cope with.

'I wouldn't say I'm nervous – I just dislike dentists.'

'Not all dentists,' I laughed.

'I hope not,' said JP.

'I had trouble with the previous one, and it put me off.'

'You went to . . .' He glanced at her card again. 'Ah, Cunningham, Pope and Fisher. And who treated you there?'

'Mr Fisher.' As Tina said it, I braced myself.

Mr Cunningham had been our dentist during childhood and had been perfectly nice – as nice as a private dentist would ever be to a family losing its toehold and sliding bumpily down the social ladder – and we'd enjoyed his gentle rebukes and jokes about us eating too many Spangles and we liked his glamorous eyebrows. I must say he put in an inordinate amount of amalgam into our hundred or so teeth and had sold my mother all sorts of mini-brushes and mouthwash for the periodontal gum condition brought on by all her pregnancies, pills and alcohol, but he was nice.

In the mid-1970s, though, my family were among the first to be relegated when the practice took on a junior colleague. Mr Fisher was a divorcee, he wore his hair in a middle parting, and his tunic was so tight you could see his buttocks clench as he leaned over. I couldn't believe someone who looked as though he'd lick the gravy off a plate and tease a dog could be a dentist and be permitted to look so closely into another person's body. He seemed wrong for it.

Mr Fisher had an interest in children's dentistry, especially orthodontics, and showed an aptitude for making parents conscious of slight misalignments and crookedness in their children's teeth.

'Look at this overcrowding,' he might say, or, 'it would only take one hockey ball to smash those prominent front teeth right in.' He didn't worry about the long-term effect robust orthodontic treatment might have on the child's bite, or other details. He was only after plaudits from his colleagues for bringing in such lucrative work – and was soon made a partner. Thinking about it now, perhaps he was a Libra.

Anyway, Mr Fisher joined a list of men who exploited our mother for their sexual gratification and/or material gain. That on its own wouldn't usually provoke violence – those men were often despised by the end of it but usually got away unharmed. Mr Fisher, though, made the mistake of involving my sister's teeth.

What did he do? Firstly, he convinced my mother that Tina would benefit greatly from orthodontic treatment to bring her upper incisors back into line after years of thumb-sucking had protuberated them.

'How would she benefit?' asked my mother, looking at my sister with a cocked head, and thinking as she did that her little girl was perfect with those teeth exactly as they were, resting on her plump lower lip as if she were waiting for the answers to life's questions.

Mr Fisher insisted that the extraction of two upper teeth followed by twelve months wearing a simple appliance would catch her a better class of husband – that was how he put it. My sister quite liked being the centre of an exciting new thing – her family around her and highly attentive. I could see the attraction of it all and don't blame her for going wholeheartedly along with it.

My mother wasn't in a position to pay for the suggested treatment, having had one financial blow after another, and with us getting more and more expensive to keep. Perhaps she'd find a dentist to do this work on the NHS, she told Mr Fisher, but he wouldn't hear of it. We were loyal patients, and he'd do my sister's orthodontics on the NHS, even though the practice generally didn't. She mustn't worry her pretty, sexy, woozy little head about it.

Soon after that, Mr Fisher dropped in at our house on his way to a nearby riverbank for a spot of night fishing, only he never left our house and didn't go fishing. Instead he and our mother got drunk and had sex on the carpet. He had no dignity about it and they didn't even close the sitting-room door and our dog wandered in.

For once, we children hoped very much he wouldn't become our new man at the helm. He was a dentist with a grunty voice and a middle parting, and he wore awful tight jeans.

My sister was in the chair the following week and Mr Fisher administered a local anaesthetic via four injections; two into the roof of her mouth and two into the soft tissue under her lip. After that, he suggested that my mother and I might like to step into the waiting room, but Tina said we mustn't go. So we remained around the chair, like the family at a deathbed, as Mr Fisher extracted two of her healthy adult teeth – and it was terrible. The extractions were straightforward enough – good, single-rooted premolars, cleanly brought out – but there was something wrong in the air. It felt as if this were a tableau to symbolize every dreadful thing we'd been through, except it wasn't our mother being dragged about and manhandled – this time the evil had settled upon my sister and it was in her mouth with forceps, brutally assaulting her, but simultaneously smiling and clenching its buttocks. Tina and I did not take our eyes off each other, even as Mr Fisher twisted the teeth out. We didn't even blink. She gripped our mother's hand but looked at me. It was frightful. All the time I knew she was thinking she'd been a fool to agree to this – and I thought the same.

We drove home, the three of us in tears. My sister, changed somehow, was trembling. And my mother, knowing she'd made some awful bargain, could hardly keep the car in a straight line on the road. I suggested we call in at the Travelling Man for a cup of something – it was out of character but I felt we might otherwise die. My mother drove on, breathing through clenched teeth and occasionally saying, 'All shall be well, all shall be well,' which someone had taught her to say when things were not.

Soon after my sister's gums had healed Mr Fisher got back together with his ex-wife, Anthea, and for that reason and others, our mother was less keen to have sex with him. They had an argument in our garden. It was difficult to get an appointment with him to have my sister's appliance fitted – he was suddenly very busy. Eventually, we went to the surgery without even having an appointment because it was all beginning to seem a bit odd and my mother was feeling guilty and sick about the whole thing.

She was told by the receptionist, 'Mr Fisher regrets that he won't be able to fit Thomasin's appliance until you've settled your account for the consultation, the surgical treatment and the manufacture of the orthodontic appliance.'

The bill was over two hundred pounds, which is thousands in today's money and was millions in non-money terms, and every drop of blood in my mother's head drained away and even her lips went white. She wobbled. A strong smell of pepper filled my nose and my eyes brimmed with tears.

Mr Fisher supposed that our mother would be alone in understanding what had transpired, that only she would be able to follow this saga – its offers and arrangements and reprisals – and that she would feel ashamed and disappear. He supposed her children too young, naive, innocent to appreciate the rules. But it was not so. We'd deciphered games more complex than this one, and with higher stakes.

We retired to the waiting room and sat quietly in its regency splendour. My eyes landed upon a beautiful print of Gimcrack the grey thoroughbred on Newmarket Downs, originally painted by Stubbs. Did horses look like that in Stubbs's day? Or was he like all those cave painters, and just couldn't do realistic horse necks?

My sister got up out of her chair.

'Won't be a moment,' she said, and walked across the parquet hall to Fisher's surgery door. She was thirteen years old, tall and strong, and had held a snake, steered a horse no one else could ride, and swallowed a wasp that had stung her throat in passing and meant she had to wait at the doctor's in case her tubes all closed down. They didn't. She'd beaten bigger men than Mr Fisher. We peered into the hall as she opened the surgery door and asked him for her orthodontic appliance.

'Could you give me my brace, please?' she said.

Mr Fisher called out to the receptionist in a slightly panicked voice, 'Jean, could you help this patient a moment, please.'

'Where is my appliance?' repeated my sister. 'You may as well give it to me.'

Mr Fisher's colleagues now appeared in the hallway, scratching their heads. Mr Cunningham, our old dentist, approached him with his hand up to his face and spoke quietly into his knuckles, as if he were coughing.

'No!' said Mr Fisher. 'Mrs Vogel must settle the account first.'

'But you said, very clearly, that you'd treat me on the National Health,' said Tina. 'I heard you – we all heard you.'

'I did *not* say that.' Mr Fisher gazed around. He was a good actor, and it was almost as though he believed himself.

'You're a liar,' said my sister. 'Tell the truth or I'm going to make a huge scene.'

'I did not offer to treat you on the NHS,' lied Mr Fisher again.

And so Tina smacked him across the face with the back of her hand – it was a good-looking strike, which spun his face to the side and made the audience gasp. I think about that smack often – it's nice to be able to write about it. It must have been considerably more painful than a slap. With a slap, the travelling hand, being slightly concave, collects air, which buffers the impact. A back-handed smack is more like a punch, in terms of pain.

'Now get me my appliance or you will be sorry,' said Tina.

The nurse scampered around and then approached my sister, handing her the appliance which was clamped on to a plaster model of her upper jaw.

'Thank you.'

Tina removed the appliance from the model, dropped it and crushed it beneath her foot like a cigarette end.

She looked up at Mr Fisher – as did several people. There was quite a crowd now, as patients who'd been in the waiting room had come into the hallway.

'Men like you disgust me. You are disgusting.' And with that she threw the plaster model at his medical light and it exploded with a flash and the room went dim.

None of us ever returned to Cunningham, Pope & Fisher, our

mother never paid the bill, and my sister never got her teeth sorted. But I always hoped the gossip reached his wife, Anthea.

'And what did Mr Fisher do to upset you?' asked JP.

I butted in. 'Mr Fisher didn't do anything . . . she just found him a bit brusque.'

'I'm afraid I ended up having to hit him.'

'Oh.' JP lifted his head to recall a fragment of gossip. 'Aha, the famous slap. That was you, was it? We heard about that.' And he shot a look at me, and then at Tammy.

Tina settled back in the chair now, relaxed. She'd announced herself and knew she'd get the best of treatment. JP passed over the card and called out her tooth chart to me, quite unnecessarily.

'Your upper fours have been extracted,' he told her, as if she might not have realized.

'Yes,' said Tina, 'I know.'

7. Masonic Improvements

Things started to improve all round. I was gaining confidence in the surgery, and was now fully adept at managing the instruments and equipment. Also, I had finally learned from Tammy how to hold patients' arms down – quite forcibly if necessary – during treatments to prevent the seizing of the hand-piece, which could actually pose a risk to JP's life. I was good at wiping them down afterwards (the patients) and becoming quite skilful at reapplying lipstick and make-up to shaky-handed ladies if need be. Since becoming an avid magazine reader I'd collected a little bag of free make-up samples especially for this purpose and could sort them out in a trice. Once, in an early attempt, I'd been a tiny bit heavy-handed with Rimmel's 'Thunderclap' eyeshadow, and a patient's relative had phoned the surgery later to enquire about the 'bruising around her eyes'.

Another time, early on, I'd straightened a man's shirt and tie after a gruelling extraction, brushed his hair out of his face with my hand, and wiped the dots of blood from the corners of his mouth. I fell slightly in love with him, even though I knew that was probably wrong of me.

Surgery etiquette was soon second nature to me. I knew, for instance, never to laugh at someone's teeth, especially when they removed them. Never to heave or gasp, even at the worst, most rotten stumps. Never to underestimate how important a person's teeth were. I quickly overtook JP and Tammy in this regard even though I was by far their junior.

Also, life in the flat became a bit nicer and I was less lonely now that I had Andy popping in from time to time with his laundry. And Tammy, who'd been given a book on optimizing her fertility, was now enjoying researching ovulation and conception and wedding venues and a much calmer presence. Meanwhile my mother's novel was coming along in leaps and bounds – a whole episode of her life, involving a beagle and Princess Margaret, had come back to her in vivid detail and was now being cleverly incorporated into the middle section. Allegorically.

Just then, though, Bill Turner, JP's dentist pal from up the road, put a spanner in the works. Due to unusual plaque build-up he had started coming in every few weeks to have his teeth cleaned with JP's ultrasonic scaler. I liked Bill. He'd been evacuated to the Midlands as a teenager after narrowly escaping a bomb in the East End, and had been fostered by a well-to-do couple who introduced him to oranges and got him into medical school even though he was a cockney. I didn't know how to explain his caked-up teeth. I imagined he literally didn't bother flossing, and stuffed himself on candy prawns and Toffos all night, watching telly – his wife Jossy being the sort to demand a telly in the bedroom, and Bill the sort to fall asleep without cleaning his teeth, which was one of the dangers of tellies in bedrooms.

During these visits Bill talked freely about his life, telling us about his home-grown asparagus, his golf clubs, his three high-achieving sons, but most alluringly of all, his Freemasonry activities: the fine white gloves, ceremonial goings-on and handshakes, as well as the mutually beneficial, tit-for-tat arrangements involving golf and speeding tickets, admittance to theatres and nuclear bunkers, and so on. JP was bewitched.

'Freemasonry sounds marvellous, Bill,' he might typically say as he chipped away at the horribly caked-up teeth. 'Do you think you can get me in?'

'Sure, I'm happy to nominate you to the lodge,' Bill might say, rinsing out, 'but you'll need to clean your act up a bit first.'

'What do you mean?' said JP.

Bill spelled out what he needed to do. First and foremost, JP needed to look the part, the surgery and building needed a facelift too, and then there was his philanthropy profile to improve.

'Philanthropy?' said JP. 'Don't tell me I have to adopt a Biafran.'

'No, just some charitable work, something visible, along the lines of my garden parties for the Retired Airman's Fund,' said Bill.

'You could sponsor St Pippin's Home for Pets,' I suggested, but was ignored.

'Or do what Jacobs up the road has done,' said Bill.

'What?' asked Tammy, scribbling into a notebook.

'He's had a nuclear bunker put in his back garden. That did the trick all right.'

Tammy asked some awkward questions.

'I still don't see what's in it for JP,' she said.

'Look,' said Bill, 'imagine that, right now, JP is a fine, healthy cactus, but that after joining the Freemasons he'll flower, metaphorically speaking, in the eyes of everyone around and he'll have people queueing up to help him, if he needs help for anything whatsoever.'

However much I liked Bill, the consequences of his Freemasonry talk were profound and inconvenient. JP took on a decorating firm, two miserable old men who were around for weeks on end, burning off old paint, then scraping, sanding, priming, undercoating, and painting the whole ground floor, as slowly as possible. Sending up dust and fumes and smells. The patients were impressed though. I noticed how much they admired the works being done. Every single one of them mentioned it, and JP loved it.

'I'd do it myself, but I haven't the time,' he'd say.

New things kept arriving – surgical instruments, a top-of-the-range Flexi 400S surgery light – and ornamental rustic barrels containing laurel bushes appeared either side of the front door. Mr Skidmore put in three On-Guard battery smoke alarms, and, worst of all, two orange three-drawer filing cabinets to replace the rusty old khaki ones, which meant re-filing every single dental card. Also, because the new drawer mechanisms were fiercer than the old ones, Tammy said we must practise opening and closing the drawers as silently as possible so that we could be continually filing all day, in between jobs – even while patients were having elaborate or sensitive treatments – without causing a disturbance. Tammy was an expert at this kind of thing and demonstrated her technique – a sort of pull outward but at the same time pushing slightly, to stop the dragging vibration. And when closing (this being the real problem, noise-wise), resisting the roll on the final inch toward closure, which produced a jolting clack.

'Don't let the drawer take control – imagine it's a frisky horse and the drawer handle is your bridle.' She wasn't a rider.

Tammy invented a game. She'd hide around the corner and try to hear me opening and closing a drawer. I used to just stand there and she'd call out, 'Well done, I didn't hear a thing.'

It was the cost of everything, though, that worried Tammy the most – she'd got her wedding and honeymoon cruise to think of, and after settling well at home she suddenly started to come in more, to 'drum up business'. JP had already been in the habit of vaguely mentioning possible treatments but now, under Tammy's watchful eye, he was making patients fully aware of 'all the options' for dental restorations including expensive, private procedures – e.g. gold crowns instead of fillings, white fillings instead of silver, and bridges instead of dentures. Tammy was then quite forcefully encouraging them in a follow-up move in the waiting room, and if cost was ever the barrier to having the fancier treatment she might say, 'Think how much you spend on your hair in a year,' and if it was a man, 'Think how much your wife spends on her hair every year.' And quite soon JP was doing more than just silver fillings, plastic dentures and cleaning.

Things progressed slowly with Andy Nicolello and me. I mean, we had cups of tea while his laundry went through, and he'd shout at newsreaders on the television and criticize JP's dental impressions, and call him 'Plasticine Joe' and 'Farah-man', referring to his slightly too-small hopsack trousers.

Sometimes we might dash up to the Old Horse for the duration of the mixed-coloureds cycle but Andy wouldn't risk leaving the tumble dryer unattended because in his head all those crackling synthetic fibres would be overheating and tiny bits of fluff catching fire, and so forth. He was as wary of electricity as people in the olden days who'd had buckets of sand on standby in case of flames leaping out of sockets, and switched off their fridges at bedtime and risked their luncheon meat going off and the milk turning sour, just for the peace of mind.

The romance was beginning, I could feel it. On our walks up and down between the wash and the dry, we'd link arms, and I'd make sure we were walking along in step – right leg, left leg, right leg – and if not I'd do a little skip to correct it and he'd sometimes pull me in closer. It was slow. Slow but sure.

If I had any complaints about Andy it was his professional pride. He'd been taught to manufacture dentures by Mr Burridge – whose name in the industry was 'Mr Softee' because of his marvellously comfortable dentures – and Mr Burridge himself had apparently conceded that Andy had surpassed him in this respect and was the best apprentice they'd ever had.

It was because of this that I boasted about having filled a tooth for JP. I laughed about how the drill had almost flown out of my hand. In truth, JP had done the important drilling himself, but because of the difficult angle (upper right seven) and limited visibility, he'd had to call upon me to pack the amalgam into the cavity and, the following day, to smooth it off with a burr attached to the drill. And it served me right that Andy had a tooth that needed a tidy-up and refill and now assumed I'd be willing and able to do it for him and that, before I could object, he had trotted down to the surgery, switched on the treatment island, and sat down waiting.

'It's a recent filling,' he said. 'You need only remove the old amalgam, tidy up the cavity and refill it.'

I picked at the filling with a probe, needling it into the hairline join. Andy jumped.

'You're going to have to use the hand-piece,' he said, and using the vanity mirror pointed. 'Drill in there, and there, around the old filling, in short bursts.'

I drilled as instructed for a moment and stopped to give him a break and then started up again. It was an unexpectedly lovely encounter. Him making the most adorable, involuntary little sounds – choky little coughs and swallows, and saying, ''S'cuse me' all the time – clutching the napkin at his neck to catch the blue-black gravelly liquid that ran down his neck and pooled in the hollows of his collar bones, there being no nurse to aspirate. Eventually the filling jumped out and he spat it into his hand. The cavity was like a clean but jagged cave. I picked at the dentine looking for caries and then lined it with Dropsin, partly because it was good practice to put a barrier between the tooth and the filling, but mostly because it meant detaining Andy in the chair a few moments more. Reclining, eyes closed, black eyelashes resting on his lightly scarred cheek; trusting, friendly, relaxed, like a resting horse, and then alert again as I mixed the amalgam.

'I'll fill it now,' I said, and he opened his mouth wide. I packed the amalgam into the cavity and tamped it down. His facial expression when I said, 'Bite down now please, gently,' and his biting down so tentatively on the still-malleable amalgam, almost made me cry.

Did it honestly matter that we'd been raised and shaped by eccentric mothers?

Mine: drunk, divorcee, nudist, amphetamine addict, nymphomaniac, shoplifter, would-be novelist, poet, playwright.

His: teetotal, anti-Establishment, rabbit-trapper, alleged suicide-pact participant, television-forbidder, misery guts.

Did it make us incompatible in the eyes of the world? Plus, what did it matter what people thought?

'Does it feel OK?' I asked.

'I think it's fine,' he said, chewing gently.

'Let me check it's not high . . .' I said. 'Open, and bite again.'

And honestly I just wanted to watch him gently bite and open and bite and open and not let him up, but to climb into his lap and kiss all over his face, especially around the upper-left area where he was probably a bit sore. It was all magical and divine.

Back in the flat after I'd tidied the surgery, Andy told me he'd doubted I'd handle the drill quite so well.

'It's a powerful instrument,' he said, impressed.

I reminded him that I was a medal-holder in javelin and had won a dart-throwing competition the summer before and my winning throw had measured over twenty metres. He wanted to know what that was in feet and inches and, when I told him, whistled. Everything sounds bigger in feet. And then he wanted to know the weight of the dart and then the rules of the thing (Could you run up? What was the position of the non-throwing arm?) until I wished I hadn't brought it up. My mother had warned me about this – that men like to explore things, to understand them on their terms. If you tell a man you've mined a diamond, they might ask when, how, what tools? Did you wear the regulation hard hat? And what carat? How much is it worth? But they might not think to ask to see the diamond.

I related the whole thing to my sister on the phone later.

'I did a filling for him and it felt wonderful,' I said. She told me quite angrily that what I'd done was illegal and that my weird feelings afterwards were psychological and closely related to a dangerous mental condition called Shendyn's Syndrome where people deliberately injure other people, so they can kiss them better.

'I'd never injure Andy,' I protested.

'That's what they all say,' she said. 'So you are going out with him then?'

'No, not really,' I said. 'But I like him.'

Because of Andy's manners and gentleness, I entertained the possibility that he might be gay or asexual. Men were beginning to be so then – often the nicest ones. I examined the evidence. He liked freshly laundered clothing. He never minded me having a bowl of show fruit – in spite of his left-wing politics. In fact, he sometimes chopped up apples and oranges to make us a mini fruit salad. And he once experimented with a slice of lemon in his tea. He didn't try to rub against me, and never once got his penis out, which won't sound particularly gay, asexual or kind but, back then, the exposed penis, though often upsetting, was strangely intended as a compliment.

The idea of Andy being gay or asexual gave me the confidence to throw myself at him – thinking, if it turned out he was gay, he'd explain it to me and then we'd be able to continue our relationship as really good friends, like Tarzan and Cheetah or Alison Langdon and her Filipino manservant, Anacleto. And if not, we'd kiss and make love. And so, one night, after we'd watched an erotic episode of *Dallas*, when I'd asked him how it felt to suddenly be able to watch TV, and he said it was nice but nothing on TV beat watching spiders weave their webs, which he'd done for hours on end in various corners of his home over the years, and he began to describe spiders methodically picking up and weaving threads, I leaned in, cupped his face in my hands and said, 'Can we kiss?'

It was a real question which required an answer, so I waited and the answer was a most lovely slow smile and then the feel of his lips on mine and the gentle warmth of his nasally exhaled breath. None of the frantic head-circling that was all the rage back then. It was very nice and not wet or fast or uncomfortable.

'I threw myself at you,' I said.

'Good,' he replied.

And that was the start of it all.

8.   The Good Life

The subject of contraception occupied me for a while. I wondered if the pill would suit me. I mean, my mother couldn't have it due to vascular peculiarities, nor my sister because of her acne rosacea and fearfulness. Added to which I'd read copious *Woman's Own* correspondence on the topic and knew it to be a minefield. I might lose or gain weight or – another possibility much discussed by Jo and the team – I might feel despondent or depressed and have a drop in libido.

But if not the pill, what? Durex? I couldn't see Andy in a Durex – it seemed wrong for him and embarrassing. The Dutch cap was inappropriate for me on emotional grounds. I'd seen my mother's pinky-beige thing sitting behind the taps on the bathroom sink in the mornings after she'd had sexual intercourse with a vet or a doctor or a man of some kind, and had had to locate her cervix beforehand, and its high failure rate was why she'd had so many babies, miscarriages and abortions, and therefore misery.

I phoned Melody in Luton and Dunstable and she returned my call on the faulty phone and we had a long conversation about my situation, it being her favourite subject. Melody's main aim in life was to have sex without it making her sad or pregnant, and she was happy to advise me. Firstly, she wouldn't *dream* of taking hormones to fool her body into thinking it was pregnant just so a man could ejaculate inside her with no repercussions. Secondly, neither did she want the worry and risk of the withdrawal method, which was very popular back then, and thirdly, she didn't trust any other contraception not to fail or cause mental and/or physical anguish.

'Have you ever wondered why there isn't a male pill, Lizzie?' she said. 'Have you ever asked yourself that?'

I hadn't, but I said, 'God, I know.'

However, Melody had devised and perfected (and had shared widely) a method of arranging her inner thighs so that they squashed into a makeshift vagina, and according to her, no one in a hurry could tell the difference.

'Its weakness is that it's slightly disappointing for women who actually enjoy being penetrated,' she said, 'but not many are too bothered about that bit.'

'No,' I said.

After the phone call, I tried to imagine presenting a thigh-vagina to Andy. I thought it probably inappropriate in our case because Andy wouldn't be in a hurry, we wouldn't be in a car, and I felt I liked him too much to trick him. And in any case, I reminded myself, our mutual weirdness would reflect for ever like two mirrors, and I shouldn't even go out with him, let alone go on the pill or the cap, or present a bogus vagina. For both our sakes.

Over the weeks I began to piece together Andy's life. I tried to put the rumours out of my mind: that he lived in a bus, that his brother faked their parents' suicide (to inherit a bus?), that they lived on roadkill and beechnuts, that they forcibly tattooed people to initiate them into a bird-worshipping cult, that his brother was really his father. His parents had gassed themselves, drowned themselves off Loxton Locks, taken cyanide tablets left over from their spying days, been pushed over the edge after having a letter published in the *Leicester Mercury* which contained a disastrous grammatical error.

I let myself believe only what I heard from Andy himself and, though he wasn't a chatterer, snippets slipped out. Mr Nicolello had been a brainy dropout who'd met Andy's mother, a fellow brainy dropout, at university – both of them anti-capitalists who refused to be shackled to the banks or utility companies – and they'd bought a piece of wayside above a village and endeavoured to be self-sufficient, like Tom and Barbara from *The Good Life* but not as funny or charming. They managed to generate electricity somehow and though they'd had lighting, the power was gone by night-time and they insulated a tiny refrigerator with a beanbag and relied upon candles and home-made entertainment, such as reading and singing after dark. They had died 'close together' after Mr Nicolello had been diagnosed with an enlarged heart and then the country had voted in the referendum to remain in the EEC and the pair had literally lost the will to live.

Since their deaths Andy had lived with his much older brother, Tony, and his family, in a shack-style house behind the soap factory.

'Tony is a chip off the old block,' Andy told me. 'You know, suspicious and worried all the time – he can't help it.'

I never knew how to respond to bleak pronouncements of this kind but I did once ask if talking about his family was easy for him, knowing of my own unorthodox, riches-to-rags childhood: menace of a mother, homosexual father running off with a bloke from the Vogel factory, then the whole business crashing, and all those redundancies, and so forth. But he denied having any previous knowledge of me or my family, except that I had a grandmother in one of the posh bungalows who grew her own marrows and drove a Volkswagen.

Andy's eccentric upbringing – the thing that made him seem unsuitable for me – was probably what made him the perfect companion. While most boys of his age liked to roam from pub to pub, guzzling Brew X1, and kicking empty boxes noisily along the street, fighting other boys, pulling fish out of the river for the hell of it, Andy just loved lounging around after a hot bath, watching telly, shouting at the news, listening to cassettes with the lights on and boiling up water for endless tea, coffee and Lemsip – making the most of all the hot water and electric light.

And though he was breezy about it, I imagined that being in the flat must surely have felt like coming home after a cold, rainy fortnight camping in Derbyshire – only it had been twenty-odd years. For me it seemed like the beginning of a love affair, a really nice one, but I tried to ignore that feeling.

My mother used to pop in between visits to her Snowdrop Laundry customers and dropping and collecting Danny from Curious

Minds – though mostly to work on her book. For years she had been writing 'Three-Quarter Sleeves', which she called a novel but which was largely based on her emergence from girlhood to womanhood in the late 1950s. A time when, instead of advertising her wifeliness, she'd developed a taste for freedoms such as drinking coffee with ice cubes and showing her arms, and her parents had been at their wits' end.

She'd sent a synopsis and sample chapter to her favourite publisher (Faber & Faber) and, one afternoon, showed me the reply she'd had from an editor there – Patience Tidy. The novel had been rejected.

Patience Tidy thanked my mother for her submission but added, *There is a lot of this type of women's writing around now*, and suggested she might consider other genres, since she had such an intriguing voice.

'Other genres indeed!' said my mother. 'Patience Tidy just wants to keep the whole of realism clear for her existing authors.'

'She says you have an intriguing voice,' I said.

My mother read me an excerpt of the book.

'What do you think, Lizzie, honestly?' she asked afterwards.

I told her I couldn't agree with the editor. People would always want to read about a teacup overflowing into a saucer while a man looks distractedly at the meat on a woman's forearm (in a tea room). I would, anyway. My mother might not have been a very good mother, laundry representative or wife but she was an avid reader and an intellectual and she knew, probably better than Patience Tidy (not meaning any disrespect), what women wanted to read.

'Forget Faber and Faber,' I said. 'Try somewhere else.'

'Well, maybe.'

But I knew she wouldn't want to give up on her preferred publisher. She'd already written the acknowledgements, including, *I'd like to thank my editor, Patience Tidy at Faber & Faber, for her thoughtful interventions*, because she loved the name, and thought it'd be just her luck to end up with an editor called Dick.

My mother had always been a writer – of plays, poetry and

letters to newspapers – but it had been more ideas than actuality. Now ambition was being matched by words written, and order imposed on chaos, and it was nice and very cheering, especially after years of seeing her sleep through whole days only to come wide awake just as everyone else (including the television) was retiring for the night. And the knowledge that she might appear, silhouetted, in my bedroom doorway, woozy but conscious, at II p.m., wanting company, forced me to invent a fake snore so unpleasant that she'd leave me alone and try my brother Jack, who was less strategic and kinder.

My siblings put our mother's sudden sobriety down to a bout of influenza she had in the spring of 1979 that had put her off spirits, and it may have been that, but I thought it was more to do with the acquisition of her new dog. Angelo was a smooth-haired, patchy, white-and-brown dog with only three legs and one working eye who, for a while, needed the constant care a drunk could never give.

My mother had found Angelo after he had been hit by a car on the Mayflower roundabout, just along from Curious Minds. No one had been there to claim him and he had no tag, so she scooped him up and rushed him along the London Road to Mr Swift's veterinary surgery, and when asked by the vet nurse what name they should give him, she had suggested 'Angelo' – it being her favourite name and the one she'd meant to call baby Danny. But on her way to the Leicester Royal Infirmary to give birth, she'd heard 'Daniel' by Elton John on the radio and it put Angelo out of her mind for a few weeks, by which time we'd all got used to him being Daniel, or Danny for short. So it was nice for her to have this naming opportunity.

Mr Swift the vet was an ex-lover of hers. Their relationship had ended when Mrs Swift had intervened and told him to choose between them. My mother had insisted that he remain with his wife but the wife had said, 'No, it has to be Roger's decision' (his name being something along those lines). 'He might prefer you, with all your animals and wacko children.'

'No, he's sure to prefer you,' my mother said, 'with your wacko tea towels and wacko Crimplene blouses,' batting 'wacko' back at her, even though she'd never heard the word before and was unsure of its actual meaning.

Anyway, Mr Swift probably felt that remaining with assorted wacko blouses wasn't so much of a worry as taking on a bunch of wacko children and he chose to stay with the wife, and though my mother had been glad really, she never missed an opportunity to dash over to his surgery with a sick animal – because of his kindness and in memory of all the wonderful sex they'd had.

'Honestly, Lizzie, if he hadn't had such bad breath I might have made a real play for him,' she once told me. But this was all before Mr Holt – to whom she was more or less faithful, if you didn't count jolly friendships and poem-sending.

A week or two later she'd popped back to Mr Swift's surgery to find out what had become of Angelo the dog and was informed that he'd had to have a front leg amputated at the shoulder, and that because no one had come forward for him in spite of the half-dozen notices posted in the vicinity, he was now about to be sent to St Pippin's Home for Pets near Market Harborough.

'At the shoulder?' my mother had cried, and the veterinary nurse had told her that dogs couldn't be left with stumps, like human beings, 'or else they lean on them and walk on them and the stump can't take it'.

She had been about to leave when the nurse put her finger to her ear and said, 'Listen, that's him, he hasn't stopped crying.' My mother had cocked her head and heard the persistent two-note whine. 'He's going to need a saint,' said the nurse, which might have been a strategic thing that they were trained to say in order to offload injured dogs. Anyway, it worked. My mother took him to live with her and Mr Holt, their wacko children, Sue the dog, and their cat – knowing he was going to be the hugest nuisance and burden and so grotty looking he'd put people off their lunches. She helped him learn to walk on his three legs and put butter on his pads so that after a walk he'd content himself with licking his three paws and not feel the pain in the phantom fourth. He went to work with my mother and everywhere else besides, and she would tell his story ('He was at death's door, but now he can run again') to anyone who showed an interest and soon Angelo became my mother's badge of decency, her Jiminy Cricket. Angelo was her good deed that would last for ever.

And he was so visible.

'Aren't you a good person,' people might say, and, 'Golly, that's so kind of you.' She became addicted to the praise – like an actress or writer being constantly applauded. If Angelo wasn't allowed somewhere, like Twycross Zoo, or the Fish & Quart, my mother would simply say, 'Come along, Angelo, if you're not wanted, I don't want to be here either.' And the zoo or the restaurant would have to watch him hobble away.

Being a sober person with a disabled dog to care for changed my mother creatively. It gave her time to write. She became expert at making up limericks really quickly, on the spot, such as:

> There was a young lady from Tring,
> who only wanted to sing,
> the tragic thing was,
> her husband got cross,
> So she strangled the bastard with string.

And she was also able to concentrate, to write methodically and for longish periods of time without falling asleep. She changed as a human being, seeming to understand, all of a sudden, that people were tired at night, sometimes exhausted, and didn't always want to stay up talking, or looking for poems in old books or for descriptions of certain men in Jane Austen. And she now knew how important it was not to run out of milk or bread or honey. The only downside to her new zeal being that she felt everyone (including me) should be working on a novel and, if we weren't, we should be reading or rereading the classics, such as *Silas Marner* or *Lolly Willowes* – and if not, we were missing out. She was like a Christian who wasn't happy just loving Jesus but wanted everyone else to love Jesus too, or a drunk wanting to be surrounded by other drunks, or women in high heels wanting others to be similarly crippled, or people dwelling on nuclear war wanting to make others worry too, and so on.

Returning to the letter from Faber & Faber, another difference was my mother's acceptance of Patience Tidy's idea, and after only the mildest, tiny tantrum and some name-calling, she took it as a compliment and a challenge.

'OK, then,' she said. 'If that's what you want, Patience.'

And she stopped writing about herself and her mother and started instead an exciting feminist sci-fi thriller. Not only that, she was going to introduce a dental theme – inspired by my new job – and its title would be 'Winter Green'. I was perturbed to hear this, it being the name of my boss, and protested quite neurotically but she said it was only a working title and not to worry, and anyway, there was no copyright on names. And nothing that awful was going to happen, not in a realism sense anyway. Probably. Although there was going to be at least one death and lots of outdoor sex.

'Let's see how that goes down with Patience Tidy,' she said, and eventually asked, 'Anyway, how are you? What have you been up to?'

I told her I was on the brink of entering a loving relationship with Andy and she said he had seemed a very nice person and suggested I go to see Dr Gurley about birth control.

And then I told her that Andy was a Nicolello and she said, 'Nicolello, do I know them?'

And I said, 'The Flintstones.'

And she said, 'Oh, Christ, not those people who lived in that encampment behind Granny's house, whose parents had the letter in the *Mercury*?'

'Yes, them.'

Tammy wasn't pregnant yet but JP was keen that optimum conditions for conception should be constantly maintained and he was suspicious of her tight trousers, Jazzercise classes and red-wine consumption.

'Look, Jape,' said Tammy, 'if jazz dancing and drinking wine were a problem there'd be no babies in Italy, France, Spain or New Orleans.'

One day, one of the instructors from the Jazzercise classes came in for his six-monthly check-up and JP grilled him. The instructor was unfazed and gave out some impressive statistics about the number of women who didn't have heart attacks who might have had them had they not been committed to Jazzercise. And how many felt really alive who'd previously been dead inside, and so forth. This only exacerbated JP's anxieties and, afterwards, he had a word with me.

'Go with her, will you, nurse?' he said. 'Make sure she's not overdoing it.'

Jazzercise was fun, I must admit, even though I was the only one in tracksuit bottoms. Tammy was very good at it and really looked the part in her leotard and neckerchief.

Ann-Sofie from the Lunch Box was there and Jossy Turner, wife of Bill, as well as the girl from the Raj Restaurant, whose name was Pritiben – Priti for short. It didn't look as though Tammy was over-doing it, though she was doing some incredibly high kicks.

The second session went less well but only because Tammy accidentally kicked Priti in the mouth and almost knocked her out, so we finished early to walk her home just to be on the safe side. As we walked along, Tammy pretended to be interested in Priti's life, partly out of guilt and partly, I suppose, to prevent her slipping into a coma. Thus, we discovered that she was studying for A levels and was hoping for a place at a London university the following autumn. Just like my brother, I thought, but didn't say.

Tammy was surprised. 'But I thought you worked on Patel's housewares stall on the market – didn't I buy a salad spinner from you last week?' she asked.

'That's part-time, only until I finish school.'

'Gosh, I just love spinning that salad spinner.'

Priti seemed alarmed to hear this and advised her to use it with care, and certainly not to spin it just for fun – they'd had a couple of them returned, broken. Tammy thanked her for the tip but assured her she wouldn't dream of spinning it just for fun, which was obviously untrue. No one spun a salad spinner just for salad. We dropped Priti outside the Raj Restaurant and Tammy told her she must come to the surgery to have JP look at the tooth – an upper incisor that stood proud of her arch and would have taken the brunt of Tammy's kick.

A couple of days later, she appeared in the waiting room wanting to make an appointment as per Tammy's suggestion and Tammy squeezed her in the following day between a family of four and a man known for lateness.

'So you've had a blow to the mouth, have you?' said JP the next day, making it sound as if she'd been in some kind of ruffian-type punch-up.

'Yes. A kick in the teeth,' said Priti, not sounding at all like a ruffian.

'It happened at Jazzercise class,' I added. 'Tammy kicked her by accident.'

'Well, I think this tooth might flare up and need root filling,' said JP. 'And I'm sorry but since you're not one of my patients I can't offer you treatment on the NHS.'

Priti looked surprised. 'Oh, why not?' she asked, albeit politely.

'You are presenting with a mouth injury that might need extensive treatment, and I don't provide that on the National Health except for my existing patients.' He dropped his probe and mirror into the sink with a loud clang. 'I suggest you go up to the Family Practitioners Association who will give you a list of NHS dentists.'

In the waiting room I apologized and reiterated the information about the Family Practitioners Association. Priti was bemused but philosophical.

'Do you fancy coming up to watch some telly later?' I asked.

She said she couldn't – she had a hundred tea towels to fold and press. I told her to bring them along, and I'd help her.

'That wouldn't work,' she said and left.

I could really imagine Priti in London. In my head I saw her and my brother Jack, laughing together on a rain-drenched, tree-lined London street, books under their arms, dashing into a white concrete building for coffee and going to a piano recital or joining the Fabians. Jack was the type and Priti might well be too for all I knew. I felt a stab of envy. I should be looking forward to laughing in rain-streaked concrete coffee bars as well but I was stuck researching the best sex positions for conception for my senior colleague, and sex-proof hair.

9. Angelo

When my mother next came round to collect Danny she had Angelo the dog under one arm.

'You can't bring him in,' I said.

'What do you mean?'

'Angelo can't come into the flat,' I said, petting him. 'I'm sorry, but Tammy's allergic to dog hair.'

'That's ridiculous,' said my mother. 'It's your flat now.'

'JP goes up there sometimes,' I explained.

'What for?'

'The bathroom.'

'What's he doing in your bathroom?' asked my mother, aghast.

'Going to the toilet.'

'For crying out loud, Lizzie,' she said, barging in through the door, 'you live here now and they can't suddenly announce a dog ban, especially if the dentist's shitting in your toilet.'

'They haven't suddenly announced it, they said so from the start.'

'Said what?'

'No dogs or cats.'

'You can't live in a place with a dog ban,' she said. 'What about Angelo?'

'Well, I know but . . .'

'It's fucking ridiculous,' she said, and marched up the stairs followed by Angelo, who was remarkably good at getting up the stairs for a three-legged dog (though not down again).

My mother soon started leaving Angelo with me whenever she went to the theatre or to have a shame-counselling session with Abe. And though I objected to start with because it was flouting the rules, in reality I was glad. I began to love his calm serenity.

He'd get as close to me as possible without being actually on me and would lie down quietly, in a circular position, while I watched *Dallas* or did a face pack. Imagine Qizong Zhang's *Dog Beneath Bamboo* – that's just what Angelo looked like. Not that I knew that at the time – I'm adding with hindsight.

Occasionally he'd worry his phantom leg that was gone from the shoulder, looking confusedly at where it should be, and I'd imagine he had paw-ache, like humans had with missing limbs. I'd give him a sliver of his favourite cheese (Edam) to take his mind off it, and sing to him about the old lady who went up in a basket, seventeen times as high as the moon. I have to admit that Angelo's bulging eye put me off my food slightly, and if I was eating, say, spaghetti hoops on toast, I'd sit facing in the other direction. I could manage an apple, sitting right next to him, no problem, but not an egg. In fact, I'd never even think of having an egg if I had him with me. But that was about eyes and eggs, definitely not about Angelo.

I worried a lot about who had owned Angelo before, and so did my mother. We used to discuss it at length.

'Imagine how Angelo's real owner must feel,' she'd say, 'wondering about him, and worrying.'

'I know, it's unbearable.'

'It's too, too unbearable.'

'It really is.'

'Unbearable.'

'Poor thing.'

'If only they knew how happy he was.'

To give my mother her due, she did sometimes deliberately walk Angelo around Victoria Park before collecting Danny from nursery – just in case the real owner might be out there looking for him. But she was always relieved when they came away without having been approached, and however much we worried about it, and how unbearable the thought of his grieving owner, the last thing we wanted was for Angelo to be found.

★

It was some weeks later that Miss Gwendolyne Smith of Victoria Park came in for her six-monthly check-up.

'Just a scale and polish, nurse,' said JP and I handed him a manual scaler, pasted up a rubber cup, and put a bib around Miss Smith's neck. I'd been admiring her perfect conduct. Open mouth. Tissue ready in hand, efficient rinsing on command, spitting into the centre of the spittoon, no drips or spray or strings of saliva, and resuming the open-mouthed treatment pose afterwards. No trying to talk.

As I took her card from the marble table, the note jumped out at me: *Relation of Oscar Wilde*, it said, and, *Lost dog*.

JP had also seen the note and was asking her about it as he jammed the scaler between her lower incisors.

'Did you ever find your dog?'

She turned away so she could answer properly. 'No, never.' Bloody saliva was now coating her lower teeth.

'Oh, I am sorry.' JP pushed her by the chin back into the treatment position. 'I lost a dog once,' he said, 'very sad.'

Miss Smith blinked and looked wretched, her mouth beginning to droop slightly now.

'Open wide,' said JP. 'Or was it a cat? Yes, I believe mine was a cat – no, tell a lie, it was a dog.'

'It was a cat,' said Tammy from the desk, not even looking up from her paperwork.

In the waiting room afterwards, filling out the forms, I brought the subject up again and knew it was Angelo before she had even described him. I'd known that Miss Gwendolyne Smith – the perfect patient – was bound to be Angelo's real owner, the moment I'd seen the note on the card. He was so well-trained.

I checked that her contact details were up to date, charged her the £2.70 and made her an appointment for six months' time.

At coffee break I asked Tammy and JP about Miss Smith and her missing dog.

'When did she lose him?' I asked.

JP had no memory of the patient even mentioning a lost dog,

of course, but Tammy thought it was 'about two check-ups ago, I guess'. She measured time like that. 'Why do you ask?'

'I'm just wondering if I might know the whereabouts of the dog.'

'Oh, my gosh,' said Tammy. 'You mean that three-legged dog of your mother's – wow, hang on, when did she find that dog?'

'About two check-ups ago.'

'Don't go getting Miss Smith's hopes up, nurse,' said JP. 'What are the chances it'll really be her dog your mother found? And even if it is, I can't see Miss Smith wanting it back now – not with three legs.'

JP was wrong. Miss Smith would always want her dog back, however many legs he had, or none, but it was true that coping with a three-legged dog wasn't plain sailing. People stared and commented, laughed, cringed. You needed to be the type. And his eye was worse (as previously mentioned) but less noticeable. Miss Smith, I felt, would find it difficult. I needed to think it through.

If I were to approach Miss Smith, she would have the upset of finding out that Angelo (or whatever his real name might be) had suffered a life-changing accident. And have the agonizing decision of whether or not to take him back. My mother, whose life had been improved one hundred per cent by Angelo, might lose him for ever and have the misery of knowing he'd returned to a less exciting life. She might go back to drinking too much and ruin her chances with Faber & Faber.

And Angelo himself, who was happy and settled with my mother, might suffer in another upheaval – but equally, might he be even happier with Miss Smith, his original owner? I had myself to think about too. I liked having him about. I loved him.

In the end I had to face up to it. If Miss Smith had got herself a new pet or even had a busy, sociable job, I might have let sleeping dogs lie, but she lived alone and was an editor of poetry and drama who worked from home. Angelo had been her constant companion before his disappearance.

'Oh, God!' said my mother, head in hands. 'What makes you think Angelo belongs to this woman? People lose dogs all the time.'

'He might, he might not. I just think we should rule it out, that's all,' I said, 'just in case.'

'OK then, ring her up and rule her out. If you must.'

I played it down on the phone. I didn't want to get Miss Gwendolyne Smith's hopes up.

'Oh, no, that doesn't sound like Oscar,' she said. 'Oscar has four legs.'

'Yes, but so did this dog once, before he was run over near the Mayflower roundabout.'

'How do I know this isn't a hoax call?' Miss Smith barked.

'Because I'm the dental nurse at the Wintergreen practice and I'd never do anything like that.'

She wouldn't let me bring Angelo to her house but said she'd meet us at Victoria Park, in front of the arch of remembrance.

My mother and I set off. We walked slowly, partly so Angelo could keep up and partly to delay. My mother was quiet, playing with a scene in her head, or planning a new sticker for her car. As soon as we turned on to the path I saw Miss Smith ahead.

'Is that her?' my mother asked.

'Yes.'

She scooped Angelo up in her arms and went nose to nose with him. They blinked at each other.

'You're such a silly dog,' she said, 'nothing but trouble anyway.' And she snuffled into his neck for a moment before setting him down, handing me the loop of his lead, and walking away.

I approached Miss Smith. Angelo ambled along the path, sniffed at a discarded daisy chain, then stopped and looked ahead. He wagged his tail frantically, then stopped, then went again. I unclipped the lead.

'Oscar?' called Miss Smith. And Angelo hobbled hurriedly towards her and sprang up in a most excited way – a way I'd never seen before – as if he were on a pogo stick. Then he spun around in a frenzy.

Miss Smith shielded herself and laughed.

'Yes, yes, it's me, it's all right,' she said, and joined in the dance.

I stood silently and watched. Miss Smith looked at me, red-faced.

'Yes,' she said, 'this is Oscar. This is my dog.'

I patted Angelo and hugged him and said what a lovely outcome and that kind of thing. Then I glanced back at the retreating figure in the distance and said, 'That's my mother, she's a bit upset.'

'Oh,' said Miss Smith.

'Do you want to take him?' I asked.

She looked at me, confused. 'Of course I want to take him,' she said. 'He's my dog.'

Back at the flat my mother was deeply engrossed in looking busy.

'So,' I said.

'What?'

'That's that, then.'

'Yes.'

'It was the right thing to do.'

'Yes, he seemed very pleased to see her. Thank you for handling that. Now shush, I'm working.'

I made us some hot chocolate and my mother told me she'd known upon waking that morning that something bad was going to happen, something she'd been preparing for her whole life.

'Angelo going back to his rightful owner is the bad thing you've been preparing for your whole life?' I asked.

'Yes,' she said. 'Without him my shame is back.'

'Perhaps you'll find another thing to rescue?'

Priti called round then and was probably the best possible visitor under the circumstances because, not being a dog-lover, she didn't encourage us to ramble on about Angelo. She asked if my mother had another dog, and I had to say yes, she had Sue, but Sue didn't travel well (was how I put it), and then she changed the subject and asked if I'd mind if she did her homework in the flat – only she'd had an argument with the meat chef at the Raj, and had stormed out.

'Do you work there as well as on the housewares stall?' I asked.

'Sometimes, when they're busy.'

My mother was impressed.

It was all very *Woman's Own* – a female friend, all het up after a domestic or work tiff, needing some moral support and a cuppa. I was thrilled.

After my mother had gone Priti arranged herself at the dining table and hardly looked up from her biology textbook for what seemed like hours. It was like having an industrious, clever, grateful husband and I went the whole hog and did some baking and called a tea break. Priti was almost overwhelmed by the tray of hot biscuits and I trotted out the recipe (basically, sugary pastry with an ounce of cocoa powder added) so she could throw some together at home, but Priti feared she'd never rise to them because of a fear of ovens. In return I revealed how little I knew about the internal workings of the human body. I should have been worrying about my mother and the loss of Angelo, but the day went by in a stream of sweet drinks and snacks, smoke rings, impressions of Barbra Streisand and Prince Charles, and oven-glove demonstrations.

Andy settled into a routine of coming round twice a week, once with laundry and once without. I liked the visit without laundry more than the one with it – being proof that he liked me just as much as he liked the Hoover Aristocrat – but then it occurred to me that he might be making the second visit out of old-fashioned decency. We'd play cassettes – his Leonard Cohen, Van Morrison and Kate Bush, which, though lovely, never suggested sex, and my Rickie Lee Jones and Blondie (who did) – and we'd roll around on the sofa, but nothing much happened after a certain point. We were couplesque, that's the only way I can describe it. Andy was like an alien – gently curious and adorable – and I was eager but demure, but neither of us was rampant, which was the word I had in my head – I'd read plenty of Jilly Cooper and Jackie Collins – to describe the force required.

I realized we'd got into what Claire Rayner might describe as a 'tedious rut' and I phoned Melody for advice. She referred to it as a classic case of 'top half only' which was when the girl wasn't slaggy (rampant) enough to move things on, and the boy was either too nice, or being 'fed by two owners'.

' "Fed by two owners"?'

'You know,' said Melody, 'getting it from someone else.'

'Oh.'

'What does Andy look like?' she asked, as if there might be a clue there.

I thought for a moment and then said, 'Like Kevin Keegan, but with straight hair, taller, with a bigger nose and olive skin.'

'Yeah, you see, boys that look like Kevin Keegan can get trapped into sex affairs with the boss's wife.'

I thought of Mr Burridge, imagined his wife, and dismissed it.

'So, what should I do?' I asked, her being the expert.

'Ask him his favourite sex position – that might set him off – or put a Donna Summer tape on, or "*Je t'aime*", and do a striptease. But honestly, I wouldn't rush things. I'd just enjoy it. God, once you've gone all the way, it's over pretty much, unless you get engaged.'

Though Melody was usually more *Spare Rib* than *Woman's Own*, her advice on this occasion seemed to reinforce the sense of womanliness I was developing – enjoy life but be sensible and practical, wear a crazy jumper but be a grown-up, open a savings account, take up a sport, rinse and reuse yoghurt pots to freeze tiny leftovers, lose weight without dieting, join a book-of-the-month club, relax in a Radox bath, and take vitamins, because as a woman it's likely you'll cook five hundred meals, make a thousand beds and carry three thousand pounds of shopping over the following year. *Woman's Own* wouldn't want me doing a striptease to Donna Summer. Keenness on sex was as unattractive as too much make-up, and as unappealing as mentioning periods. And since I'd lured Andy in with the Hoover Aristocrat in the first place, and then thrown myself at him, I was probably already keen enough. I needed to act cool, look good, and not be too clingy or enthusiastic. It was his turn to make the running.

'Be sure to make the best of yourself,' said Melody, meaning clothes-wise.

There was a certain look that I liked, which fitted with the attractive but not-too-keen; this was 'busy city woman', dashing around in coloured trousers and chunky but short sweaters (mustard, burgundy and dark green) and leather boots, carrying things, lots of things, bags and picture frames, and almost dropping them but laughing as if slightly shocked and so forth, and wearing hats, floppy hats, caps, trilbies etc.

'Yes,' I told Melody. 'I'll go shopping, I'll buy a hat.'

'Hats are good but not a trilby or other women will hate you,' she said, and we said goodbye.

With this in mind, I bought a beret. I didn't go all the way and get a black one in case it seemed as though I was trying to look French, but instead I went for a shade of browny-green, which I later regretted because Andy asked if I'd joined the Green Berets and, not knowing what the Green Berets were, I said in all seriousness that no, I hadn't.

I felt I should be enjoying living in the city more – or at least looking as if I did – and having a little gaggle of pals popping in all the time, different types of people who all knew me really well and shared my jokes. And a boyfriend who couldn't keep his hands off my bottom half as well as my top half. I began to wonder if I wouldn't feel better at home – more relaxed, more 'me' in the family setting, where I wouldn't be responsible for every tiny thing. Where sex could occur naturally and I wouldn't have to run around pretending to be busy in a beret so as not to appear too keen.

10.   Going Home

The building refurbishments that had been initiated by Bill Turner were lingering. The staircarpet had had to come up because of suspected dry rot and though it was a pain in the neck it presented me with the perfect excuse to go home. No one could call me a sissy or accuse me of being lonely – I'd simply be escaping the nuisance of the building work. So when my mother next called round to collect baby Danny, I casually brought the subject up.

'Ugh! This building work is throwing up a lot of dust,' I said, running my finger along a shelf.

'If it gets too bad let me know,' said my mother. 'I'll get you a dust mat from the laundry, they're most effective.'

'Thanks,' I said, 'but it's probably best if I just come home for a bit.'

My mother was dead against it. 'You can't,' she said, 'we're taking a lodger.'

My mother had had a series of lodgers over the years. A woman who used to cry if the Beatles came on the radio, and couldn't use tampons. A doctor who let a mature spider plant die of thirst and had a problem swallowing, and a student who invaded the treehouse.

'Why?' I asked.

'We need the money.'

I questioned this. 'Really?'

'Yes, really.'

Mr Holt was working seven till seven through the week, she said, and doing paperwork all weekend, and she was having to cheat on her call sheets just to save a couple of hours a day for her novel. They were living on Heinz soup now that she'd been cured of shoplifting and had to pay for alcohol and cheese. She had cancelled the newspapers and the window cleaner and, if they didn't find some money somehow, she might have to take Danny out of Curious Minds.

Having Danny at nursery up the road was important to me. Not because of the preschool number-knowledge and self-esteem apparently promoted by the Montessori method, but because I liked knowing he was close by every week day and that, in the event of a nuclear attack, I'd be able to rush and get him, and barge my way into Jacobs the accountant's shelter; and though we'd be amongst only a few humans left alive in the county, we'd have each other and one of Mr Jacobs's rifles to defend ourselves. I couldn't see a nuclear attack happening on a weekend somehow.

'Are you saying I can never come back?' I said.

'Well, you've left home,' said my mother. 'I suppose you could – in an emergency – but I can't keep rooms for all my offspring, like shrines.'

'So I'm stuck living here for ever, working for a man I really dislike?'

'We all have to work for horrible men. Leaving doesn't make them any less monstrous. In fact, staying can sometimes make all the difference, especially in your job.'

Later that week, Abe appeared in the waiting room. He'd broken a filling at the back, and wondered if he could see the dentist. I went to ask JP if he could fit him in.

'It's Mr Abraham. He's a client of the Snowdrop Laundry,' I said, 'and a friend of my mother's.'

'And I'm expected to see him, am I?' said JP.

'Well, yes. He's broken a filling and he does have a dentist, but he's based at the Government Dental College of Bangalore.'

'Well, get a deposit off him first,' he said, annoyed, 'and tell him no NHS.'

I took a deep breath and went back out to the waiting room, where I found my mother too.

'The dentist will fit you in,' I told Abe, 'but he won't be able to offer you NHS treatment.'

'That's OK, I don't want NHS.'

'Hang on – yes, you do,' said my mother.

'He says he doesn't,' I said.

'But why shouldn't he get NHS?'

'He's a casual patient.'

I turned to Abe. 'And you will have to pay a deposit of twenty pounds beforehand.'

Abe seemed to understand and put his hand in his pocket, but again my mother objected.

'What? No,' she said, 'absolutely not.' She pushed Abe's wallet away. 'We'll go elsewhere.' When they left I wanted to cry.

It gnawed at me. That I worked for a man who was prepared to exploit people's misfortune was sick-making. The idea that Abe understood it all too well, and was quite prepared to ignore it in order to get his tooth fixed was mortifying, and my mother's outrage only highlighted the awfulness of the situation. In the surgery, clanking about with no patient and nothing to do, I did cry a few angry tears and glared at JP who stood picking at his teeth in the mirror.

'Let's have a cup of tea, nurse, shall we?' he said.

I clomped upstairs and, after producing a filthy brown drink made with a teabag and a spoonful of Maxwell House, I buzzed him to come up. I watched him swallow it down, sigh, and wipe his mouth. He lit a cigarette which he passed to me and I fed it to him, puff by puff. Sometimes I left it in his lips too long and he had to turn away to let go and inhale; other times I pulled it away before he'd got a proper lungful, and then I stubbed it out before he'd finished. Best of all, I decided that the next time I'd turn the hot end round and burn his hideous lips. Making that plan soothed me.

At the end of the day my mother returned. Alone. I told her to go up to the flat, and I'd follow in a minute. On the way she met JP on the stairs and blocked his passage.

'Can you explain what happened earlier?' she said.

JP tried to deflect her.

'I can't help wondering what your husband thinks of your gallivanting about with a client of the laundry.'

But my mother was from a family of solicitors on the male side and bitchy liberals on the female.

'That's irrelevant,' she said. 'I want to know why you refused to treat Mr Abraham as a National Health patient.'

'I think you'll find I offered him exactly what I offer all casual patients,' said JP, barging past.

'I think you're a xenophobe.'

'You can think what you like, dear,' he said as he swung out of the building.

'Xenophobe!' my mother called after him.

'He won't even know what that means,' I said.

'He'll know enough Greek to work it out.'

'What happened to Abe?'

'He went up to Bill Turner, which worked out very well,' she said. 'They're both Freemasons and members of the Leicester Flyers.' She touched her nose.

'What *does* xenophobe mean?' I asked.

JP and Tammy were quite surprised my mother came in for a private check-up – it being soon after she'd called JP a xenophobe on the stairs. I wasn't surprised, though. She disliked JP, but she disliked most people and didn't mind doing business with them. It actually made it easier for her to consult him, dentally. This might seem strange but it's true. It's something to do with knowing where everyone stands, metaphorically.

JP greeted my mother too warmly and told her I was getting along very well, which was a nice, jolly thing to say but she replied, 'Well, why shouldn't she be?' and then made an icy quip about having written my application letter for me.

'You look different,' she told him. 'I almost didn't recognize you.'

Tammy, fastening the bib, whooped, 'Oh, my gosh, see, Jape? People are noticing. Doesn't he look distinguished, Mrs Vogel?'

Tammy had been smartening him up on the cheap as part of what we were calling the 'Masonic Improvements'. The long, cotton surgical smock my mother had last seen him wearing had been replaced with a tighter-fitting 'Latimer space-age' tunic, which came in a fine, drip-dry fabric, buttoned at the shoulder, and reached to mid-thigh. The sockless Mediclogs that had given me athlete's foot had been ditched in favour of proper lace-up brogues. And over the weekend her DIY hair trim left him looking more like Leonard Parkin than Reginald Bosanquet, with a low side parting and some kind of grease keeping it neat. Men often looked like one newsreader or another back then, hence their horror at Angela Rippon coming along. JP also had the look of a child after a barbering – ruined and untrustworthy – and complained that his exposed neck felt vulnerable and cold. Off duty, Tammy draped it with an untied silk cravat, which made him look like a drunk on the prowl for women and made me want to punch him in the face. As well as all that, he was trialling contact lenses and his eyes were red-rimmed and weepy.

'Yes, very debonair,' said my mother.

'He's trying for the Freemasons,' Tammy blurted.

'So I hear.'

JP gave my mother a thorough scale and polish, proclaimed her dentally fit, encouraged her gum-health endeavours, and said he'd like to see her in three months' time.

My mother told JP that if he had no objections, she'd like to occasionally sit in the waiting room for inspiration. JP supposed that would be fine but didn't make any enquiry as to why she might want to do this and she was obliged to reveal a thing that no writer wants to reveal – without seeming to be forced.

'I'm a writer,' she said, 'and working on a book.'

'Righty-ho,' said JP. 'See you in three months. Keep up the good interdental work.'

My mother and Tammy were the exact same age and would both be turning forty around then – my mother's birthday was later that week, Tammy's in a couple of months. My mother's response to this was to occasionally wonder, aloud, if she'd have to stop wearing knee-high boots and to remind us not to mention it. Tammy, on the other hand, was planning a dinner party where the theme would be 1940s fashion because she had been born in 1940; she suited the clothes of the era and had been practising styling her fringe into a victory roll.

'So what's your mother's book about?' JP asked after she'd gone.

'It's kind of John Wyndham meets Jilly Cooper.'

'Well, just as long as I'm not in it,' he said, laughing.

11. Mildred Quietly

After lunch one day, when Bill Turner was in the chair for his regular scale and polish, JP suddenly remembered that Bill must know the result of the secret ballot regarding his (JP's) nomination to the Freemasons, and though he'd deliberately drawn a line through the rest of the day so the pair of them could discuss the outcome on the golf course, he was impatient, and while he scaled Bill's caked-up lower incisors, he pushed him to reveal the outcome.

'Let's get out on to the green,' said Bill. 'We can chat there.'

'Come on, old man, put me out of my misery. Am I in or out?'

Bill spat and said, 'Ah, I'm sorry, you were blackballed, I'm afraid.'

JP let his head hang for a moment and exhaled. 'What? But why?'

'Who knows?'

'How many?' asked JP.

'Two, only two, so we can go again. It was a "no", not a "never",' said Bill.

I liked JP's golf afternoons, in fact I looked forward to them. It was a chance to sterilize everything, clean all the drawers and cabinets and have a really good sort-out; also, to use the phone, pluck my eyebrows, and clean my teeth with the rubber cup and prophylactic paste. But what should have been a lovely clear afternoon turned into a detailed analysis of the result and the compiling of a list of further improvements to be made before JP's next attempt.

My mother called in to collect Danny. It was her birthday but neither of us mentioned the date. It wasn't the fact that she was forty that bothered her, she just hated birthdays. She always had – and not just hers. She told me about the two possible lodgers who'd shown an interest in my old room. One was a young woman with a gerbil, and the other was a salesman in his mid-thirties who'd only need the room Wednesday to Sunday because he spent Mondays and Tuesdays in Cambridge.

What were my thoughts?

I wasn't keen on a gerbil in my room, scattering wood shavings and sunflower husks all over the carpet, and I guessed my mother wouldn't want the salesman.

'Exactly,' she said. 'I've read too much Flannery O'Connor. I'll wait for more responses.' She gathered up Danny's things but before she could leave I pushed her birthday gift across the table to her. It was a box of Tempo felt pens in assorted colours with a sketchpad and a little bottle of liquid paper. She was delighted with them and immediately showed me a neo-cubist drawing method she'd learned from the Curious Minds parents' manual. She drew a horse, then a face and then wrote *Mildred Quietly* in many different ways and colours – a nom de plume she was trying out. I wondered if it might be a bit close to Patience Tidy in style. But she thought not. Then she wrote, *Angelo Angelo Angelo*, and we talked about him briefly before she drew a picture of him, and eventually I said, 'Perhaps you could have another baby?' meaning as a replacement.

'Mr Holt has said we're to have no more,' she said, and told me she'd dreamt the night before that she'd rescued a baby koala but Mr Holt had objected and the koala had heard his harsh words and run away to St Pippin's Home for Pets. She was livid with him for his behaviour in this dream.

She then wrote, *Andy Andy Andy*, in swirly writing. I must've looked puzzled because she said, 'How are things going with Andy?'

I told her how much I'd taken to him.

'What's he like?' she asked.

So I told her how unusual he was. That he knew every card game and board game from rummy to beggar-my-neighbour, pick-up-sticks, Go and backgammon. He could fold paper into swans, dogs and yachts, was good at Meccano and Airfix, and could knock an apple out of a tree with a catapult. But he had never heard of Ker-Plunk or Operation due to never having seen television. ('Crikey,' I told her, 'I saw him eat a four-finger KitKat in great bites, as though it was any old chocolate bar.' He didn't know the correct way was to snap one finger off at a time, because he'd never seen the advert.) That he'd never seen *Blue Peter*, and therefore hadn't heard of John Noakes and Shep. He'd missed out on *The Goodies*, *The Monkees*, *The Jacksons*, *The Osmonds*. He'd not seen *The Yellow Rolls-Royce*, nor the film about the rogue truck, nor *True Grit*, nor *The Sound of Music*. And that now, on his evenings with me, he'd be glued to the television, constantly getting up to change channels and see what was on the other side. He found *Dallas* 'enjoyable and intense' but couldn't take to *Coronation Street* after seeing a vicious slanging match between Bet Lynch and Elsie Tanner, which Bet won.

'Golly,' she said. 'Does he read much?'

'He's definitely read *Animal Farm*.'

'Christ. And do you ever talk?'

'Sometimes, but not if the news is on, or *Blankety Blank*,' I said, 'or *Not the Nine O'Clock News*.'

'How frustrating.'

'Or *Wish You Were Here*.'

I told her how handy he'd be after a nuclear attack – if anyone survived – how he could tame a duck, start a fire with a stick, knew how to make a barrel float, and that he didn't mind talking openly about things.

'That's good to know,' said my mother.

This led us to wonder what we two might contribute, in a post-apocalyptic scenario. I said I knew where my friend Melody's parents, the Longladys, had buried a stash of coffee granules and tins of fish. My mother talked about good places for wild berries and the importance of music in bad times, which didn't seem to amount to much. We wondered if our animal skills would be use-ful if no animals made it, and had anyone made a shelter big enough for animals – in the Noah's Ark style? We didn't know. And then, on that bewildering note, the doorbell went and it was Andy. I hadn't been expecting him, but was overjoyed to see him especially after the conversation we'd been having, and feeling that war was imminent. He was in a world of his own, though, sorry to intrude and so pink in the face, I had to ask if he was OK. He wasn't really, he'd had a terrible argument with his brother Tony after he (Andy) had criticized him (Tony) for going owling at night – with a torch.

'You remember my mother, don't you?' I said.

Yes, he said, he did.

'What do you mean, "owling with a torch"?' my mother asked, worried.

'Shining a torch up into the trees, at night, to see the owls,' Andy told her.

'Is that a bad thing to do?'

'It's very bad. Torch beams dazzle the owls,' he said, 'and it can send them into blind flight.'

My mother and I just stared at him.

He repeated, 'Blind flight,' quietly; his voice cracked and he seemed truly disturbed. 'I can't trust him to do the right thing.'

'How upsetting,' said my mother.

And then, with no consultation whatsoever, she offered him my bedroom for £5 per week, negotiable. And he accepted.

My mother went home with Danny and her new felt tips and left me with Andy. It all felt very strange.

'So,' I said, 'are you serious about wanting to move in there?'

'Yes.'

'But what about your brother?'

'He'll be glad to be rid of me. We don't get along.'

'So you're really going to move in?'

'Yes, if your mum's offer was serious.'

I assured him it was. That was how she did things.

'But I warn you, she'll read your diary and walk around in the nude.'

I was furious that she had failed to consult me before making the offer. How did she know I wasn't about to offer to take him in? He was my boyfriend and she had literally snatched him. However, it wasn't my style to make a fuss about people ruining my life. Yes, my boyfriend had suddenly become my mother's lodger, but I'd just have to get over it and look on the bright side. If there had to be a lodger, Andy was better than a stranger, and it meant that I could still go to the house and have a nice time without having to worry that some grotty old bloke might suddenly plonk himself down at the table and start eating duck pâté and pontificating about British Steel. But Andy being the lodger did present other worries. What if he and my mother became embroiled in some way or read the same book at the same time, or took country walks together? Would they? Could they? She might but he wouldn't, was my guess. Would she still walk around in the nude? Would she still wee in the sink? Would she sing 'Dido's Lament' at the top of her voice and remind poor Andy of his dead mother?

Later, the telephone rang and I ran to the landing to answer it. It was my mother wanting to make sure Andy understood there would be no meals provided or cooking done for him whatsoever and she had no intention of catering in any way, shape or form. There'd be no mealtimes – as such – no serving up of gravy-filled pies or jacket potatoes oozing with butter. Nothing. It was entirely every man for himself.

'It's fine, he gets it,' I said.

'Good. Just as long as he knows the score.'

'Yes, he does,' I said quietly, 'but he wonders if it's OK for him to bring girls back.'

'OK to do what?' asked my mother.

'Bring girls back,' I whispered again.

'What girls?'

'Well, me.'

'I suppose so,' she said, 'just as long as you don't put cigarette ends out of the window, or expect any catering.'

Some days later, Mr Holt and I went to collect Andy and his belongings from the shack behind the soap factory. We'd gone in the Snowdrop van which hadn't been necessary as Andy only had a battered suitcase, an old John Collier carrier and a motor-cycle helmet. He was sitting on the suitcase by a five-bar gate as we pulled into the lane and it was like a *Play for Today* because one small muddy child sat on the gate and another watched from a tree.

I didn't get out of the van in case Tony appeared with a Stanley knife and started a fight, which is what would've happened in a *Play for Today*, plus I was recalling my own home-leaving when the stolen spoon had been discovered. Tony didn't appear and Mr Holt opened the back doors. Andy said his farewells to the two boys, clambered in, and then sat on the floor, silently crying, all the way home. I got up to comfort him but Mr Holt asked me to sit down again, for safety reasons. If I'd been driving, I'd have pulled over, but Mr Holt knew that wouldn't have been what Andy wanted, and by the time we got back he seemed a bit better.

The whole family helped Andy feel at home. My mother changed the curtains from ones with huge daisies to a more manly abstract design. Danny made him a picture of a teapot with tea coming out, I gave him a Pagan Man deodorant, and Jack didn't make a fuss about having to switch to the daisy curtains, he simply turned them the wrong way round so that the daisies faced out-wards. Andy had brought his own duvet cover and a rolled-up poster but apparently very little else interiors-wise.

We had corn on the cob for tea, which was a treat in those days, especially the amount of marge we were taking, unchecked, and Andy made a comment about sweetcorn being one of the five main problem foods for the denture-wearer.

'Well, let's enjoy it while we can,' quipped my mother.

In the end we all stared out of the window at the enormous hawthorn hedge that ran the width of the short back garden and was alive with birds. Soon, I went to get the bus back to my flat and, though it was a wrench, it seemed more normal than staying at home with Andy there, counting sparrows and looking sad.

When the bus came, it was empty. The driver was surprised to have to stop and seemed curious. The bus was only really scheduled at that time to get into town to bring people home. I felt strangely upset to be going the wrong way and sat near the back, in case he tried to chat.

What would Andy be doing now? I wondered. My mother might be at the shelves, choosing a book to lend him – a book he probably didn't want but would now have to read and then discuss. This thought – of Andy having to read *Moby-Dick* – cheered me up no end. I laughed quietly to my reflection.

He would try to be a good kind of lodger. He would entertain everyone by peeling an orange in one piece and describing birdsong. He was a quick learner and would soon realize that the best, most helpful thing he could do would be the feeding of people. I imagined him heating up spaghetti for Danny, searching the kitchen drawers for the can-opener, not spotting the wall-mounted one in a silly hidden place near the boiler. He'd put slices of bread under the grill, and take a while to notice that the pilot light doesn't work and have to search for matches, which were kept out of Danny's reach in a little red tin, where Andy would never think to look. Then, once he'd lit the grill and the toast was toasting, he might take hold of the grill-pan handle without the oven glove and, it being burning hot because for some reason it was made of highly conductive material, would drop it with a God-almighty crash – the noise and chaos making him seem (unfairly) a clumsy idiot, which he wasn't. And then my mother would appear and ask if everything was OK and how was he getting on with *Moby-Dick*, or *Tell Me How Long the Train's Been Gone* or a Pamela Hansford Johnson, to indicate that, though he was a clumsy idiot, she didn't really mind just as long as he was reading a book that she could chat about.

I regretted my decision to not leave a *Things to Watch Out For* list, which would have included:

Make sure your bedroom door is firmly shut or else it might pop open whenever anyone opens or closes the hall door. Check the latch bolt has fully entered the strike-plate throat. Test by trying to pull the door open – if you hear a click, that's it. But don't trust by just looking.

The thing about giving this kind of advice outside of a journalistic context, though, was: A) people don't actually listen, B) they think you're fussing, or mentally ill, C) what's in it for you? D) it's not sexy to worry about practical things.

I hadn't left him entirely without advice on survival, though. I'd warned him not to show any disrespect to the piano, which was an easy thing to do – situated as it was in a sort of passing place between the kitchen and the lounge, making it an easy target for a perfunctory plink.

By the time my bus pulled in, I had concluded that Andy would be fine. And that though his living there would expose us all in some uncomfortable ways, it somehow put us on the map and made us all exist more, especially Jack with those daisies facing out on to the street.

I waited a whole fortnight before going home again, and when I did, it was all change. My brother Jack had grown, probably to his full height of six foot one inch, and towered over my mother who was five foot six inches. He'd got a moustache too and was outside the front of the house tinkering with a Suzuki AP 50, which was, if he was to be believed, the second-fastest moped in Flatstone.

The biggest and most noticeable change of course was that Andy Nicolello was there, and now seemed settled and happy and showed every sign of belonging. For instance, filling the kettle through its spout, shaking coffee powder into the mug without a spoon and kissing the dog on the lips.

I can't emphasize enough just how strange and exciting this was for me, and how distracting. I mean, notice that I barely mention my little brother's moped – a thing that was totally against the rules in our house because of the likelihood of the novice rider being run into by bigger, more powerful vehicles. The story of how Jack got this moped was a heartbreaking one, and though he survived, I will tell it, but later because now I have to describe how wonderful it was to see Andy Nicolello there, at my house, eating a slice of toast and Dairylea and laughing at the photographs in the parish magazine.

Not everything was rosy in the garden, though, I heard, e.g. my mother had thanked him for not playing a certain LP that he'd got from his brother, containing golden oldies such as 'Runaround Sue', which she considered unpleasant, saying she'd rather hear Sue's side.

Also, my mother's habit of having the gas fire going the whole time was bothering Andy's throat. He wasn't used to the dry air and had developed a persistent cough. Though he'd lived in a shack, it had been well-built and with insulation and ventilation and none of the spent-gas dryness of my mother's house – a flimsy type put up in a hurry. Andy told me in confidence that he'd suggested my mother wear a cardigan over her vest instead of putting the fire on, and that she'd been most annoyed by the suggestion and told him he didn't get to decide who wore what in her house for £5 a week. If he wanted those kinds of rights, it would be more like £15 a week. She always liked her arms out, still does.

Also, Andy was occasionally thoughtless about my mother's sensitivities (and mine, come to think of it). There'd been an incident, my mother told me, at the depot, earlier in the week, that was keeping Mr Holt over there practically all weekend. The incident involved two old boys Mr Holt had under him – Stan and Clarence – brothers who'd shared a Jack Russell called Scamp which came to work with them. Stan had taught Scamp to take titbits from his mouth at dinner break. Clarence thought the trick uncouth and had put in a formal complaint against his brother. Before Mr Holt had had a chance to conciliate, Clarence had accidentally run Scamp over in the forklift. The two had been on compassionate leave the rest of the week, Clarence in a terrible state. Mr Holt was exhausted, having done the work of three men and attended a dog funeral.

Hearing this, probably for the second or third time, Andy let a snort of laughter escape. Anyone who knew my mother at all would have known not to snigger at that point. She swung round and stared at him for a moment and I knew for certain there'd be no way of making up for that.

My mother changed the subject.

'I'm exhausted and in need of a chamomile tea,' she reported. 'I've just written a gruesome strangling scene – I feel like Anthony Burgess.'

Andy went out then, which I suppose was polite of him but disappointing. I watched him loping down the street, then wandered around looking for further signs of his living there. It was a small house so it wasn't long before I'd looked everywhere and was at the door to my (his) room.

Andy Nicolello had a duvet cover of autumn leaves in oranges and browns – I noticed this through the open door. I entered and snooped. I opened every drawer and held his clothes to my face, the Daz fragrance still detectable but competing with the sawdusty smell of my bedroom furniture. I closed the drawer and lay on the bed. My collage of Smirnoff adverts had been covered over with an enormous poster of Africa, made up of animals. The zebra, the lion, the elephant, the gazelle and others. I clacked through his cassettes. Ian Dury, Paul Simon, Bach, the Sex Pistols. I wrote *Scamp* in the layer of light dust on his mirror, thinking it quite funny, then changed my mind and wiped it away. He might assume my mother had done it and think her mischievous, and that was the last thing I wanted.

I snooped deeply. I noted a framed photograph of Pablo Picasso and a pretty woman, both in their bathing costumes, smoking.

Later, Mr Holt arrived home and was delighted to see me. 'Please tell me you've made an apple pie,' he said, with praying hands, and I said, 'I'm just about to.' And I did, albeit a crumble. And when we ate it later I began asking about Scamp and the old boys but my mother stood behind him frantically signalling, 'No,' which was a habit of hers to keep everything sweet.

Andy returned and we took a cup of tea up to his (my) room and chatted. I thought I might take my top off but, just as I crossed my arms and took hold of the bottom edge of my shirt, Danny walked in wanting to tell us that his lorry was articulated, which was impressive but not conducive to sex.

12. 'Bright Eyes'

Around that time, maybe a few weeks later, JP surprised me horribly with an invitation to join him and Tammy for lunch at the Golden Fleece – a pub run by a Freemason called Kenneth Benn. We were to be ready to leave at one o'clock, he said, as he was playing a round of golf later with Bill Turner and couldn't hang around.

'The noisettes of lamb are highly recommended, I hear,' JP said.

I politely declined the offer. It wasn't just the thought of watching him arrange bits of food on his cutlery, nor my suspicion that either they were trying to entice me into a *ménage à trois* or that JP wanted to present me to Kenneth Benn as the daughter of city tycoon and Freemason Edward Vogel, it was also that eating out wasn't a favourite occupation. I hadn't quite recovered from the realization (at a young age) that the sight of me eating made my mother hate me – an idea born around the same time that my divorced father was very prone to taking us for long restaurant lunches to prevent the possibility of a visit to his new life.

Things happened during those lunches – dramatic and troubling things. For instance, the time my brother, Jack, pretended to be a dog and ran around under the tables barking, and bit my father's hand in front of everyone. The time we were seen by our mother's cousin in a restaurant with our father and she reported back to our mother that we'd seemed to be having 'a fine time' and our mother had been terribly hurt by this and surprised because we always, *always* told her what a terrible ordeal it was. And the time, early on, when we went to Fenwick's of Leicester's dining room to be introduced to the wife our father had just married and the waitress gave us too few bread rolls.

We'd seen the marriage announced in the newspaper and sent them a home-made card. None of us was very good at drawing women and so our mother had had to do the bride and she made her a bit grotty with a huge neck but none of us dared complain. And here the wife was, in Fenwick's – the new Mrs Vogel, in real life looking like Shirley Partridge, smiling and touching her earrings. She wore clip-ons and told a funny story about one falling into the soup on their honeymoon cruise and splashing the captain.

Although captivated by my new stepmother's charming story, I'd noticed that everyone except me had taken a roll from the bread basket, and now there were none.

'Yes,' my father was saying, 'the captain's smart white uniform was covered in green spots,' and I interrupted him with the news about the rolls.

'Don't worry, Liza,' he said (he called me that sometimes), 'call the waitress over and ask her to bring you one.' Everyone paused to watch me do it but I didn't, I couldn't – I was just a small child and not ready to call waitresses over. My father drummed his fingers, waiting so that he and Shirley Partridge could continue with their honeymoon tales and maybe even burst into 'I Think I Love You' – him singing, her on tambourine. After a while, my siblings resumed chattering, tore into their rolls and attacked the butter. I wished I were dead.

Suddenly, in the distance, a door swung open and there, all in white – half-surgeon, half-saint – was the waitress holding a roll in a pair of silver tongs, as carefully as if it were one of my vital organs.

'Madam,' she said, placing it down, 'I'm so sorry.'

I cried two tiny tears of relief that no one saw but Shirley. I'd have loved to fall into her arms, but obviously never would. And neither could I relate the whole thing to my real loving mother because she'd dig around in the details and find a version of the event in which she was being personally snubbed.

'Oh, won't you come with us to the Golden Fleece, Lizzie?' Tammy pleaded. 'Don't you want to?'

'I *do* want to,' I said. 'It's just I don't usually eat in public.'

★

When JP and Tammy got back from the Golden Fleece at two-ish they were snarky. I asked how the meal had gone and Tammy told me I'd been sensible to decline – she'd ordered the noisettes of lamb and it had been like eating rubber bands, and Kenneth Benn had been smarmy as heck.

'You dodged a bullet, Lizzie,' she said.

JP denied it angrily, and said his lamb had been perfectly tender and Ken most hospitable.

Tammy faffed around in the utility room for a few moments and then, realizing she was running late for her hair appointment, asked me if I'd mind moving the cactuses out of the waiting room to the shaded bench in the garden.

'They need their outside time,' she said.

I said that would be fine.

JP went upstairs to the empty surgery for a rest. He was good at taking naps and often had twenty minutes. Sometimes he'd have a cassette of Neil Sedaka or *The Mikado* going and I'd hear him shouting along to 'Oh, Carol', 'Tit Willow', or 'Three Little Maids'. This particular afternoon, it was Art Garfunkel, and soon he was singing along to 'Bright Eyes'. It's a dreamy kind of song, as you might know, with a lovely melody and compelling lyrics (dreams, rivers, fog, eyes) and I couldn't help but sing along and harmonise. Before we got to the last chorus though, the waiting-room door interrupted us and I was surprised to see Priti. She looked ghastly – a terrible swelling around her mouth was dragging her lower eyelid down, giving her a zombified appearance. I was reminded briefly of Holly the buck rabbit arriving at Watership Down, after escaping the Sandleford warren and being nursed back to health.

'My God, Priti, what's happened?' I said.

'I've got such pain,' she murmured. 'Can the dentist help me?'

JP hated seeing casual patients, especially just before golf – when he apparently really needed the rest. But after my mother had called him a xenophobe, seeing Priti in this state, and knowing JP had at least thirty minutes before he had to leave, I ran upstairs – after settling Priti with a *Woman's Own* and a tissue – knocked assertively and put my head round the door.

He wasn't napping, he was fiddling around with a screwdriver adjusting the chair.

'*Da-de-da-da-de burned so brightly, la-da-da-da so pale . . .*' JP sang.

'JP, there's a casual with toothache, will you see her?'

'Is he coloured?' he asked.

'She's Indian.' I looked him steadily in the eye.

'*Da-de-de-de-da burned so brightly . . .*' he sang.

Then: 'It's not one of your mother's friends, is it?'

'No,' I said, 'it's the girl Tammy kicked in the face – she's in a lot of pain.'

'Her again, is it? I haven't got time – send her up to the FPA,' he said, and turned away. '*Bri-ight eyes . . .*'

'I think you have got time.'

'I beg your pardon?'

'You're meeting Bill at three – you've plenty of time.'

'Oh, yes, you're the boss here, I forgot,' he said.

'She's in agony,' I began, 'and feverish.'

'Off you go now, nurse, please,' he said, turning up the volume on his radio-cassette player.

I returned to the waiting room and told Priti that the dentist was unable to see her but that he'd strongly suggested she go up to the FPA and they'd give her a list of dentists who might be able to fit her in. I explained where she needed to go.

'I could walk up there with you,' I offered.

'Why won't the dentist see me?' Her mouth was paralysed with pain.

'He's too busy.'

'But there's no one else here,' said Priti, her voice trembling, gesturing around the empty room.

'*How can the light da-da-da-da-da suddenly burn so pale?*' drifted down through the ceiling.

'It's his golf afternoon,' I said, unable to think of anything better to say.

Priti's response to this was shocking. She grabbed a tentacle from one of Tammy's most impressive *Schlumbergera*, pulled it off, dropped it to the floor and silently broke down. Tears began dripping down her face, wide, glossy tears that ran along her jawbone and dripped off her chin.

I picked up the cactus tentacle and stared at her. She tried to speak but the words were lost in a dry, harsh moan that came unbidden from her crumpled mouth. She covered her face with her hands and her body rocked with quiet sobs.

Upstairs JP had rewound the cassette and as 'Bright Eyes' came on for a third time my sadness turned to anger. How dare he not help her? How could he let someone suffer like this while he tinkered with a screwdriver and played Art Garfunkel? Maybe if he could just see her he'd have a change of heart. I remembered my mother's words about making monsters less monstrous.

'Come on,' I said, ushering Priti into the hall. 'I'd like the dentist to see just how much pain you're in – and maybe he'll be able to help.'

We ascended the stairs one step at a time, and at the door to the spare surgery, I knocked.

'Ye-es?' said JP. I pushed Priti gently into the room before me.

'Erm, sorry to bother you again but this is the patient. I thought you should see how poorly she looks.'

I was shocked to see JP now lying on the dental chair, in swimming trunks and protective goggles, under a sunlamp. I tried to retreat, pulling on Priti's sleeve, but JP shot up, pushed his goggles on to his forehead, turned and looked at us in disbelief.

'*There's a high wind in the trees, a cold sound in the air, and nobody ever knows when you go, and where do you start? Oh, into the dark,*' sang Art Garfunkel.

JP squirmed in the chair and flicked the cassette player off.

'What the hell do you think you're playing at, nurse?' he shouted. 'Get her out of here at once.'

Back in the waiting room I apologized profusely to Priti. 'I didn't realize he was under the sunlamp.'

We heard the front door slam and through the window I saw JP dart across the road with his club bag bashing against his hip.

Priti started to leave but I told her to wait. It was ridiculous. If her pain had been in her toe, her arm, her leg, her stomach, she'd have gone to the GP and had it cleaned up, looked at, fixed and medicated for free, but because it was in her mouth, she was turned away. It was insane.

I went to the front door, looked out, and then locked it and left the key in. It was ridiculous, I told myself again. I knew what to do. It wasn't rocket science. I took Priti through to the surgery. I switched on the water to the spittoon, flicked the light on, put the bib around her neck and washed my hands.

'Rinse out,' I said.

There was an abscess above the upper right two. Taking a Mitchell's Trimmer, I lanced the abscess and stroked the gum downwards until it drained. I made up a warm saline wash and Priti rinsed while I wrote a prescription, copying exactly the duplicate of the last one JP had written.

'Remind me, what's your full name?' I said.

'Pritiben Mistry.'

'Get this made up,' I said. 'Take the tablets according to the instructions, keep rinsing gently with warm salty water, and come and see me tomorrow, in the flat, after surgery hours.'

JP was quiet and embarrassed the next day. At the usual coffee break time he made an excuse and left the building. I celebrated this outcome with a hot chocolate using the practice milk and helped myself to one of his cigarettes.

Priti duly called the following evening.

She felt much better, she said, and was very grateful to me for treating her. Although I avoided looking too closely at her face, she definitely seemed improved.

'I'm sorry . . . about the plant,' she said, meaning the cactus that she'd ripped.

'Oh, no,' I said, 'don't worry, people always take it out on the plants.'

Priti looked puzzled.

'Do they?'

'Yes,' I said. 'Well, occasionally.'

We chatted about life. She talked about her two jobs and I told her about my one job. We met again at Jazzercise a couple of weeks later and afterwards she came up for a cup of tea and I told her all about Andy and she told me about her boyfriend, Dhann, who was a Punjabi and whom her uncle thought 'flashy'. She also told me that her family had left Uganda when she was young, but she could still remember their old home.

'It was nothing like Leicester,' she said.

They'd had a small field behind the house, in which they'd kept a few farm animals. The sheep had been so agile and clever they'd been able to clamber up into small trees and help themselves to fruit. It sounded magical to me but Priti said they were just a nuisance. She could remember her parents working all day in a shop and it being hot, and having a nasty school uniform. She was sometimes homesick even now. I said I knew how she felt.

For the next week or so JP sang 'Bright Eyes'. I too sang it, though unwittingly, and therefore Tammy sang it as well. Mrs Skidmore, the cleaner, sang it and because we all sang and hummed it constantly, the patients picked it up and they whistled, sang and hummed it. 'Bright Eyes' was no longer anything to do with *Watership Down*, nor Art Garfunkel. It was a musical reminder for my having treated a patient, and forged an NHS medical prescription.

'What's that song we all keep humming?' said Tammy, humming it.

' "Bright Eyes",' said JP. 'Smashing song.'

This reminded Tammy of the book. And she told me how much she liked seeing what books people were reading because it gave her ideas.

'What do *you* like reading?' I asked, realizing I'd only ever seen her with a book on Consultative Selling and magazines about weddings and houses.

'Oh, I'll read anything,' Tammy told me. 'Romance, whodunnits, thrillers, biographies, memoirs, you name it . . . but not poetry.'

She'd particularly noticed the book I'd been reading when I'd come for my interview.

'It made me think how lovely you must be,' she said, 'and to be truthful, that's partly why I really wanted you to get the job.'

'Oh, really, what was it?' I said, pretending not to remember.

'That one about the rabbits.'

I can't tell you how long my mother and I spent selecting a suitable book for me to be seen with at my interview. A book reveals more about you – as a person and a colleague – than anything else, barring what you actually say and your qualifications and experience. That was what my mother thought. She suggested I take a book which combined scientific curiosity, adventure and literary merit, something like *Moby-Dick*.

'Not that,' I said. 'I don't want any whale talk.'

'Why on earth not?'

'I couldn't finish it.'

'You didn't finish *Moby-Dick*?' said my mother, scandalized.

'You know I didn't,' I said. 'It made me feel sick – all the sperm oil and beheaded whales.'

My mother tutted. She used *Moby-Dick* as a measure of people.

'How about *Jaws* by Peter Benchley then?' she said. 'It's basically *Moby-Dick* for the less able reader – it has the teeth connection, and not quite so much harpooning.'

'Yes,' I said, 'perfect.' And we scoured the house unsuccessfully for Mr Holt's copy, which as it turned out had come from the library.

We went through the bookshelves. We rejected *Black Beauty* by Anna Sewell because it seemed childish, Edna O'Brien in case it made the dentist angry, Wodehouse in case they thought me prone to pranking. We almost chose a Jane Austen but my mother worried that they might think me overqualified for the job. I wondered briefly if I might take the book I was actually reading at the time – *The Millstone* by M. Drabble – but my mother said, 'Are you mad?'

In the end I settled for *Watership Down* because of its natural-history elements, wide-ranging appeal, and because I wouldn't mind some rabbit talk, having read it twice and seen the film.

Now I hated it. I hated JP, and I asked my mother if I should hand in my notice. She repeated her view that 'staying can sometimes make all the difference'.

I became wilfully less conscientious, though. Not with the patients, or the instruments, of course – I didn't go crazy and risk anyone's life. But I watered the cactuses and African violets with tap water and splashed it around a bit haphazardly. I was less careful about the staircarpet – JP had asked us expressly not to tread on the nosing – and I was very sloppy with the appointments book. If a patient asked to make an appointment in advance for their next six-monthly check-up, I'd say, 'No need, just give us a ring nearer the time.' And if they asked, 'Do you send reminders?' I'd say, 'Yes.' Even though we definitely didn't – because of the cost of postage. And when it came to making tea and coffee, I made half-tea-half-coffee, and I didn't warm the milk as I was supposed to. I used the coffee spoon in the sugar, and soon there were brown clumps in the bowl – and I really couldn't have cared less.

I occasionally set the smoke alarms off with my cigarette lighter, especially if I suspected JP was resting under his sunlamp, in his trunks, so as to inconvenience him. And I'd chuckle to myself hearing him stumble around, trying to get his trousers on quickly in case there was a fire.

13. Sex

I decided I was going to have sex with Andy (and had the Durex ready), but I realized it couldn't be in my family home. Especially with an unreliable bedroom door that might swing open at any time, the paper-thin walls, and Danny wandering around looking for someone to play with. But it wasn't just those things, it was the atmosphere, too.

My family home just wasn't conducive to sex – not to me anyway. It was to my sister and my brother who had it there frequently over the years, I gather, and my mother, etc. But I was sensitive. So many things made it impossible for me to have sex; if the other person was laughing, annoyed, acting sexy, or watching telly, or wasn't freshly washed, or if we were standing up, or on a bus, or in a bus shelter, or in a dark street, or on a bridge, or in a phone box, and definitely not in a car. I know that will make me seem fussy but there was a whole list of things I couldn't do, and though my reasoning seemed sound, I appreciate now that these abstinences made me an odd teenager.

I rarely drank alcohol, in case my face and neck went blotchy, or I lost control and said things I'd regret the next day or had sex with someone who hated me. I was happy to have smooch/ kissing sessions but I'd never yet allowed anyone to touch my breasts or vagina (Christ), the reason being that I didn't want anyone who'd *want* to touch them to touch them. I rarely put my tiny cleavage on show because if/when people looked at it, I wanted to hit them. I never used to bring anyone back to my house in case my mother was naked or tried to talk to them or to lend them a book or tell them her favourite names – while naked. And so on. I never ate in cafés in case I burst into tears. I never left the tap running while brushing my teeth because it seemed such a waste of water – and that was before people even cared about water. I never let any of my friends babysit baby Danny for my mother in case she changed her mind at the last minute and didn't go out and just sat there chatting to them.

Because of all the above, if I was to have a sexual relationship with Andy, he'd have to come to my flat for it and, since he'd been living with my mother, he didn't seem keen. He'd come in for a cup of tea, telly, chat and cuddle, but then he'd suddenly have to leave. He might be babysitting Danny (see above) or cooking a pie, or just wanting to get back for an early night. So I had to address the subject head on, and I did so one evening at my flat.

'I can't have sex with you at my mother's house,' I said.

'Can you have sex with me here?' he asked.

That led to a most lovely, exciting hour of love – though not quite sex – and then him suddenly wondering if we might go out for dinner and me declining abruptly and, instead of explaining my complicated feelings about eating out, I said I needed some time alone to work on my dental journal.

In my imagined life, we'd have rushed out joyfully to a bistro and picked at each other's plates, laughing, and looked at each other full in the face while chewing confidently, and I'd have been wearing his shirt, and I'd have stopped laughing after a while and told him about JP refusing to see Priti – in a straightforward manner, angry but mature – and he'd have been outraged and impressed that I'd taken action.

Instead, he went home and I remembered a girl friend from the past, whom I'd considered a numbskull, once telling me in all seriousness, 'Your problem is you think too much.' And so, in response to that long-ago thing, I wrote a long, clever article for *Woman's Own* called 'Do You Think Too Much?' which concluded that conscientiousness was nothing to be ashamed of and thinking things through, philosophizing, pondering, considering – call it what you will – was a good thing, as long as it didn't turn into procrastination and stop you living a full life.

*

Around that time, my mother received a written warning from Mrs Danube, principal of Curious Minds nursery. It was mostly concerning her lateness.

You are frequently late to collect your child and this is inconvenient and against the rules of Curious Minds, she wrote. It was true, and quite polite under the circumstances. My mother was never on time; once she'd been so late that Mrs Danube had taken Danny with her to Oadby because Mr Danube needed her home, and she'd had no alternative. My mother had said that in a different narrative it would have been kidnap. The letter went on to say that Danny often arrived at school without required items from home and she gave examples of things that had recently been requested but were still absent: *A photograph of his family, 10p towards the materials for his lentil rumba shaker, a change of clothing, an overall or apron, some slip-on gym shoes.*

My mother was blasé about it. Mrs Danube was in the wrong job, she said.

'She should be a prison guard or a swimming-pool attendant.'

I wasn't, though (blasé). I didn't like to displease Mrs Danube and it wasn't just my fear of authority, it was my worry that Danny might get it in the neck if she was rubbed up the wrong way. Anyway, I redoubled my efforts to do things right on my Danny days.

And so it was most alarming when, just days after that, it looked as though I might be delayed at the surgery and therefore late for Danny. It was the day that JP was going to fit himself with a new upper denture (a key item from the Masonic Improvements list) and first had to extract his two front teeth. For anyone not dentally aware, dentures can be fitted immediately afterwards to replace extracted teeth (this technique, called immediate restoration, is very popular for people not wanting to go around with missing teeth while their gums heal). The procedure, in JP's case, should have been quick and easy, the teeth in question being single-rooted incisors, old and slightly loosened. However, he managed to bungle it by snapping one of the teeth off at the gum line. He then couldn't extract the root because his allergy to the local anaesthetic had caused a mild but incapacitating reaction, leaving him unable to grip the instruments.

'You might have to call Bill Turner to get this root out for me,' JP said, and I looked at the clock. It was almost time for me to leave to get Danny. I stared at JP, who was leaning on the treatment tray examining his shaking hands. He tried to pick up the vanity mirror to look at the mess in his mouth but it only slipped through his fingers.

'It's no good, nurse, you're going to have to call Bill.'

In the time it would take for Bill to arrive, I could sprint up to Curious Minds, return with Danny on my back and put him in the waiting room with a copy of *Playhour and Robin*. 'OK,' I said.

I picked up the receiver and dialled. Bill's nurse Rhona answered and said Bill had gone home. I began to dial Bill's home number but hung up. We hadn't got time. I was against the clock. I'd seen JP extract roots many times. Incisors were straightforward – all you needed was a tight grip and a steady hand.

'Sit down,' I said.

He understood – it made sense to him too – and he sat. I washed my hands, selected a clean pair of straight-beaked anteriors from the pile on the draining board, and held them up for his approval.

'Yes,' he nodded.

He sat back in the chair, opened his mouth wide, and curled his lip. I approached but he suddenly sat up.

'Get a really tight grip on it, won't you, nurse.'

I pushed him gently back.

'I know.'

Holding his temples between my thumb and fingers, I was surprised at the slimness of his skull and the slipperiness of his hair. The heel of my hand pressed his brow. I located the root – more by feel than by sight. JP's clumsy digging around at the gum line had made it bleed quite heavily. I pushed the beaks up around it and, pushing some more, gripped it, relaxed and let the forceps slide down the root – just to get the feel of it. I needed to get a hold further up to avoid breaking any more off. I jammed the beaks up quite hard and JP grunted.

'That's it,' he seemed to say.

I pushed up further and then gripped, hard. My thumb joint hurt. I rotated one way, then the other and kept that up for a while before increasing the force until I felt the bindings break and then there it was, the root, perfect, pinky-yellow in the beaks. And JP sat up.

If the police had burst in and arrested me at that moment for quackery, I'd have pleaded temporary insanity, and my lawyer would put it to the court that I'd had no choice. That, just like the women in *Woman's Own* and *Titbits* who'd pulled communication cords, jumped off trains, run along train tracks, abandoned cars, set off fire alarms and made hoax calls to the emergency services, etc., there'd been no other course of action available to me. Not because of maternal instinct, involuntary familial love, or a sense of duty, but because of the cuntish look on Mrs Danube's face when I or any other guardian or mother arrived a minute or two late for pick-up.

JP examined the root.

'It's all there,' I said, with pride.

He continued looking at it. And then, shielding his mouth with his hand, said, 'Yeah, I must've loosened it.'

I hadn't given it another thought until I saw JP again the Monday after. He was in bright and early even though his first patient wasn't due until nine-fifteen.

'How's the new denture bedding in?' I asked.

'Nurse, I need to talk to you about that,' he said, with some stress, I thought.

'Oh, is everything OK?'

'The thing is, I never should have let you do it.'

'Do what?'

'Extract my tooth. It was unprofessional and irresponsible and just plain wrong.'

'OK. Sorry.'

'Look, I'm not blaming you for what happened, but I have to impress upon you just how seriously wrong it was.'

'OK.'

'Had I not been suffering some kind of allergic reaction I never should have allowed it.'

I was a bit surprised by this, to be honest. It was his tooth, after all, and he was a dentist. It was up to him what he did with his teeth, wasn't it?

'Is the denture bedding in OK?' I asked again.

'Yes, thank you, it's fine.'

'May I have a look?'

'I don't think that would be wise.'

I felt a little peeved. I had taken the tooth out and, whether or not it was wrong ethics-wise, I had every right to see how it was healing.

'I'd like to see how it's healing,' I persisted.

'Oh, all right then, quickly, but then we must never speak of it again. And never tell a soul.'

Andy called in late one day with a drop-off and came up after surgery for tea and telly. He had a bath – even living at my mother's house, baths were a luxury – and stayed in so long I honestly wondered if he'd drowned. He hadn't but he had gone woozy. I told him about Priti's abscess. I'd tried not to because the last thing I wanted was to discuss JP's awfulness when I was planning to have sex, when sex was already fraught with off-putting possibilities, but I couldn't wait.

'She was obviously in agony,' I said, 'and I confronted JP with her, and he just waltzed off to play golf with Bill.'

'What a cunt,' said Andy.

'I treated her myself,' I said.

And Andy looked shocked. 'What?'

'I couldn't see what else to do,' I said. 'She was in no state to go trailing around town, begging for treatment.'

'God, no, you did the right thing,' he said, 'but you must be careful.'

Then I told him how I'd extracted JP's root – I couldn't help myself. He was shocked and impressed, couldn't believe it, and wanted all the details.

'Was it difficult?'

'Not really, only like getting an awkward eyebrow hair – once I'd got hold of it, I just wiggled it out.'

'You're a real little dentist now,' he said, with pride.

14.   The American Sabbatical

The surgery was going to be closed while JP and Tammy had a week in Dubrovnik with Bill and Jossy Turner. This closure coincided with the Mercurial Laboratory also being closed – it being one of the weeks of the so-called 'Leicester fortnight', during which many factories and businesses closed down and the city became a ghost town. The point being that Andy would have the week off too. I had been on the point of asking if he fancied going away together for a few days, maybe to Blakeney or Wells, and mentioned this to my mother.

'Perhaps,' I said, 'if Mr Holt is planning a trip over to Norfolk to visit his mother he might give us a lift.'

I was imagining a week of beach walks, sea dips, birdwatching and sex. Andy roaming, gazing at swooping seabirds through his binoculars, and then spying me in the dunes, wearing my parka with nothing underneath. But my mother advised me against bothering Andy.

'I believe he's planning a solo birdwatching trip along the coast of Suffolk,' she said.

'Oh,' I said, 'but I'd like Suffolk too.' I could write some articles about life on the east coast, I thought, and maybe do a watercolour or two, and relocate the sexy games to Walberswick dunes. But my mother felt the word 'solo' was a clue to Andy's intentions.

'I think he's planning to have some time alone,' she said. 'You know, solo.'

This irritated me no end, Andy Nicolello thinking he could just crash into our lives, cause ructions and necessitate the swapping of curtains. And now the holidays were here and he thought it fine to just disappear on his own.

'I could still go with him,' I said. 'He'd have plenty of time alone – the two of us need only meet up at the end of the day and have a rudimentary supper in our digs.'

'I think Andy really needs some space.'

How was my mother the expert on what Andy wanted and needed? What about what I wanted and needed? Or was it that she secretly planned to whizz up the A14 in *her* parka with nothing underneath?

I didn't suggest anything to Andy for that week. He went off on his own with his binoculars and a notepad and a book about pere-grine falcons. And with nothing else available to me, except going to stay in Andy's empty bed to spy on my mother, I invited myself to my father's house for a couple of days, to see them and also to investigate their USA plan, which suddenly seemed quite interest-ing. For the remainder of the week I'd do DIY jobs in my flat while listening to music, and possibly write an article entitled 'Mothers'.

Before going to my father's, I met up with my sister at the Hun-gry I Pancake House. She was full of Massachusetts.

'Whoever gets to go to the States will be eating lots more pancakes – they practically live off them over there and fill them with cherries and ham and God knows what.'

The more we discussed Massachusetts, the more I felt I should be the one offered the opportunity – my sister and brother were already so successful and I was very much in a rut with nothing much on the horizon, only Andy, and to be honest, where was that going?

'Why would they pick you to go with them?' I'd asked my sis-ter. 'You've never shown any interest in them before.'

'I'm the obvious choice. I'd help them settle and then get a job and be a perfect role model,' she'd replied, and continued, 'The USA is crying out for trained nurses who speak English and have a psychology diploma.'

'Nonsense,' I said, 'the USA has its own trained nurses. You'd seem very old-fashioned over there compared to American nurses.'

'What do American nurses have that I don't have?'

'Confidence!' I shouted, which was a bit low of me.

My sister laughed. 'So what skills could you take over there?' she asked.

'Dental nursing. I'm in training, plus I'm working on my A to Z of Dentistry.'

'You must be fucking joking,' she said. 'Have you seen their teeth over there?'

'What about them?'

'They're light years ahead in dentistry. You'd never get a job in a dental clinic over there with your teeth – they'd laugh in your face.'

That rang true, actually. I'd heard JP and Bill Turner marvelling at the veneer work Brits were getting done in the States and coming home with. The dazzling white teeth literally shone out of the mouth as if they were illuminated from within. Unnaturally white teeth were a thing some people were particularly keen on, I'd noticed, especially middle-aged men. So perhaps dental nursing wouldn't be an option for me, but I could go anyway – in the first instance as a kind of daughter-cum-au pair and then launch myself as the USA correspondent for *Woman's Own*. I could pick up all sorts of American lifestyle tips that would enchant and enthral our British readers.

How does Rosalynn Carter keep her trim figure in spite of a peanut addiction?

How do American women cope with the modern problems such as indecent exposure, sexual betrayal, the side effects of the contraceptive pill, and creasy eyeshadow?

Do they mind not having a queen/king?

Do they get French cheeses and if so, how, and what do they serve it with?

Why do American women like English men so much when they sound so stuffy?

Why do Americans serve such big lunch portions?

How do they keep their turkey moist during cooking?

Why do their cars have to be so big?

Racoons?

The history of that double-wink, with the right eye, then the left.

And all the above was without even going there and seeing it for myself in real life; there would literally be no end of things to report on. It gave me butterflies and goosebumps just thinking about it.

By the end of our pancake lunch, my sister and I were in a race for the USA but we agreed on one thing – we'd keep it between the two of us. If Jack got wind of it, he'd go straight to the head of the queue, being a boy, and clever.

'If anyone gets to have a year in the USA with Dad it should be one of us girls,' said my sister.

'And we must stop saying "queue",' I said. 'It's "line".'

'And you must learn to drive,' said my sister, which was true.

It wasn't going to be difficult, I thought, to get ahead of Tina in the race for America. She seemed to have forgotten the impact of the face-to-face encounter and only made the odd phone call reminding them how medically qualified she was becoming, with new courses and modules stretching a year ahead. This would mean nothing, though; if they had to choose between the two of us, they'd only remember her as a needy vegetarian with a habit of speaking the truth at the worst moments. Whereas I was going to stay with them, in person, and my jolly presence and tips on how to make frothy coffee, and combat bad breath and dental sensitivity, would be at the forefront of their minds for weeks afterwards.

Knocking on the door of your father's family home is a horrible thing. Anyone who has done this will know. You knock, he lets you in and goes overboard with how welcome you are. His new children's intimacy with him hits you every time. They talk to him, call him an old silly and they burp but he doesn't mind really. And then it turns out your half-siblings play Beatles records at the wrong speed just for fun, and your half-brother knows all the words to 'Yesterday' and 'Sergeant Pepper' and they have all the records, in their sleeves, and this is all heartbreaking.

Of course, the 'American Sabbatical' – that's what they were calling it – cropped up. Firstly, that they probably wouldn't be going until 1982, which was months and months away; a child in a straw boater piped up, 'It's because of my Latin classes.'

'Why, do they not have Latin classes over there?' I asked, and my stepmother moved in to shield the girl from my question.

'Timing is important,' she said, 'educationally.'

My stepmother mentioned that my father was very much at home in the USA.

'He seems to go down very well there.'

'Why is that?' I asked.

'It's his very Englishness they take to, coupled with his funny Americanisms.'

She and my father then told various anecdotes about people being delighted at my father saying, 'Howdy y'all,' and so on, but in his royal voice.

My father's house was most charming, with rickety patterned floor tiles that knocked together under your feet. Mrs Penrose wandered about with beeswax polish, and an old apple tree creaked by a flaky red-brick garden wall. To have an old apple tree seemed such a delightful thing – I thought of our spindly young trees, put in by Mr Holt after Dutch elm disease had done for every tree on our estate and beyond, which still showed no sign of fruit, only papery blossom.

The youngest child clambered up the tree as if reading my mind, and I watched my father, amused but fretting that she might fall out. It was a curious scene; the child was barely four feet up and perfectly able-bodied. I thought of all the trees I'd climbed – some seven foot at least, not to mention the roofs and windowsills – if only he'd known. If only *I'd* known this was all it took. I imagined all the confidence I'd ever had swirling about in the branches of all the trees I'd climbed, disappearing in the breeze like petals, because no one had stood at the bottom calling, 'Be careful, Lizzie.'

When the child protested that she couldn't get down, my father called, 'Oh, you silly nitwit,' and fetched a ladder.

★

In the morning I heard my father move through the bedroom swishing the curtains back and waking the children, one by one.

'Good morning, [name], it's another lovely day.'

And I imagined their sleepy little eyes opening on the new day. How lucky they were. I imagined hearing this every morning in Massachusetts.

I stayed in bed until nine even though I'd been wide awake since seven and by the time I got downstairs they were all togged up for a walk in the woods. I went with them but I couldn't get the morning greeting out of my head. 'Good morning, [name], it's another lovely day.'

One of the children saw me smoking and another saw me not smiling — and all the things I did or said, or didn't do, meant so much to them but nothing to me because I was only acting — for Massachusetts. And then, to cap everything else, my father and his wife's friends, Gita and Prideep, came for supper and talked about the danger of aerosols to the environment, poor old Robert Runcie having to drive up and down the Dover Road, and Mrs Thatcher writing to Mr Carter asking for missiles — and I had nothing to say except that my colleague might have a test-tube baby.

I felt Massachusetts slipping away and I'm ashamed to admit that, before I left, I went to the velvet-lined cutlery box they had in the dining room and helped myself to a silver rat-tail teaspoon.

15. Woman's Own

Intuition told me I wouldn't be going to Massachusetts with my father. My brother wouldn't go either – he'd be too busy dissecting crabs or watching zebra gallop patterns at the University College. I doubted my sister would be invited; she'd ruin the family vibe with awkward comments like at a recent dinner where the middle child had played Vivaldi in plaits and a Victorian blouse, and my sister had said, 'Do you know "Ring My Bell"?'

If I wasn't going to become the *Woman's Own* USA correspondent, based in Massachusetts, I'd go to London instead and get a job and become a writer in my spare time, which would be considerable. Writing was one of those careers that needs no qualifications – a thing my mother endlessly mentioned – but to have written reams and reams of stories, essays, articles and poems, which would be doable in London, the city being so conducive to it.

'Writers just have to write, like artists, musicians and criminals. They just need to keep going at it,' she'd say. And, 'The old writers are falling like flies – Barbara Pym, C. P. Snow, Elizabeth Bishop, all gone this year.'

And you see, I had the benefit of my mother's innate knowledge of the publishing industry. Quite how she knew so much, I don't know – but she seemed to know more than the actual professionals. I wouldn't be bothering Faber & Faber and trying to write a literary masterpiece to beat all the grotty old men to the prizes and recognition, though. I shouldn't even want to write a book, as such. I'd write my column for *Woman's Own* and try to bring it up to date for the younger reader, and if *Woman's Own* didn't want my column (it being too young in tone) I'd offer it to *Woman* which was that bit younger.

I'd research which toothpaste was actually best for fresh breath, not which was the most advertised (Colgate) or had the nicest name (Crest) or the nicest colour (Aquafresh) or was the gentlest (Sensodyne). I'd conduct a fresh-breath test – feeding a bunch of women garlic-and-herb cheese on toast with spring onions and chilli powder, and then getting them each to clean their teeth with a different brand, and finally asking a really fussy man, say JP, to declare a winner.

I say a man like JP because he was extremely anti smelly foods and had banned his previous two wives and now Tammy from eating onions unless they were Whitworth's dried variety (and you know my views on dried veg of all kinds), and frequently complained that my cooking made the building smell 'like Calcutta'.

Extrapolating, I might research an article about all the things men don't like women doing. ('He'd Rather You Refrained From . . .') I could interview women in London and produce a league table of worst things. My own limited experience suggested that men disliked women driving, eating onions and spices, having a dog, talking about sport, laughing loudly, spending money on fripperies, disagreeing with them, chatting on the phone, climbing trees, talking about dogs, mowing the lawn in flip-flops, wearing too much make-up, being too fat, being too keen, worrying and reading the news on TV.

The readers could decide for themselves how they might react to the findings. One woman might stop talking about dogs to please her husband, another might suddenly take up laughing and golf just to make hers suffer. It would be entirely up to you, the individual.

I'd already been working on a piece about the brain entitled, 'Who is in Charge Here?' about how never to read the newspaper when you're eating your lunch because your brain – focused and worried about the news – can fail to notice that you're also eating . . . and even after a huge cheese-and-pickle cob it will stop worrying about nuclear war and start wondering, 'Where's my lunch?' even though you've just eaten it. And how sniffing lemon peel can help you remember people's names. And how chanting can soothe period pain. And how giving your brain a name could raise your intelligence and what are good names for brains and that ninety per cent of women asked to name their brain called it Brian. And only ten per cent of men did. OK, I made up the brain names thing, but I bet it's fairly accurate. That's how suited I was – and still am – to magazine journalism.

On a dull but serious note, I thought I might write about how to avoid athlete's foot. I might test all the preparations on the market. But then, I thought, maybe not. Maybe athlete's foot is just too unattractive a subject. But then again, maybe that could be my specialism ('The Uncomfortable Truth') and I could implore young women not to waste so much money and time on cosmetics and bubble bath and instead buy their own car with the money they saved. I'd urge all woman to get a car. For I had noticed a link between women with their own car and other good things.

Or I could stick to the same old stuff: which soaps go soggy in water, why baths are safer than showers, why showers are more healthy than baths, why baths are better at cleaning intimate areas, why showers are better at preventing thrush, how showers cure depression, how baths are good for reading, how showers save water, how will we bathe after a nuclear attack, why some people hate pulling the plug out while they're still in the bath (feelings of desolation and loss), and why some people like it (the sense of toxins being dragged away down the plughole).

16. A Good Bash

Tammy's birthday came round on the Friday before her party and she and JP had a full-blown argument. In front of me.

JP had asked Bill's nurse Rhona to walk on his back.

He'd asked me as well but I'd refused because I hated him and, even if I didn't, I'd seen this kind of thing before and knew never to do anything physical with anyone except in a life-saving scenario. I'd seen things go horribly wrong, like the time my mother pulled a man's head sharply round to relieve a muscle ache – and the man has had to wear a neck brace ever since, except when in the bath, and can only cross the road on a zebra.

Anyway, Tammy was terribly upset when she found out about Rhona's back-walking.

'What's the problem? She walked on my back,' JP said. 'I've got lumbago.'

'You know that back-walking is highly erotic!' Tammy shouted. 'I used to walk on your back, and then look what happened – you left your wife.'

JP seemed genuinely puzzled. 'The two things weren't connected.'

'Well, you definitely used to get aroused by it.'

Later, she apologized for this all going on in front of me but went on to say she felt vulnerable because of the 'breeding programme'.

'It's really changed everything, you know, having to have sex in the mornings when he's most likely to be fully able, but I feel like heck and haven't even had my sugar-free Alpen.'

I told her I didn't mind. I wasn't really listening.

'You are coming to my party, aren't you?' she said.

I had been keeping quiet about it because I really didn't want to go but felt guilty because, well . . . poor Tammy.

'I don't think so – I mean, I won't know anyone,' I said.

'Bring someone,' she replied, 'but please, please, come.'

Later she checked that I knew not to bring Andy Nicolello because he and JP would lock antlers over something and ruin the atmosphere. So I asked my sister.

It was late notice but I rang her.

'It'll be a good bash,' I said.

She laughed at my saying 'a good bash' but agreed to come.

The party started out quite promisingly. JP was in a good mood because his son, JP Junior, had shown up unexpectedly and told JP that he and his girlfriend were having a trial separation. This meant he'd moved out and was living in professional quarters at the infirmary.

My sister and I wandered about the house and garden. It was a strange mix of lovely things that anyone might admire, such as the espaliered quinces along the side of the house and a most attractive vegetable garden, which was like something from Beatrix Potter – including a rustic wheelbarrow and some cloches and even an old sunhat on a spade handle. Inside was less lovely but contained items of interest nonetheless.

Tammy hadn't invited many of her own friends but Ann-Sofie from the Lunch Box (and Jazzercise) was there. Ann-Sofie was very much in charge of the conversation and the subject was sandwiches – a favourite.

'Customers come into the shop,' Ann-Sofie was saying, 'and they ask themselves, "Do I deserve mayonnaise today?" Not out loud, obviously, but in their heads – because sandwiches are a kind of reward for their hard work.'

JP listened with his eyes half-closed. He resented Ann-Sofie getting so much attention. He didn't like her very much anyway, and had once marked her dental card with two stars just for bringing up an article on toothbrushing techniques she'd seen in *The Times* newspaper. One star meant 'difficult patient', two meant 'nightmare' and three meant 'difficult, nightmare and a bad payer'.

'I read this week in my paper that we're not supposed to brush up and down any more,' she'd said. 'Can you comment on that?'

Now, JP butted into the sandwich conversation to describe his dismay and his disgust at seeing a pre-packaged salmon-and-tomato sandwich on sale in Marks & Spencer.

'A pre-packaged sandwich, in Marks and Spencer!' he laughed. 'Thirty-eight pence. Good God, you can buy a whole loaf for that – what is the world coming to?'

It went against the mood so we ignored him. In fact, my sister turned to Ann-Sofie and asked her to describe her most outlandish sandwich requests. Ann-Sofie obliged with examples: a customer who regularly asked for double ham and double cheese with triple pickle. Someone asking for sandwich spread, which made everyone laugh (but I thought quite reasonable). Someone wanting chicken-and-egg. Another wanting just salt and pepper. Someone wanting egg mayonnaise on granary and roast beef on Rearsby. The list of bizarre and wrong choices went on and on. But Ann-Sofie didn't mind, it was the customer's prerogative. The only thing she objected to was people requesting 'no butter'. What was so wrong with a no-butter request? we wondered. Ann-Sofie explained that butter acts as a barrier between wet filling and bread, and, for a dryer filling, adds moisture and adhesion, and is therefore always necessary. Plus, she had all the bread buttered and ready before she opened the doors at eleven.

JP clanged a glass to get our attention.

'All right,' he said, 'I hope Ann-Sofie won't mind my interrupting her consumer research, but I'd like to say a few words about the birthday girl if I may.'

He made a little speech saying that Tammy really deserved this celebration. She'd worked hard at the surgery, coming up with fresh new ideas for the practice, and had had a most spectacular year with the cactuses.

'And, I hope she won't mind my saying, but I want you all to know, we're trying for a baby.'

The assembly made noises of surprise and uncertainty. And then, after a slight delay, called out congratulations.

Tammy made signs of coyness and JP added, 'No, look, seriously, folks, I'm just saying it because we all love Tammy so much and I know you'll want to support her efforts to fulfil her biological potential.'

Ann-Sofie turned to her neighbour and said Tammy might have left it too late. This wasn't meant to be heard but JP had ears like a hawk and responded, saying that he had no worries on that score because an old pal of his from med school was one half of the test-tube-baby duo behind Louise Brown, and if push came to shove, he'd call in a favour.

'Oh, God!' said Ann-Sofie.

Tammy was fiddling with the buffet crockery and napkins and encouraging guests to help themselves.

'Actually, I've just read the biography of the test-tube mother,' said Jossy Turner. 'The couple should be early thirties at most.'

'Tammy's young for her age,' offered JP, 'she's not menopausal, she does Jazzercise twice a week and what have you – it's highly likely we won't even have to go the scientific route.' JP fell silent after that and stared out of the window.

'There are ways of increasing your chance of conception,' Jossy Turner continued – she loved this subject so much that she reminded me of Melody in her confidence and curiosity.

'I know,' said JP, 'I've got the nurse on it,' and he nodded at me. 'Lizzie doesn't let her have liver sausage for lunch, or seeds.'

'They mustn't go to zoos or pet farm animals,' said Jossy.

'No, actually,' said Ann-Sofie from the Lunch Box, 'the best way to help things along is for the woman to climax during intercourse, apparently.'

'Climax?' said JP.

'Yes!' I said. 'I read that too – it's much more likely if the woman has enjoyed it.'

'Who asked you?' said JP.

'Ah, but women don't usually climax during intercourse,' said Jossy. 'I read that in *The Hite Report*.'

'Really?' said Bill Turner.

'Well, most can't apparently,' said Jossy.

'Yes, it was in *Woman's Own* too!' I shouted, but then remembered it hadn't been in *Woman's Own* at all, it had been something Melody had said about anatomy that I wasn't prepared to share.

'The lateral something or other,' said Jossy Turner.

Tammy was now chivvying people at the buffet table.

'Why should it make a scrap of difference whether Tammy enjoys it or not?' JP wondered aloud – troubled, annoyed.

'I suppose if the woman isn't all tensed up or furious and resentful,' I ventured, 'it might make it easier for the—'

JP broke in with, 'Christ almighty, nurse, why would she be all tense and whatever?'

'I don't know,' I said. 'I'm just saying.'

There were some sniggers and Bill Turner changed the subject and began describing the garden party he was planning to coincide with the air show. But JP was still gazing across the room.

'Look, I enjoy it, all right!' hissed Tammy, and she busied herself lighting tiny candles underneath a great tureen of stew.

'I thought we were having a finger buffet,' said Jossy.

'No, it's Sicilian casserole,' said Tammy. 'We've provided Splayds.'

As well as the possibility of a test-tube baby, JP presented Tammy with a Polaroid picture of a portrait of herself – painted in oils by Jossy Turner. The real thing hadn't been dry in time to unveil at the party.

'It turns out oil paint takes for ever to dry,' said Jossy. 'Literally days!'

But it would be delivered by the framers to the surgery in a week or so.

Tammy seemed thrilled and passed the Polaroid around. The picture was blurry but seemed to show her holding a real live fawn in front of a nice sky.

'It's not a great photo, but I think you'll like my interpretation of you when you see the actual painting,' said Jossy. 'And you'll be glad to hear JP haggled hard and got it for half what I asked for it.'

'She'll love it,' said Bill and JP in unison.

A week or so later JP was away at a BDA event and Andy had come up to my flat at lunchtime. He laughed at my descriptions of the party, especially *The Hite Report* and reproduction talk, but was most interested to hear about JP's collection of antique barometers. I'd been about to send him out to the Lunch Box for sandwiches when he suddenly, alarmingly, suggested we go out for lunch. He'd suggested going out for meals a number of times before and, as usual, I rejected the idea.

'A sandwich is fine,' or, 'We could have soup,' I might say.

And he'd always say, 'Or we could go out.' Meaning, go to a café.

And I'd say, 'No.' Forcefully, and with no ambiguity.

It occurred to me then, that lunchtime after Tammy's party, that my continually declining Andy's offers of going out for a meal might be the thing that was preventing our relationship from flourishing. Could Andy be taking my reluctance to dine out as reluctance – might he equate eating together publicly with commitment? I don't suppose he thought in those precise *Woman's Own* terms, but maybe something along those lines.

I explored the topic.

'You really like eating out?' I said, in the style of a question.

'I haven't done it much, but yeah, it seems a nice thing to do.'

'But it's so expensive.'

'Yes, I suppose, but you don't have to be flashy about it.'

He told me he'd never eaten out as a child, not anywhere, ever, not even on the motorway, nor at school, nor in a hotel, and so it was a huge treat. His first time had been the Mercurial Christmas lunch on his first year there, and it had been so much fun, he'd been almost overwhelmed by feelings of joy and well-being. He rambled on about this rather too long. It was clear that dining out was his idea of bliss, and while it wasn't exactly my idea of hell, it was far, far from heaven.

'Why?' he said. 'Aren't you keen?'

'We used to go out with my father a lot, as children,' I explained. 'It was quite stressful sometimes.'

We'd often dine at the very top of Fenwick's of Leicester, as previously mentioned, with its low attic windows, which afforded no views and nothing to pretend to look at, except clouds, while my father read his paper. Once we'd settled, without consultation, the waiters would appear in a great procession, shake out our napkins and set down enormous, hot white plates full of meat slices and baby vegetables, and a lamp-shaped jug of gravy. My sister and I hated meat but didn't then have the courage to refuse it. We weren't inclined to chat, at the start anyway – we were shy of our father.

One time, my brother Jack, when he was still the littlest brother, had a tickly cough and the waiter marched over specially to ask if he would like some lime cordial, which he said was good for throats. And then, on the same mission, turned to the man on the next table and asked – most apologetically – if he'd mind refraining from smoking his pipe during the luncheon period, and presented him with a silver cigarette box in compensation. The man nodded, helped himself to a cigarette from the box and put his pipe into his pocket. The waiter produced a lighter and the man began on the cigarette. I smiled over a little thank-you, and he smiled back and poured himself coffee from an elegant pot.

After a few tiny bites of my lunch I noticed the man's jacket smouldering, and turned to alert my father. First, though, I had to swallow down a troublesome piece of beef I'd been chewing round and round for some while. I gulped half of it down, but the other half remained in my mouth – connected by a string of gristle to the piece that had gone – and I began to choke, great silent churning heaves that seemed to turn my throat inside out, and I reached for my brother's, now empty, glass of lime cordial.

The man's jacket was smoking quite thickly and I hadn't known whose life to save first, the man's or my own, and in the end had no choice but to turn to my sister for help. She remembers that my face was white, that I had probably already slightly died. She then put her fingers down my throat and removed the beef(s) and, before she could tell me off for not chewing each mouthful properly, I pointed to the burning man at the next table and soon waiters were at the scene with soda syphons and towels. And though it had been, as always, a perfectly nice occasion and no one had died, there was always a sense afterwards of having disappointed my father, of having failed to engage with the man, to matter. I tried to describe this to Andy.

'And that makes you unhappy in cafés?' he asked.

'Not unhappy exactly, more undeserving,' I said.

Andy seemed to understand and said he'd be pleased if I'd try a café with him, to put the past away, etc. and though the whole thing reminded me horribly of *Tender is the Night*, I agreed to have a go at going out for dinner – that evening.

Later that afternoon, I'd been catching up on admin, wiping the cactuses down, and plucking my eyebrows, when Gadsby's the framers delivered Tammy's portrait wrapped in brown paper. Soon after that Andy returned and asked if he might have a bath before going out for our dinner. I was only too pleased because this meant we could have an attempt at sex before trailing around the town to find somewhere I could face.

However, soon after that Tammy appeared and was about to ring for a taxi to take the parcel home when my mother also arrived and coaxed her into opening it.

'I'm an art historian,' said my mother. 'I must see it.'

I tried my best to describe the portrait to avoid the opening, thinking there'd be no chance of sex with everyone here looking at paintings, which would lead at least to coffee if not wine. But my mother was adamant. I locked the front door and we went upstairs to the flat where Tammy carefully unwrapped the painting and balanced it on the television table. We gazed at it. It depicted Tammy holding a baby deer, because that's what Tammy had been doing in the photograph JP had given Jossy to paint from. Tammy explained that the deer – orphaned in the Bambi style – had the run of a bed and breakfast in the Ardèche. The hosts hadn't given it a name and so Tammy had called it Gleem after a favourite toothpaste she'd had as a child in the USA.

I could see that everything about Tammy in the portrait would be pleasing to JP. The white blouse with a ruff neck, the tousled hair that had a touch of Marilyn about it (tousled due to not trusting any French hairdressers). But the fact was, she was completely eclipsed by the fawn, whose warm brown eyes, sweeping black eyelashes, dark ear tips, fine bone structure and cute nostrils reduced Tammy to nothing but a beige blob with a bitchy, slightly lobotomized expression.

My mother sat cross-legged on the sofa. Tammy remained standing. Nothing was said for a while. The painting was awful. Naive but not impressionistic. You could sense how hard the artist had tried to copy the image, but Tammy's hand supporting the fawn's body was huge, like a cartoon squid.

My mother didn't think much of it either. Not that she said so, but I could tell. She kept saying, 'Mmmm,' and leaning further and further back, and tilting her head, as if to get a better look.

'Who did you say painted this?' she asked.

'Jossy Turner,' said Tammy. 'A friend.'

'Hmm,' said my mother (obviously thinking what I was thinking, 'Some friend!'). 'She shouldn't have included the baby deer.'

Tammy abruptly admitted to hating it.

'I hate it,' she said simply, whereupon my mother started trying to be kind about it but only succeeded in being odd and disturbing.

'It reminds me of a classic painting from the eighteenth century – the restfulness of your face, dense-looking, expressionless, dumb and inscrutable and like a ruined child, like Luisa of Naples.'

I implored my mother, with my eyes, not to say any more because it couldn't be anything but upsetting to hear such things.

'Do you think so?' Tammy said. 'Maybe I'm being a bit harsh.'

She told us she had actually asked JP for an intimate session with a photographer called Bobby Shotz for her birthday but he'd commissioned Jossy Turner instead, who'd just been on a short painting course and had all the kit and a lot of leftover paints.

'I would have preferred Bobby Shotz,' she sighed, 'but JP says photographers are all total perverts.'

'That's true,' said my mother.

Tammy seemed upset.

'Let's have a glass of wine,' my mother suggested and she opened a bottle of Mateus Rosé that I'd got for show. Andy was still in the bathroom; he'd taken a James Baldwin novel in with him and was, as usual, taking his time. Thank God.

Tammy began unburdening herself. The painting seemed to have unleashed some feelings. She wasn't happy with the fertility programme, she told us. She was fed up with having to lift her legs and cycle in the air after sex, and doing it at the crack of dawn just because that's when JP got the urge. It had put her right off sex. Now, because of her ovulation calculations, she sometimes had to do it on a Friday, which ruined her hair for the weekend. I'd heard much of this before, of course, only now she sounded serious.

'It's not like I even want a child,' she suddenly announced, and seemed to have surprised herself.

'Oh, of course you do,' said my mother. 'Do have one.'

'But I don't want one,' said Tammy. 'I don't like kids, and I like my life the way it is.'

'Look, just go with it, have one, and if you decide after a few weeks that you really can't stand it, I'll take it.' My mother actually said this.

'Mum!' I said. 'Don't say such insane things.' I was glad Andy was still in the bath while this conversation was going on.

'Could that actually happen?' asked Tammy. 'Do people give them away to pals?'

'No, it couldn't happen,' I said.

'I'm sure I saw something like that in *Titbits*,' she said.

'But why are you continuing with the fertility programme, then?' I asked. 'All the fruit juices and pelvic exercises, etc.'

'I've been living a lie ever since Junior had that vasectomy and JP got it into his head that he must continue the bloodline. But I hate babies. I've never wanted one and I'm the sort to leave it outside the butcher's or accidentally pick up the wrong one.'

'And only know because of its turtle-shaped birthmark,' I added.

My mother was sympathetic (and excited by all the revelations) but warned Tammy that she might live to regret not having one. She herself was a novelist, poet, member of the Institute of Advanced Drivers, accomplished car mechanic, in possession of a clear soprano voice, grade seven piano, proficient horsewoman, and had always been thin, she said, but those things counted for nothing in the eyes of the world.

'The only thing that ever got me any acknowledgement is giving birth,' she said, and she didn't say it lightly or philosophically, but with a tinge of resentment in her voice. 'And that's why I keep having them,' she continued. 'I mean, who in their right mind *would* want babies, I mean, really? But have you thought how you'll feel in ten years' time?'

Tammy seized my mother by the upper arms.

'Look, I don't want a baby or a child of any kind,' she said, 'and if I had wanted one I'd have tried to have one already, and if I wanted one now I wouldn't have a secret cupboard . . .' She tore out of the sitting area and trotted down a half-flight. We peered over the banister and saw her yank open the door to her secret cupboard, rustle about manically and then stomp back upstairs waving a fan of foil-and-plastic packs. 'And I wouldn't have these, would I?'

'What are they?' I asked.

'Pills – she's on the pill,' said my mother.

We drifted back into the sitting area, somehow needing to have the painting in view, for reference, and found Andy standing in front of it.

'This is cool,' he said. 'Cute deer.'

'What?' shouted Tammy. 'What the heck are you doing here?'

'Umm, I'm just waiting for Lizzie.'

My mother gave Andy a stern look and he retreated into the kitchenette. I followed him and left her and Tammy mumbling and finishing the wine while I put the kettle on.

'Oh my God,' I whispered to Andy, 'did you hear all that?'

'Not really. I wasn't listening.'

We discussed our dinner date. I claimed not to be hungry and Andy suggested we walk round the long way to the Fish & Quart to work up an appetite – but even talking like that made me uneasy.

'Oh, shit!' shouted my mother, suddenly remembering she was late to collect Danny. She got her things together and Tammy went with her. We said awkward goodbyes.

'Have a great weekend,' I heard myself say, and they were gone. Andy and I took our coffee to the lounge and there, propped up in front of the television, was Tammy with Fawn, irreparably, horribly defaced in thick black marker pen.

PART TWO

17.   Lessons

I was going to have to get my driving licence. It was the one quali-
fication I could get, after all. In the unlikely event of my going to
Massachusetts, I'd have to ferry my half-siblings around in a huge
Cadillac, and equally, if I stayed in England, I'd need it for any of
the positions advertised in the *Lady* magazine (that I'd have to take
up in order to begin my writing career), all of which demanded a
clean driving licence – and no clever words could make up for not
being able to drive.

My sister had called round to get her teeth polished and afterwards we had coffee and honey buns while I leafed through
the *Yellow Pages*. I couldn't decide between Asquith's School of
Motoring – jolly-looking – and the Fosse School of Motoring –
serious-looking but guaranteed to have you *Test-ready in 12 weeks or
your money back**. Their advert featured an L-plate ripped in half
which was quite strong. We mulled it over. My sister had recently
passed and was opinionated.

'What about the Harry Janis School of Motoring?' I said, tapping his tiny entry. 'He's never had a fail and he's cheap.'

'Harry Janis?' said Tina. 'God, no, that's the bloke I had who
got his penis out, remember?'

'Oh, yes. I couldn't have him.'

'No, I reported him to the police,' she remembered slowly, pic-
turing it in her mind's eye.

'Was he arrested?' I asked.

'No, but he was warned that there'd been a complaint, though,
so he might bear a grudge.'

Tina did the sums and told me how much it was going to cost,
which was so ridiculous, I doubted her maths. Driving lessons
were out of the question unless I asked for a pay rise, which was

also out of the question, or moved back home and used my rent money, but that was out of the question too unless I was prepared to share my old bed with Andy Nicolello, which I wasn't, even if he would, which he wouldn't.

Later, on the phone, Melody suggested I ask my mother to teach me. This made sense to Melody because I'd repeatedly flagged her up as a great motor-woman compared with her own mother who used to abandon the vehicle if required to reverse.

Being taught by a relative wasn't the way I wanted to learn – I'd had my heart set on proper lessons – but now, knowing the cost, I had to admit Melody was right. My mother was a good bet and the Flying Pea the perfect little car to learn in – highly visible, easy to park, and with a fitted radio-cassette. Plus, I assumed, my mother must long for an opportunity to make up for our awful childhood.

'Or, even better,' said Melody, 'what about Mr Holt? He's a super driver.'

That was true, he was an exceptionally good and careful driver – always used the handbrake and frequently checked the oil, and so forth – but I wasn't planning on being that sort. I was hoping to be a driver more like my mother – a relaxed, one-handed type, with Snoopy stickers on the back, eating lollies at the wheel, listening to Cat Stevens and tooting at my friends. But safely. No. I ruled him out. I'd recruit my mother and after I'd finished talking to Melody, I phoned her and put it to her:

'I really need to learn to drive to widen my career options,' I said.

'Well, don't look at me.'

'I am looking at you,' I said, 'metaphorically.'

'Well, it's no good.'

'But you've always said we girls must learn to drive and be independent of tyrants.'

'And so you should, but leave me out of it.'

She was terribly sorry, she said, and she blamed Abe's counselling. He'd made contact with her subconscious again in a recent session and it turned out that she was weary of being at the beck and call of her children who were draining her energy – she needed to cut the apron strings wherever possible.

'So, you see, giving you driving lessons is out of the question,' she said. 'I need to minimize my maternal obligations.'

I asked to speak to Mr Holt, but was quite relieved when he said he didn't feel he could commit to the plan either because of his working hours. He put my mother back on.

'You'll have to save up or ask your grandmother,' she said.

So that was that, I had no choice but to go cap in hand to Granny Benson. I didn't ask for driving lessons from her, but for money to put towards some. I told her I wanted to better myself and she was pleased to hear it, feeling there was much room for improvement. She agreed to pay for a whole course of lessons but on the condition that I agree to attend confirmation classes with Reverend Woodward at her village church in order to get the official pass into the Church of England.

'I was confirmed as a baby,' I told her. 'There are photographs.'

She told me that had been my christening and that I had missed my confirmation at the age of twelve or thirteen because I'd renounced Christianity and become a druid.

'Oh, yes,' I said. I'd forgotten all about it, but couldn't deny it.

Anyway, I agreed to see Reverend Woodward for confirmation classes and get my Christianity back on track in return for driving lessons. It was a deal and I told her I'd phone with the details of the driving school and the fees and so forth.

'No need,' said Granny Benson. 'Reverend Woodward's wife can teach you.'

'The Reverend's wife? You mean Mrs Woodward? Is she a driving instructor?'

'No, dear, she's a crossing sweeper,' replied my granny, who was always quick with a joke.

I tried to picture Mrs Woodward teaching me to drive and I found I couldn't. I could only picture her gagging as JP took her dental impressions. She didn't seem the type to teach a person anything as dynamic as driving.

'But I was hoping to go with the Fosse School of Motoring with their "test-ready in twelve weeks or your money back" promise,' I said and described the advert featuring the L-plate ripped in half.

'No,' said my granny. 'Mrs Woodward's more appropriate. You'll be able to chat about Jesus when you're not negotiating traffic, and it might reinforce your confirmation classes.'

I'd never known my granny to be so keen on Jesus and suspected she was just enjoying reining me in, like someone spinning a salad spinner just because they can.

I later found out that, far from never having had a fail, Mrs Woodward had never had a pass – barring her husband Reverend Woodward and he'd pretty much stopped driving after swerving to avoid a peacock in the car park of a stately home and hitting a statue.

'He still has nightmares about the Earl of Richmond coming to life just as he hit him,' Mrs Woodward told me, 'a kind of resurrection gone wrong.'

After making my bargain with Granny, I called in at my old house, my old home, what I should now call my mother's house, or even Andy's house. I rang the doorbell, which felt strange. Andy answered the door – even stranger – and asked if I'd like to walk up to the King's Head for a game of darts. I said I wanted to talk to my mother first, but yes.

My mother was typing up a chapter for the new novel. She looked exhausted, with her hair all over the place and an unlit cigarette in her mouth. Seeing me, she stopped dramatically, pulled a sheet of paper from her typewriter, scrabbled around among other papers strewn over the dining table for her lighter, found it and flipped the lid up.

'You look exhausted,' I said. 'Shall I make some tea?'

'I am! I've just written a strangling,' she said. 'Jack, put the kettle on will you?' she called through to my brother, who as well as having a place at the University College London, was known for making good tea.

She then told me that on top of her rejection from Faber & Faber, she'd now had one from Penguin Books – for 'Winter Green', her sci-fi feminist thriller.

'Penguin have feminist sci-fi thrillers coming out of their ears, according to the letter,' she said and she reached round to pick it up from the sideboard.

'Idiots,' I said.

'I wouldn't put it past them to give my idea to one of their worn-out old has-beens,' she said.

'God, no, like that thing that happened to Maurice Morris.'

'Oh, fuck, yes, poor Maurice.'

My mother's old friend had written a brilliant television series, sent it to the BBC who rejected it outright, saying they had something just like it in the pipeline, and then, the following year, the exact series had come on the telly and Maurice died of disappointment.

Finally, there was a pause in which I could tell her about my driving/confirmation lessons plan. She didn't consider it good news at all. On the contrary, she called it oppressive. She was very angry with her mother for cooking up the plan and went into the hall to phone her. They had a short conversation and she came back in a fury, saying that I was being indoctrinated. At which point Andy joined us.

'I don't care, I can handle it,' I said. 'I just want my driving licence – I'll put all the other stuff out of my head once I've passed.'

'You think you will,' she said, 'but they're clever, they make you imagine you're having epiphanies left, right and centre, and awakenings and visits from God.'

'I'm not the sort. I'll set the agenda.'

'How will you do that? The agenda's already set.'

'I'll change the subject at every possible opportunity.'

'You can ask the vicar for his thoughts on Darwin,' suggested Andy.

'Yes, exactly, and Robert Thingamabob,' said my mother.

'Oh, but I don't want to offend him,' I said. 'I just meant I'll talk about pop music, or my favourite flower, and go off on tangents.'

My mother told me that if I saw a shooting star or heard my name whispered on the breeze, or saw God's face in a pie crust, etc., I mustn't make any mistake.

'Those things are nothing to do with God – it's just that you're a human being with an eye for magic and a poet's imagination.'

'I wouldn't recognize God anyway,' I said.

'He looks like Jesus, but older,' said Andy.

It seemed my mother and Andy were egging each other on in a joint dismissal of my plan and, though I was thrilled at having a boyfriend who was able to say, 'Ask the vicar about Darwin,' I felt slightly crestfallen. Luckily Mr Holt stepped in.

'Look,' he said, 'she's found a cheap way to get driving lessons and if anyone can handle the missionaries, Lizzie can.'

'Thank you.'

'Ask the vicar if he's heard of Charles Darwin,' said Mr Holt.

'Andy's already said that,' pointed out my mother.

'Alfred Russel Wallace, then.'

A few days later, my grandmother informed me she'd made arrangements with the vicar's wife, so I was to expect a call or a letter. But before I was allowed to start my driving lessons, my confirmation lessons with Reverend Woodward must be under way – these were to be one-to-one meetings in his lounge at the vicarage. I was to start that week.

Reverend Woodward was very pleasant and a good deal younger than I'd expected, knowing his wife. I arrived ten minutes late and said, 'Sorry, I'm a few minutes late,' to which he replied, 'As are all polite guests,' which was unexpectedly reasonable and pleased me no end because, in addition to not believing in God, I also had (have) a slight ecclesiaphobia. Vicars having been on the whole rather disturbing up until then and had so rarely lived up to expectations. Demanding we live like Jesus – always turning the other cheek, walking in another man's shoes, and never abbreviating

Christmas to Xmas. Never understanding or forgiving but always disappointed – particularly when it came to divorced mothers – and there was all that dandruff on the cassocks.

There was the one, Reverend Derrick, years before whom I'd seen in my mother's sitting room. I'd been in the garden and he inside, gazing out. I remember waving a toy panda's paw at him and him waving back. But when, a few moments later, I peeped in to give him another panda encounter, I saw him – still gazing out – being robustly fondled by my mother on his bottom half.

That was a previous vicar, though, not Reverend Woodward. Reverend Woodward was exactly as a vicar should be. Kind, open, intelligent, and therefore a pleasant surprise. He was a patient of JP Wintergreen's, having rushed there after a trampolining accident in 1977, and eventually been fitted with a partial upper denture. I couldn't help staring at it. The front incisors, slightly on the large side and a shade too white, were typical of JP's work – pre-Andy Nicolello.

Reverend Woodward couldn't help detailing the accident, the way people do.

'I went into the foetal position rather forcefully and hit myself in the mouth with my knees,' he explained, and imagining him in this somersault-gone-wrong, I remembered my mother's trampolining accident – it was quite a time for trampolining.

I began the first confirmation session pretending to be a Christian, which proved difficult. Reverend Woodward asked me some awkward questions about my conversion to druidism at the age of eleven, which he'd heard all about. I started to explain but it made me sound like such a stupid eleven-year-old, which I assure you I was not. My eleven-year-old self was special to me, still is, and I didn't like to besmirch her. In the end I just told him the truth – that my mother invented the whole druidism thing, so that she didn't have to take me to the vicarage once a week for the confirmation lessons. Because, A) she couldn't be bothered, and B) she was afraid of being caught drink-driving by a village policeman who seemed hell bent on it.

'How do you feel about your mother denying you entry to the Kingdom of God?' he asked.

'Well, I'm pretty annoyed, of course,' I lied.

Around that moment, I noticed smoke creeping under the door. I pointed and said, 'Holy Smoke,' and Reverend Woodward said, 'Damn,' and ran from the room into the kitchen. I followed. He grabbed a flaming pan and flung it into the sink, then clanged around burning his fingers, throwing stuff into the bin and fanning the air with a tea towel. I opened the window.

It turned out he'd forgotten I was coming and had put his tea on just before the doorbell went, and then he'd got settled with me and forgot all about his chop and cabbage. Mrs Woodward, who would usually have done the chop, had gone to play chess with some prisoners, he said. I'd thought of Mrs Woodward as a kindly old soul who dropped her denture and did good deeds, but the absolute terror in Reverend Woodward's eyes when he mentioned how cross she'd be about the burnt chop made me wonder.

The kitchen emergency was a blessing, though. It broke the religious ice, so to speak, and meant I could relax and say, 'I'm not a regular churchgoer, as such.'

And he could say, 'You don't say.'

And I could laugh and blush, and he could smile broadly.

Actually, it seemed for a tiny moment that we might be about to kiss. But we didn't and it never again seemed that way, far from it. It was interesting, though, and it occurred to me afterwards that a lot of relationships must start with the strange sudden possibility of a wrong, inappropriate kiss, and it made sense of all my mother's awful affairs. Especially the ones with vets and doctors and policemen and people who do something very, very brave or clever, or exciting.

I told him I was having confirmation classes only as part of a deal with my granny Benson (of this parish) in return for driving lessons. He surprised me by saying what a very good granny she must be. I said she could sometimes be quite crushing and mean, and he said he'd never seen that side of her, and I said I bet his wife had. And he laughed.

Reverend Woodward began the actual lesson then and explained his role to me.

'My job is to guide my flock. Not as a shepherd because my flock are people, not sheep, but nonetheless I must guide them and help them find meaning and purpose and reasons to strive in the world.' Something along those lines.

'You're a cross between Claire Rayner and Ian Dury,' I observed, and he agreed.

'Exactly,' he said, 'except, instead of being able to pick up a magazine or put a record on, you have to come to church on Sunday.'

'It seems outdated,' I said.

We went quite philosophical and I said I didn't think we needed miracles, and epiphanies left, right and centre, awakenings and visits from God – we needed to appreciate the actual, ordinary things around us. I gave him the example that I was thankful for the sandals Jesus wore because they'd helped me cure my athlete's foot, not because they'd walked on water. Reverend Woodward said he felt that a bit simplistic.

I saw an opportunity to change the subject for a few minutes and grabbed it.

'Athlete's foot should not be ignored or taken for granted and neither should verrucas, corns, bunions, gout, or swollen ankles,' I told him. When Reverend Woodward tried to butt in with Jesus, I resisted and continued, explaining that I knew this all too well from my days working as an auxiliary nurse but since I had a high tolerance to pain and discomfort, I had simply got on with life. After reading an article in *Titbits* entitled 'First Foot Forward', which linked foot health with professional success, it occurred to me that I had athlete's foot – probably caused by the Swedish surgical clogs supplied by the practice. And I set off to Clark's shoe shop, and had to reject an array of breathable sandals – one with a high heel and another in a patent leather with a flower buckle – before finally purchasing a pair of flat, unisex, tan ones.

'Don't put them in the box,' I'd said. 'I'm going to wear them.' I strode home and, except for slightly wishing I'd gone for the navy version, I felt on top of the world. I told the vicar, and I paused there but he didn't interrupt and seemed to be genuinely interested, so I continued. When Tammy (my colleague, I explained) noticed my socks and sandals she wished I hadn't worn them in front of her. She didn't care that my feet were now getting fresh air and had the support of two buckled straps and a slight heel, which promoted good posture in the upper body, I told the Rev – she was appalled that I'd let something as trivial as foot health spoil my whole look.

'Couldn't you have at least gone for a pair of Dr. Scholl's?' she said.

I said, 'No, I couldn't,' and frankly thought it a bit rich coming from someone who had caused the whole practice to switch to decaffeinated Maxwell House in order to support her ovaries – but I didn't say that.

Reverend Woodward did interject at this point but only to say he'd got a very nice pair from the island of Crete, which had been hand-made by a widow, and were probably quite authentically like those worn by Jesus. And so an hour passed quite bearably and I went away with the name of Reverend Woodward's preferred foot powder, Daktarin.

Andy was wary of Reverend Woodward, having been hounded by him after his parents had died.

'Honestly, the guy never stopped calling round.'

'He was just doing his job.'

'What *is* his job?'

'To guide his flock. Not as a shepherd because his flock are people not sheep, and to help them find meaning and purpose and reasons to be happy – and so forth.'

'He sounds like Ian Dury,' Andy said, and I shrieked, because hadn't I said exactly that in my lesson?

The following week, I repeated this observation to Reverend Woodward – and though it seems controversial now, it went down surprisingly well – in fact, I realized Reverend Woodward was constantly on the lookout for things to preach about the following Sunday and, making no pretence that ideas came to him from on high, would jot things down to expand for a sermon. He'd had a few recent flops, he told me, in particular a sermon describing Wilfred Thesiger being humbled by illiterate desert herdsmen, which had been met with some confusion and a little anger. He needed to work on tone and style, he said. And saying that, he reminded me so much of my future self – in London or Massachusetts – seeking inspiration for my column and wrestling with my desire to write about dogs and cars when my readership would prefer cats and nail polish, and by the end of the hour we'd sketched out a sermon for the following week, based on 'Reasons to be Cheerful'.

In the third week, I was supposed to hand in some homework on the basics of the seven sacraments, but took him instead a list of things to have up his sleeve for sermons – if he got stuck one week.

> *Jaws* by Peter Benchley – authority and guidance.
> *Hitchhiker's Guide to the Galaxy* – the meaning of life.
> *On the Buses* – humiliation, cruelty, how not to treat your wife.
> *Watership Down* by Richard Adams – survival and adventure.
> *Kramer versus Kramer* – perils of marrying the wrong person.
> *Grease* – loyalty, fashion, friendship, birth control.
> *The Generation Game* – anti-materialism.
> *Roots* by Alex Haley – slavery.
> *Oh, Brother!* – monks, perseverance.
> *The Thorn Birds* – travel, farming.
> *This is Your Life* – ambition, success, failure.

He looked at the list, thanked me, and said he'd probably do something about *This is Your Life* that coming Sunday, recalling an episode in which a factory worker from Wales who had become an international superstar is reacquainted with her ex-colleagues from the factory and they all get along like a house on fire in spite of the gulf between them. He invited me to come along.

And, you see, we got along like that from then on. I wished I wanted to be part of his flock, but I didn't, and he didn't mind anyway, that's how good a vicar he was. I never knew a person who didn't love him, apart from my granny – and even she admitted to being quite fond of him.

18.   The Road Ahead

Mrs Woodward telephoned in advance of our first lesson to ask me to wear comfortable clothing and stout shoes. I mentioned my athlete's foot and asked whether I might be permitted Jesus sandals. She supposed it would be all right as long as I fastened the straps properly, and went on to suggest a powder, 'far superior to the others'. I explained I was beyond help from a powder and was using an aerosol so powerful it made my eyes water. She changed the subject abruptly, and told me she'd never passed a driving test herself because she'd learned in the military and therefore was exempted.

'It can throw people,' she said, 'hearing that, so I like it out of the way.'

'That's fine,' I said, 'it hasn't thrown me.'

'Good. Now, have you driven, at all, yourself?'

'No.'

'No mules, donkeys, go-karts, trikes?' she chuckled.

'Well, horse-riding and I had a kiddy-wheel for a while.'

'What's that?' she asked.

'A fake steering wheel you fix in a car, so the kid can pretend to steer. It's very realistic.'

'Perfect,' she said. 'Yes, that's going to make a big difference.'

Mrs Woodward was to collect me from my grandmother's house and just before she arrived my granny handed me a pair of gloves, which would prevent wheel-slippage and thumb-chafing. I thanked her for these – and in advance for the lessons.

'Driving instructors are like gods to me,' I said, in an unguarded moment on the driveway. 'Turning non-drivers into drivers seems more divine than anything in the Bible.'

'I hope you're taking your confirmation lessons seriously,' she said.

Mrs Woodward reversed in and parked on a hosepipe. I went to the car window and introduced myself. I couldn't help noticing that her driving spectacles made her look like the Dalai Lama in a wig, and that being just the kind of observation my granny made all the time, really wanted to whisper it to her. But I didn't and later I was glad I hadn't because Mrs Woodward turned out to be the nicest person I'd ever met.

The first lesson went very well. Mrs Woodward said a prayer before we drove off but I think that was just for the benefit of my grandmother, who remained standing in the driveway watching. I didn't take the driver's seat until we were safely in Woolco car park.

As I got to know Mrs Woodward's life story I found it to contain moral guidance and principles for living a good life – much more so, say, than her husband's or Jesus' for that matter, because she hadn't had Jesus' luck or Reverend Woodward's expensive education and she'd had a shocking mother, worse than mine, who'd basically sold her into a marriage aged twenty-one, and she'd had most of her upper and all of her lower teeth removed before the wedding – a prenuptial requirement. Now, thirty years on, her lower jawbone had all but dissolved even though she was only about fifty. God-wise, she was somewhere between Reverend Woodward and my mother. She believed Jesus had probably been a really nice person with good intentions and that his teachings were basically worthwhile, but she didn't think we were all going to meet up again in heaven.

'I mean,' she said, 'what a terrible thought.'

But driving – oh, Lord, I loved it straight away. I loved the feeling of acceleration and the car's response as I raised one foot and pressed down with the other – the smooth negotiation. I felt I must have been born to drive – albeit, we were still in the car park and Mrs Woodward was saying, 'Let her bite,' and that kind of thing. To my delight, at the end she declared me 'a natural'. It wasn't just the confidence I had gained from my kiddy-wheel, it was that I loved small spaces with travel blankets, and I loved moving, going places, stopping, and knowing I could go again at the twist of a key. The idea that I could literally drive to the sea seemed miraculous, and now I was the driver, it felt all the more so. I wasn't a car lover, mind you. I loved what cars could do, not what they were. I suddenly understood my mother's comment that she only felt truly safe with her own vehicle parked nearby, with a full tank of fuel, the ignition key hidden in her shoe, and her shoe on her foot or in sight.

I told Mrs Woodward, that first day, of my exhilaration, and she nodded and said that was the sign of a true driver.

'You're going to be my first pass, I just know it,' she said.

In some ways she was a very thorough teacher. She had a strict 'no high heels' rule and insisted on her pupils learning arm signals even though there was no requirement to demonstrate them on the actual test. There was her seat-belt rule, her regular eyesight checks, and her chanting of 'read the road ahead, read the road ahead'. However, she also had a habit of falling asleep. The first time this happened I was surprised. I only realized she was asleep because of her snoring and I drove round and round the same little triangle of streets so that she wouldn't wake up confused. After that I got used to it and pretty much expected her to be fast asleep for most of the lesson. When I mentioned this to her she apologized. It was a combination, she said, of her sleeping pill and the motion of the vehicle. I had her permission to shout at her whenever she nodded off, and if that didn't work, I was to hit her with a rolled-up newspaper. I knew I wouldn't be able to hit her and said I'd just shout more loudly. She agreed but asked me not to shout, 'Wake up!' in case anyone heard. I suggested, 'Read the road ahead,' and she called me a genius. She was easy to impress.

We talked a lot about driving, as you might imagine. I told her about my sister's driving lessons with Harry Janis, who'd got his penis out.

'Oh, that's very much against the instructors' code of conduct,' said Mrs Woodward, 'but to be fair, he's never had a fail.'

'Even so,' I said, 'I'd rather have you and know that the worst that's going to happen is your denture popping out.'

'But I've never had a pass.'

She always said that, but it wasn't actually true. Reverend Woodward had passed, eventually, under her tutelage and during the two years it took him, the two of them had fallen in love, left their respective unpleasant spouses and married, and Reverend Woodward now only drove in an emergency so she never counted him as a pass.

During my second driving lesson the following Saturday, I mentioned to Mrs Woodward that Andy Nicolello was not only my boyfriend, but was also lodging with my mother.

She was flabbergasted and said, 'The lad whose parents gassed themselves because of Mr Callaghan? The one who made my denture?'

'Yes. But I think that was just a rumour.'

'Well, I never.'

And I asked if we might end the lesson outside my home. She said yes, of course, but needed clarification as to where I wanted to go, and I explained that when I said 'home', I meant my mother and Mr Holt's house, and when I said 'the flat' I meant my actual home.

'And you're happy about him moving in with your mother, are you?' she asked.

'Yes. Why wouldn't I be?'

So we drove out that way, circled the village to use up the hour, and then I pulled in behind the Flying Pea, which I must say looked very green. Mrs Woodward said she'd come in for a quick cup of tea.

Andy Nicolello was there at my house, eating a slice of toast, this time with home-made raspberry jam. He loved toast – grills being a new thing for him, and bread now usually available.

My mother had been watering a neighbour's garden as a favour and invited to help herself to the soft fruit.

'I made jam,' she announced.

'And how is it?' I asked.

'Yeah, it's nice,' said Andy, 'but I think you should strain the pips and detritus out.'

Detritus. I saw my mother beam at the word.

'Yes,' she said, 'one should really.'

'What? Are you a jam expert or something?' I said to Andy.

'Yes.' And of course he was. (All those hedgerow fruits.)

Mrs Woodward suddenly remembered that it had been a jam pip that brought her and Andy and me into contact, via the surgery, and we stood for a moment and appreciated the oddness of that fact. Mrs Woodward finished her tea and then had to dash. She was visiting Gartree Prison to talk to a murderer who'd found God but hated vicars.

'Aren't you terrified?' my mother asked.

'No, he's a very nice man, apart from that one murder, which he bitterly regrets . . .'

On approximately my fifth lesson with Mrs Woodward, I got trapped in a bus stop near the racecourse and was overtaken by a number of cars including the Flying Pea – being driven erratically. I tried to go after it but somehow stalled the engine.

We saw the Flying Pea again further along the bypass, when it shot past us on a dangerous bend, and saw my mother sitting in the passenger seat. I gasped.

'It's my mother's car, but who's driving?' I said to Mrs Woodward, but she was asleep. I sped up and beeped as I drew behind them.

Mrs Woodward woke up with a jolt and said, 'Read the road ahead,' and adjusted her specs.

I told her it was my mother in front.

'Well, that was an unwise manoeuvre on her part.'

'It's not her driving!' I said. Was she giving my brother driving lessons? Was that why she'd refused me? If not him, who?

I roared after them and the Flying Pea came to a halt behind a milk float, I overtook, and Mrs Woodward strained round in her seat.

'Who's at the wheel?' I demanded, fully expecting it to be Jack.

'Good grief,' said Mrs Woodward, 'it's the lad from the surgery.'

'What lad?'

'The one whose parents gassed themselves. You know, your young man, your mother's lodger.'

'Oh, my bloody God,' I said, 'she's teaching Andy Nicolello to drive.'

'And they're not displaying L-plates,' said Mrs Woodward.

Mrs Woodward dropped me at the flat and I went in despondently. I thought about phoning my mother to ask why she was giving driving lessons to Andy Nicolello when she had refused me. It was the two-bar electric fire all over again (I won't bore you with it), only worse – and with my boyfriend.

I planned to make a speech which presented the major let-downs of my late childhood and highlighted her selfishness / my abandonment.

'First, you interrupt my Christian development and tell people I'm a druid, then you ruin my nursing career by threatening to report my ex-boss at Paradise Lodge to the tax man, then you refuse to teach me to drive, abandon me to Mrs Woodward, and possibly start having sex with my boyfriend.'

But I didn't phone.

The very next day Andy dropped in with our dental items. I heard him trot up the steps, whistling 'Runaround Sue'. JP and Tammy had left already, so I went out to the hall and I asked him, point-blank, how he thought it was OK to accept driving lessons from my mother after she'd refused me – when I was having to sell my soul to God.

Andy looked surprised and I had to repeat my question. He thought about it for a moment, puzzled, and said he thought it was perfectly acceptable.

'She can't teach you,' he said. 'You were jettisoned because of her parental-obligation thing – apron strings.'

'But it's not fair.'

'Life's not fair,' said Andy. 'Your mother is redressing the balance.'

'What do you mean?'

'She's doing the morally correct thing, probably for the first time in her life.'

'How dare you say that about my mother when she's taken you in?' I considered adding, 'And you swan around together and make her look like a nymphomaniac.' But I didn't.

'I'm a paying lodger. My being there is helping her financially, after she made a hash of her life.'

'Not as much of a hash as your parents made,' I said. (Childish, I know.)

'What do you know about my parents?'

'Nothing. But I think you're exploiting my mother's generosity.'

'What, you think I shouldn't have accepted driving lessons because you weren't offered?'

'It seems disloyal,' I said, realizing I should have rehearsed this better.

'Disloyal? How?'

I wanted an analogy. An 'imagine how you'd feel' but it was pointless.

'You know what you are, don't you?' I said.

'What am I?'

'You're her replacement Angelo.'

Andy looked confused and put both hands up in a gesture of calm.

'OK, see ya,' he said and walked smartly to the door.

'And a cuckoo,' I said, though so quietly I wasn't sure he heard.

On my next driving lesson, I confirmed with Mrs Woodward that she had been quite right – my mother was teaching the lab technician to drive.

'I saw it with my own eyes,' she said, 'but maybe she's just giving him practice and he's having driving lessons with a professional?'

'No, she's teaching him. He's had a lifetime of driving around on various motorized vehicles – and, knowing him, he'll pass first time.'

'Well,' said Mrs Woodward, 'you'll just have to pass first time as well.'

'I'll try.'

'And I'll stop taking my insomnia tablets,' she said. 'I need to be more alert.'

Andy and I had split up. Had we? Or had we not quite ever got together? I wasn't sure. But now he was at my house, in my room, and with my mother. I felt uneasy and trapped and then laughed it off and then back again. I wanted to pass my driving test before he passed his, or asap afterwards. That was going to be my focus as far as Andy was concerned.

I needed all the driving practice I could get and I asked everyone I knew with a car, including JP.

'Are you telling us that your mother's giving the lab boy driving lessons?' he asked, puffing away one afternoon at tea break.

'Yes,' I said, 'she is.'

'You don't think they're involved, do you?' asked Tammy.

'I wouldn't put anything past the pair of them,' said JP, and to give him credit, he immediately apologized. 'Sorry, nurse, but you must admit, it's rum.'

I looked at JP, puffing away and exhaling through his curled-up, hammy tongue, and then at Tammy, sipping at her teacup and flicking the ash off JP's cigarette.

'I don't know,' I said.

'Well, I'd be very suspicious if it were my mother, but then she can't drive, and she's not like that, so it wouldn't arise,' said Tammy.

I picked up the receiver on the telephone extension.

'Let's find out,' I said and dialled Mercurial.

Tammy and JP looked alarmed.

'Mercurial,' answered Mr Burridge at the other end.

'Hello, Mr Burridge,' I said. 'Is Andy around? It's Lizzie from Wintergreen.'

'Hold the line.'

'Yes?' came Andy's voice.

'Hi, sorry to bother you – it's our tea break and JP and Tammy were just wondering if there might be anything untoward going on between my mother and you.'

'She's teaching me to drive.'

'So you're not embroiled or anything?' I said, holding the receiver outwards so JP and Tammy could hear.

'No, we're not. Is that all?' Andy said. 'And why are you interested in what that fucking twat thinks anyway?'

'Yes, that's all,' I confirmed and hung up.

'Apparently not,' I said, feeling slightly like Sue Ellen Ewing.

The following Saturday afternoon I did the mature thing and went over to have dinner with my family. Andy was there watching sports on the telly with Jack and it all felt a bit awkward but he did brew up a pot of coffee and we all sipped and chatted politely. The moment we'd finished, my mother announced that she'd be taking Andy out for a drive before dinner and that dinner would be cauliflower cheese and oven chips – if anyone felt like cooking. I must say a word here about McCain oven chips; they'd just come on to the market and were a miracle for people who loved chips but didn't want to have a chip pan going. I didn't love them per se, but benefited nonetheless via the life-changing joy and convenience they brought. The availability of McCain's meant, overall, more chips but less fuss. I remember grilling them, for speed, but I can't guarantee that was included in the official instructions.

'Lizzie, come driving with us,' Andy said. 'You might pick up some tips.'

It seems sarcastic written down, but that wasn't his style – he was being generous. My mother wasn't so keen, though. Andy's lesson was an official teaching and learning scenario and therefore if I insisted on coming I must be invisible and not speak. 'Andy has his test coming up. He needs to concentrate and not have you giggling in the back seat.'

My mother's cars were never just vehicles. The Flying Pea, for instance, contained two smart, closeable ashtrays stuck to the dashboard via suction pads. There were assorted nylon blankets and cushions, fruit drinks and peanuts and snacks for Danny such as raisins and crisps. There was a cassette player that worked even if the engine was switched off, and lots of stationery in a polythene bag. My mother often did her paperwork in the car, parked up in field gateways. This was a trick to avoid going home that she'd learned from Mr Holt who also did his paperwork in the van – and more than once he had pulled into a favourite gateway to do a couple of hours' work only to find she had got there first.

Once they'd had a row. Mr Holt, claiming to have much more to do, had asked my mother to find another gateway, or go home and do hers there.

My mother had had to quietly explain to him that the moment she stepped through the door, the young of the herd would drag her down, pull on her, cling to her, and demand that she feed them, and so affecting were their cries and grabby hands that she might as well take her stock-check forms, dockets, contracts, daily call sheets, complaints and orders, and smear them all over with Alphabetti Spaghetti and kid wee because that was the effect of the home on her work.

Whereas, the moment they heard the telltale throb of Mr Holt's van outside they'd turn down the volume on the television, do a hasty tidy-up, and at least one of them might greet him at the door, asking if he'd like a cup of coffee.

I sat back and marvelled at my mother's teaching style; she was much better than Mrs Woodward.

'No!' she'd yell. 'Stay in third.' Or, 'OK, overtake that tractor – if it's safe to do so.'

Andy looked adorable, thoughtful, slightly anxious, pressing his lips together in concentration, and after my mother said, 'Take the next left,' he'd repeat, 'Left.'

The cushions and blankets made the back seat cosy. I noticed there were new blankets – dark pink, fringed, and therefore erotic-looking. And I began thinking how well they got along, like mother and son, but a mother and son where the mother has never called the son a greedy little bastard or said, 'Well, if you like your father so much, why don't you just go and live with the fucker?' And then I was asleep all among the erotic blankets, lulled by the smooth motion of Andy's expert driving, and the mumbling voices.

I woke to hear my mother's voice.

'OK, pull in over there, we'll have a short break.'

And as Andy faffed around positioning the vehicle, she lit them a cigarette each. It seemed less mother-and-son-like all of a sudden as she chugged down a blackcurrant-and-apple juice and wiped her mouth on her hand.

'Look at that view,' she said.

I looked out and saw giant water-filled tyre tracks in the verge beside us, and a lichen-covered, wooden gate held shut with a loop of plaited baler twine, and then the gentle valley beyond. To my surprise Andy started saying how much he hated the city.

'I mean, it's great for work, but I hate the bustle, the grime, the stress,' he said. 'I could never live there.'

'I know,' said my mother. 'You belong here among all this.'

'Yes.'

'I love to visit cities, but for life, I'd miss the hedgerows too much, the frozen ditches, the steaming cows,' she said.

'The fresh air, and the birdlife,' continued Andy.

'The puddles in the lanes, and the angry jaybirds shouting in the branches.'

'The darkness of the night.'

'Yes, unadulterated darkness. You never see the stars properly in the city.'

'What about cultural opportunities?' I interrupted. 'And the live-and-let-live attitude?'

They both jumped slightly.

'Christ almighty, Lizzie!' My mother turned to face me, hand on chest. 'I'd completely forgotten you were there.'

'If the city is so terrible, how come you encouraged me to go and live there?' I asked. 'I miss the frozen ditches too.'

She laughed. 'Everyone needs some time in the city.'

'Not me,' said Andy.

'No, men don't have to worry about such things in quite the same way,' said my mother, and while we pondered this, she continued, 'Actually, shall I leave you two to walk back, and Lizzie can get some fresh air?'

'Yes,' said Andy, 'great idea.' He grinned at me and we got out and watched as my mother sped off.

Andy linked arms with me and we strolled along the lanes I knew so well, and loved and missed, and which were now his lanes, and after a while Andy pushed his hand gently up into the back of my hair, fingers splayed. And I let my hand rest inside his waistband and felt his buttock muscles moving, one at a time. It seemed about as erotic as a walk could be without stopping to have sex. It seemed we were still on intimate terms.

'How would you be able to live in London,' I asked, 'if you can't even cope with Leicester?'

'I don't think I could live in London.'

'But I thought you might want to, later on.'

'It might seem bearable, later, but I doubt it.'

'But I definitely want to go,' I said. 'Would me being there make it bearable?'

'I don't know.'

And instead of going straight home, we called in to the King's Head and played darts. I got an accidental bull's eye and wanted to celebrate but a bull's eye is only a cause for celebration if you're aiming for one and I hadn't been. I'd been aiming lower.

'Let's get something to eat here,' said Andy.

'No, thanks,' I said. 'I'd better get home and put the oven chips on.'

Walking home I told Andy I didn't like him having driving lessons with my mother. It wasn't because she'd refused me, I told him, it was a different thing now I'd seen them together.

'She might try something on,' I said.

'Like what?'

'She might throw herself at you.'

'Oh, does that run in the family?' said Andy, laughing.

'No, seriously. You should be on your guard, especially on driving lessons, when you park up in gateways, like just then.'

'Actually, a friend of mine said the same thing.'

'What friend?'

'Willie Bevan.'

'Who's Willie Bevan?'

'Oh, just this bloke at work.'

'And what did Willie Bevan say?'

'That she's a bit of a goer and might have ulterior motives.'

'A goer? What's that?'

'A goer – someone who goes.'

'Oh, God,' I groaned, imagining Fenella Fielding and Ernie Wise.

'Well, you said the same thing yourself, just now,' said Andy.

'Yes, well, now you know.'

It all felt too awful. My mother was turning into a sex rival. Willie Bevan knew it and I didn't even know who Willie Bevan was.

At home, dinner was fried-egg-and-chip sandwiches. My mother wasn't hungry but smoked through the meal and kept saying how important it was to know the Highway Code, even the obscure road signs.

'They're never going to ask you the obvious ones,' she said.

'Do you know a bloke called Willie Bevan?' I asked her.

'No, I don't think so.'

Jack didn't know Willie Bevan, nor did Mr Holt and neither did I. Willie Bevan is of no consequence to this story whatsoever and yet Willie Bevan had warned Andy that my mother was a goer.

I looked at Andy.

'I'm off,' I said quietly.

Andy, surprised, jumped up with a mouthful of food and followed me to the door.

'Byeee!' I shouted to the others.

'Bye, see you,' came the reply.

'Bit sudden?' said Andy, hand over mouth, polite as ever.

'I can't stand it any more. It's all too weird.'

Andy swallowed his mouthful, blinking, sad, puzzled.

'Shall I come with you?' he said, frowning, hands upwards in dismay.

I made an emotional sigh of sadness and looked at the ceiling.

'Of course not,' I said. 'You belong here.'

19. Crystal Deep

Improving the appearance of the waiting room had been at the top of the list of 'Masonic Improvements' and now it had been freshened up and had a new, more clinical-style mirror and a bucket for umbrellas, but JP still wasn't satisfied.

'How does it compare with the waiting room at Cunningham, Pope and Fisher?' JP asked one day as he gazed in scornfully from the surgery. In truth, Cunningham & Co.'s was like something out of a stately home – velvet chairs, oil paintings and tables with knobbly legs standing on a Turkish rug, all with an aura of graceful opulence.

'They have a Turkish rug,' I said.

'OK, I'll get one,' he said.

It was just plain bad luck that later that day a patient called Mr Gillespie came in. Mr Gillespie was proprietor of Fur, Fin & Feather – a fact that was hinted at on his dental record. ('Owns pet shop.')

By the end of the fifteen-minute appointment JP was all for getting an aquarium.

The 'Crystal Deep' aquarium was delivered a week later and the fish shortly afterwards. Soon I came to love seeing the shoal of pretty neon tetras, swimming in a loose dart formation, the light glinting off them, making the African violets and cactuses look like the boring old plants they were.

It was disappointing but typical that after his urgency to acquire them JP had so little interest in the fish. He never looked at them nor asked after their welfare. He was like a divorced father failing to turn up at parents' evening, sports day, school fete or sickbed, not knowing what his child's dog was called, or his child's new baby brother, or that he'd given her origami paper for her last birthday and the one before that.

I asked JP one day if he was pleased with the Crystal Deep.

'The what?'

'Your aquarium,' I reminded him.

He glanced through the doorway at it and said, 'Well, I always think it looks a bit dull, don't you agree? Maybe we should get one of those angelfish.'

This was a bad idea and I put him off, explaining that he shouldn't introduce more fish at that point, certainly not an aggressor like an angel – I'd read the manual. An angel might worry or kill the other fish, I told him. But he bought one anyway, plopped it into the tank and marvelled at its elegance. I watched the tetras dart around the new fish – silver white and still except for its tiny pectoral fins vibrating, ominously, like wasp wings. I felt a great sense of dread and wished I could reach in and remove it.

'He's a calm fellow,' said JP, 'don't you agree?'

'Yes, for now, but according to the experts, he might turn nasty.'

I got down the following morning to find the angel had eaten most of the tetras.

When JP arrived, I shouted the news at him in a tearful and judgemental way, and then heard him on the phone to Mr Gillespie. The fish were cannibalizing each other, he said (no mention of introducing the angelfish), and after finishing on the phone he told us the problem was most likely caused by patients tapping on the glass.

Later that morning, while Tammy made the tea, JP wrote a sign reading, DO NOT TAP ON THE GLASS, and asked me to help him heave the admin desk out of the surgery into a corner of the waiting room. When, after tea break, Tammy noticed the desk gone, and when JP explained that she was going to have to police the aquarium, she objected strongly.

'Absolutely no flipping way am I going to sit out there on my own with those fish,' she said.

'Just do it, Tammy, for the fish, for Christ's sake,' said JP. 'It won't be for ever. Just until they settle.'

'I couldn't care less about the fish,' said Tammy. 'Can you imagine how humiliating it'll be for me, stuck out there asking patients not to tap on the glass?'

'What kind of mother do you think you're going to be if you can't make this tiny sacrifice?' JP asked. 'Eh?'

Tammy was furious. Her face went dark red; she let out a loud cry of anger and swiped a cactus off the console. It landed at JP's feet. The pot and the plant remained intact but dry soil spilled out on to the carpet and dusted his shoes. He turned and went back into the surgery.

And that was that. Tammy stopped speaking to JP, and didn't take coffee, tea or cigarette breaks with us. Everything was left to me.

Tammy and JP's relationship continued to deteriorate. The two of them didn't speak unless they had to and then one day, to punish JP, Tammy announced, 'I'm going back to the flat to stay with Lizzie – for the foreseeable.'

And the next day she did and I had to hide the portrait of her with Fawn behind the settee in case it caused her any more upset. She wouldn't take the bedroom but slept on a camp bed in the lounge, wearing her slumber shades. Frankly I'd have preferred it the other way around. This way I couldn't watch telly or have Andy over (in theory) because the lounge was now her room.

Tammy went completely off her fertility programme, including going to a delicatessen, buying an andouillette sausage so authentic it boasted about using the pig's entire gastrointestinal system, and was very much not recommended for babies, invalids or expectant mothers. She smoked, drank heavily, ate seeds, picked up cats and stroked them, went to Jazzercise three times a week – it really seemed as though she was on the lookout for fertility rules to break.

Having Tammy around was actually quite nice to begin with. I can't say it was lovely because I felt uncomfortable and she was a bit annoying and there was the awful prospect of her being permanent. But I was on strange terms with my mother, and, since she now had Andy to pick up Danny from Curious Minds, I was more or less redundant.

Also, Tammy brought some nice things with her. The salad spinner, her Elancyl body massager – a beauty secret of slim French women – and a hairdryer that made your hair smooth and sleek, and curled it under (or out, whichever you fancied). She had all sorts of cosmetics which I played with, and a foot-shaped bucket which you could fill with warm water and bubble bath and put your feet in while watching TV.

She went down to work every day though, as usual, and would sit out in the waiting room – working to rule, doing her nails, and reading Judith Krantz and Jackie Collins. She barely spoke except to say, 'Sign here, and here, and here,' and, 'Please refrain from tapping on the glass.' And if the patients asked to make a six-monthly appointment, she'd say, 'Give us a ring nearer the time,' which was one of my old tricks.

Without Tammy's support, the 'Masonic Improvements' came to a standstill. The days went by and JP's new slim-fit Latimer dental tunics began to strain at the buttons. And, because he couldn't wear anything underneath the Latimers, his body hairs poked through. He had itchy dry skin from leaning on his elbows and not moisturizing after his bath. And, to cap it all, he'd bumped Jacobs the accountant's car outside the golf club, which had not only humiliated him but landed him with an £80 bill.

20.   Mrs Greenbottle

Melody was in town for a few days visiting her parents, the Long-ladys. We arranged to meet at the Belmont Hotel, which was just around the corner from the surgery, so we could have tea in the new conservatory and then go back to mine for a scale and polish. I politely asked after her parents and Melody told me her mother was having crazy visions and uncontrollable weeping and had asked her father to take a vow of chastity. I said how sorry I was, but Melody brushed it off.

'You know what she's like,' she said. 'She's been reading Margery Kempe the mystic, that's all.'

She was far more concerned (and appalled) by the state of my life.

'How did it all go so wrong?' she wanted to know. She meant, how had I ended up flat-sharing with the dolly-bird girlfriend of my xenophobic boss? And how was it that my only friends were a vicar and his wife? And how had I let my boyfriend start having sex with my mother?

She gulped her tea and looked at me with pity.

'God, what a fucking mess,' she said.

She put it very well and we laughed. I told her Andy and I had pretty much split up, if indeed we'd ever really been together, and that I'd never had to go on the pill or use the thigh-vagina, things having never gone quite that far, and that we had always remained top-half only.

Melody and I had been friends since the age of nine when we'd lived next door to each other. Mrs Longlady had forbidden her to play with me because of my mother being divorced, but she'd done it anyway. She'd been such a funny little thing and here she was now, so self-possessed and fiery. She was wearing a soft denim pinafore with nothing underneath it. The bib and inch-wide straps were not altogether big enough to fully cover her front, and the occasional glimpse of her breasts was slightly distracting.

'And what are you *wearing*?' she said, looking pointedly at my shoes. I have never in my life known a more maligned article of clothing than that pair of sandals.

I explained my athlete's foot. She made light of it – just as she had regarding her mother's mental breakdown – and called it a minor ailment, and then asked how I thought Andy, or anyone, could be interested in me sexually, let alone rampantly, while I had those on my feet. She lectured me on 'the language of shoes', explaining that her own choice of footwear – tiny leather ballerinas – would put people in mind of a nimble young woman pirouetting or turning, or being lifted, or flitting, or dying dramatically. While mine (she biffed a sandal with her foot) only conjured a filthy old monk at morning prayer asking God's forgiveness for masturbating all night. And was that fair on the rest of the world?

'They're just sensible shoes,' I said.

'But don't they remind you of an old monk?'

'Well, OK, yes, I suppose, but mine is only gathering medicinal herbs.'

A waiter lurked and I felt suddenly quite self-conscious and told Melody we should go and get her teeth polished. Then I reminded her that I had athlete's foot and shouldn't even be out.

Her teeth were in good condition but I mentioned her unusual bite – a class three occlusion, or, to use the vernacular, Habsburg Jaw. And told her that JP was taking on orthodontic patients if she wanted, but this would necessitate a three-monthly visit and she wouldn't want to commit. We went upstairs and gossiped benignly. Melody couldn't stay long because of a dinner plan with her family, and I couldn't fully relax with Melody's breasts moving around like the sea under a pontoon, appearing one side then the other of the straps.

Tammy appeared and flopped on to the beanbag. She'd just eaten 'Biryani of the Week' at the Koh-i-Noor and a pint of wine with it, she said, and now just wanted to go to sleep. The drop down to the beanbag was greater than she'd expected and she shrieked, then laughed, and then looking up, saw Melody's pinafore and stopped laughing. She began lecturing Melody on clothing and decency. Which included, 'It just makes me feel so sad to see you dressed like that.' And continued, 'Go and look at yourself in the mirror and see how you feel.'

Melody picked up her duffel bag and went. I felt it a shame, but slightly deserved after her attack on my sandals. We heard the front door slam and then Tammy burst into tears.

'What's wrong with me?' she said. 'It's only the human body – who am I to tell you young ones what to wear?'

I agreed and reminded her she'd been on an emotional rollercoaster, and that made her feel better.

'Yeah, I'm all over the place,' she said. 'I want to go home.'

'Well, go then.'

Tammy and I decided to throw a dinner party, the main purpose being to bring about a reconciliation between her and JP. Had she been a real friend, I'd have begged her not to go back to him and listed all the things that made him untenable as a life partner and a human being. But I was desperate to have my flat back to myself and therefore I wanted this reconciliation as much as she did, or even more so. Also, I liked the idea of showing off the DIY I'd done on the flat.

Tammy was extremely excited about it, which shows just how gloomy she had become. Food-wise, she was thinking something along the lines of a Greek mezze with everyone dipping bread into different bowls of stuff but suddenly remembered a thing she'd read about passengers on a cruise ship all going down with dysentery after sharing a bowl of sour cream and chives. It only took one of them to dip and dip again to introduce the deadly germ.

So, no dipping. Grilled cheeses and salad with olives and maybe a moussaka – though we'd have to call it mince-and-aubergine bake so as not to put people off.

'The food would really go with the look you've created,' said Tammy, which was a very good point, the flat now having a bistro-cum-taverna look since my granny Benson had come back from Knossos with various olive-themed *objets d'art* and a replica fresco, and the kitchenette window had a gingham half-curtain that I'd run up myself from a pattern in a magazine.

'Who to invite, though?' I wondered, meaning other than JP.

'Let's throw caution to the wind . . .' said Tammy. 'Let's invite everyone.'

She had read an article recently, entitled 'Cortion to the Wind', in which the writer, Sali Cortion, surprises herself by doing a series of inadvisable things, and everything going well and her ending up marrying a blind cellist. I'd read this article too, and found it a bit fanciful.

'I don't think we should overstretch ourselves,' I said.

'That's just the sort of thing that Sali had always told herself. And that had been holding her back . . . from marrying a cellist.'

'Are we sure JP will actually turn up?'

'He will if we tell him Pa Vogel will be here. A Freemason, who might get him the nod.'

'Are you talking about my father?'

'Yes.'

'I'm not sure he is a Freemason.'

'But you said he was.'

'Only because you wanted me to.'

Tammy seemed disappointed. 'Invite him anyway,' she said. 'JP would be sure to come if there was a chance of getting him.'

'What if JP tries a funny handshake on him?' I asked, laughing.

'He won't try the handshake, he's not a Freemason yet. Give him credit.'

'Ah, but if I invite my father I can't really invite my mother.'

'Why, did they have a custody battle?'

'I don't know,' I said, 'but divorced people tend not to socialize together.'

'Mia and André get along just fine,' said Tammy, 'and Liz and Richard.'

Inviting my father would be fine – he was a good mixer and I liked the idea of JP trying a funny handshake on him. It would only be a problem if he wanted to bring his wife. I phoned him. He was delighted.

'And shall I bring Rosemary?' he asked, as I knew he would.

'I'd rather you didn't,' I said.

'That's a shame,' he said, but he didn't say any more.

My siblings and I had done rather well with our stepfather who only helped us or kept his nose out. Our stepmother, though, was tougher to deal with and harder to like. She believed in God so fiercely she had no faith left over for people. And we, her husband's ex-family – being unruly, materialistic, agnostic at best, and always looking for laughs – presented a constant threat to her children's moral development.

I must have been twelve when she claimed, in front of everyone, that when she had first met me, some years previously, I had had an imaginary friend – a middle-aged woman called Mrs Greenbottle, who had been by my side, advising me, from a young age. This was not true but it was difficult to convincingly deny it – because of course a twelve-year-old *would* deny such a thing. My siblings sniggered about it and my stepmother even went so far as to apologize for mentioning it – as if she'd broken a confidence between us.

I'd never had an imaginary friend, and if I had, I'd never have had a middle-aged one and I'd never have called her Mrs Greenbottle. I'd have had an assertive teenager with a passion for justice called Ruth or Justine or Toni, and I said so to my stepmother.

She explained that I had invented a sensible mother figure because that was what I was craving. But I wasn't. If I was craving anything it was a jolly stepmother to make things easier in our quest to befriend our estranged father. I soon got bored with denying Mrs Greenbottle and when she popped up (which was only ever when my stepmother summonsed her), I'd just go along with it.

One day, though, when my stepmother had overstepped the mark in criticizing my mother's latest boyfriend, pregnancy or car, I turned Mrs Greenbottle back on her.

'Mrs Greenbottle wants you to stop being horrible about my mother,' I told her.

'Mrs Greenbottle must know that I'm not being horrible. All I wish is that Mummy could be better and help you reach your potential, and stop harming herself with drink and promiscuity.'

'Mrs Greenbottle doesn't know what you're talking about,' I said.

'I think Mrs Greenbottle knows very well. She's not a fool.'

'How do you know? She's my imaginary friend, not yours. I invented her to turn a blind eye. She loves Mummy just the way she is.'

'Perhaps Mrs Greenbottle doesn't care about Mummy?'

'You don't even know her,' I said.

'I know that she's a very good woman.'

'Well, I'm sorry but she says she's not coming here again because of your nastiness and cheap bacon.'

And though that was the last I ever heard of Mrs Greenbottle, I still couldn't risk her in front of my friends and work colleagues.

Tammy felt we should not invite Andy – the whole point of the party being to get JP in the right mood (to take Tammy back, though that wasn't spelled out).

'Andy has a detrimental effect on JP's mood,' she said. 'I don't know why.'

'He knows Andy thinks he's a cretin.'

'Oh.'

I agreed it was best not to invite him. He wouldn't enjoy it and if I told him my motive, he'd think me manipulative, and if I didn't, he'd think me insane.

'We're going to have a right old mix of people,' I said.

'That was the very thing that made Sali Cortion's party a success – the *variety of people*,' said Tammy, listing them. 'A grumpy senior colleague, her piano teacher – good-looking but crotchety – competitive sister and boyfriend – whom she dislikes – a neighbour who has been known to complain about Sali's piano practice, her grandmother, the grandmother's companion and a few others.'

'Yes, but doesn't she wake the next morning thinking, "I dreamt I invited an odd assortment of people to dinner. Thank God it was only a dream," and then remembers it wasn't a dream – she really had thrown caution to the wind?'

'Yes, you read it too!' said Tammy. 'And it goes really well.'

So, as well as JP, we invited Reverend and Mrs Woodward, my sister, her new boyfriend, Melody (who stayed in town an extra day especially), my father, Priti Mistry, and Jossy and Bill Turner. In the event, Jossy was away on an artists' retreat in Norfolk, so Bill brought his nurse, Rhona, instead. My mother ended up coming because when I rang her for moral support, instead of offering advice, she asked why she hadn't been invited, so I had to say, 'Come if you like.'

And she then said, 'Thank you, I was going to come anyway,' which she did.

When I asked Priti I warned her that JP would be there.

'You know, the horrible dentist,' I said.

But Priti didn't care. She wanted a free evening out, plus she and Tammy had bonded at Jazzercise over having powdery leg skin.

On the night, the flat looked lovely. Tammy had moved all her things into my bedroom and turned the lounge back into a lounge. I'd spent £1 on a bunch of carnations, which I put in a jam jar, and it looked like a watercolour painting. We brought all the chairs up from the waiting room and lit a few candles in bottles. Tammy threw a red scarf over a lampshade so it would give a more forgiving light and I referenced Blanche DuBois, who did the same to hide her wrinkles.

JP arrived first, all dressed up in corduroys and a horrible silky shirt, holding a bottle of Bull's Blood and a box of mint Matchmakers. He was self-conscious and drifted about saying I'd got the flat looking 'very modish' but making it very clear he was the landlord by looking closely at certain things, like the knob on the heater and the window frames. Tammy, in a spotty dress, acted shy and kept herself busy cutting bread and snipping parsley and saying,

'Excuse me,' and opening the fridge. My mother arrived next, struggling with a pudding she'd been given by a friend who catered for weddings, something that looked like the phone book but was probably a manuscript, and Angelo the dog – whom she was dog-sitting while Miss Smith had her varicose veins stripped. I rushed to take Angelo's lead, picked him up and kissed him.

'Abe's going to try to put in an appearance after his dressage lesson,' my mother said, 'and Andy should be here soon.'

'But Andy wasn't invited,' I said.

JP made a half-hearted protest about Angelo the dog, or maybe Andy, and my mother stared at him and said, 'Is there a problem?' and it almost caused a scene but I think JP knew better than to start on my mother.

She then made an announcement about not feeding Angelo titbits because he was getting out of condition since being back with Miss Smith, whom she'd seen giving him ginger cake.

My sister arrived next and her new boyfriend was none other than JP's son, JP Junior.

JP and Tammy stared, open-mouthed, both too shocked to speak. I was furious with her for having this secret and not telling me.

'Oh my God,' I said to my mother, 'she's going out with JP's castrated son.'

'Oh, no,' said my mother.

'Junior?' said JP, and JP Junior gave his father a manly hug, and Tammy went over to say hello too.

My sister bundled me into the kitchenette to ask why I hadn't mentioned that JP and Tammy would be here.

'If you ever bothered speaking to me, or listening to me, or asking how my life was going, you'd know they'd be here,' I said. 'Tammy is fucking living here and I'm only having this bloody party so she can move out.'

Tammy and JP, at the opposite side of the room, probably heard most of this but only looked confused.

My mother asked outright, in front of everyone, where the

couple had met (Tammy's fortieth), before launching into a short talk on the doctor/nurse relationship and that JP Junior needn't think that Thomasin would let that cliché play out. Then thankfully, Bill Turner arrived with his nurse, and then Melody, who went straight up to Tammy to have a few private words, and they held hands briefly. Then Priti arrived with some bread in tinfoil. She was wearing flip-flops with socks, which made her look as though she'd escaped from a hospital.

Then the Woodwards. Reverend Woodward looked bizarre in ordinary blue jeans which had been pressed with a hard crease down the leg, and topped with a black shirt and vicar's collar. My mother tackled him on it.

'Why are you wearing your dog collar at a party?' she said. 'You'll put us all on edge.'

'It's my uniform.'

'No one else has seen fit to appear in their work clothes,' she said, gesturing to JP. 'You're not about to give a sermon, are you?'

'He's never off duty, though,' said Mrs Woodward. 'Like God.'

'Don't say that,' said my mother, pouring herself a glass of Bull's Blood.

My father arrived next and Tammy made a beeline for him and held him hostage in a corner for at least ten minutes. I heard numerous mentions of Massachusetts and New England and guessed Tammy must be recommending me for the sabbatical, and I regretted not being a better friend to her – and then dragged him over to meet JP who was being unbearable about people on state benefits wasting taxpayers' money on frozen convenience foods. I watched to see if JP tried a funny handshake but the doorbell went again and I looked away at the crucial moment. Melody trotted down and came back with Abe in jodhpurs and a cravat, bearing a most attractive basket of grapes. He went straight over to Bill Turner and I think they might have done a funny handshake.

And then Andy walked in with a bottle of posh fruit juice and told me it was just for me and no one else, and kissed me on the cheek. Then my mother appeared and asked what my father was doing here.

My sister overheard this and said, 'He's here because he's Lizzie's father, a man you chose to marry and have three children with, and we're sorry it's so inconvenient and you now hate his guts, but we didn't fucking choose him.'

My mother tutted and turned to me. 'What's he doing here?' she repeated.

'He's just a lure. JP thinks he can help get him into the Freemasons.'

'But your father's not a Mason.'

'I know that, but JP doesn't.'

My mother was very upset with my father. They got along all right on the rare occasions they encountered one another – at a wedding, say. But recently my father had done something to cause my mother great anguish.

It had been agreed that Jack mustn't get a motorbike of any kind. Not because they were so dangerous, though they were, but because Jack wasn't suited to that kind of risk. However, around that time he suddenly seemed keen to buy a moped from a kid in the village. It was my mother's opinion that Jack was counting on her to forbid it. Andy also tried to put him off.

'I couldn't have ridden round these roads aged sixteen or seventeen,' he said, in support of my mother.

Jack didn't care what they said. He emptied his building society account and, finding himself short, telephoned our father to ask for a loan. Our father agreed to send him a cheque and he was soon the proud owner of a Suzuki AP 50. He drove it home and parked it on the pavement in front of my mother's house. I wasn't there at the time, but Andy was. And this is approximately what happened.

My mother rushed outside, distraught.

'How did you pay for it?' she asked.

When Jack told her, she stared at him in disbelief.

'Your father?'

'But he says I'm never to go over to his house on it,' Jack told her.

'Why not?' asked my mother.

'He doesn't want Benjamin to see it.'

'And do you understand why he doesn't want Benjamin to see it?' my mother asked.

'Not really.'

'He doesn't want Benjamin to see it because he can't bear the thought of him wanting one at your age because the roads are dangerous and it's so young, and he'll be so vulnerable,' she said. 'He can't bear the thought.'

Jack went inside, but my mother stood out there in silence, looking at the moped and thinking. Then she telephoned my father. No one thought to eavesdrop.

The party meal went well, I must say; it was quite picnicky due to the number of people and the tininess of the dining table. Tammy's mince-and-aubergine bake (moussaka) with green salad and vinaigrette went head to head with my spaghetti ring and chopped-egg flan (Crosse & Blackwell recipe featured in *Woman's Own* which was nicer than it sounds) and came out an easy winner. Priti's bread was much remarked upon and then eaten entirely by Abe, who kept dipping it in everything.

Pudding was Marguerite Patten's Angel Whispers with raspberry jam (a triumph), and the thing my mother brought, which was basically blancmange. Afterwards I served real filter coffee in the tiny cups Granny Benson had given me, and JP filled the air with smoke from a slim panatella. It was strange seeing him smoke it himself – not being fed. He was all over it, sucking it and twirling the end in his lips, throwing his head back to exhale. It was like seeing a captive hyena enjoying the leg of a tiny, dead antelope. I looked away.

'Is someone writing a book?' shouted Bill Turner, patting the manuscript my mother had left in full view on the sideboard.

'Ooh, yes, how's the book going?' someone else asked.

'Oh, do read us a bit,' said Tammy.

My sister felt it probably wasn't a good time and why didn't we play Mountain River or charades instead but Tammy was tipsy and excited – and thought she might be in it.

And Mrs Woodward joined in. 'Oh, yes, do read some of your novel,' she said, with real enthusiasm. 'I've heard so much about it from Lizzie.'

'She writes it here, in my waiting room,' JP boasted.

My mother leafed through her papers, coughed and set the scene.

'So, it's 2024,' she began. 'Calipastra and Jim, a married couple, have taken a young, male apprentice, Stefan, to live with them. Calipastra has managed to coax Stefan into teaching her to drive – along the forest tracks. But it is illegal for women to drive without a husband or father in the car, so they are taking a huge risk . . .' Then she began reading.

The party listened intently to Stefan teaching Calipastra the basics of driving, and Calipastra seducing the apprentice as he stands *contrapposto* beside the huge car, taking his lower lip softly between her teeth, pushing him gently backwards on to the bonnet of the car, etc. . . . Then, the apprentice experiencing a number of troubling incidents in which his life is in danger and telling Calipastra, 'I think someone wants to decommission me.' Then the apprentice, having been fatally run over, lying at the side of the road, Calipastra reaching him just in time to see steam and sparks coming from his ears, and hear garbled nonsense and robot noises from his mouth (which is actually a speaker grille). And him conking out.

'You see,' my mother pronounced with great solemnity, 'Stefan was a robot.'

Mrs Woodward gasped. 'Is it autobiographical?'

'Of course it's not,' said my mother. 'It's set in the future, and Stefan's a robot.'

'It's brilliant,' said Melody. 'I love it.'

'Oh, my gosh, it's so moving,' said Tammy, in tipsy tears. 'It's like you and Andy Nicolello.'

My mother and I looked at each other.

'But where's the science?' asked JP. 'I could hear all the fiction but no science.'

'Are you caught in a temporal loop?' Tammy wondered, and I was proud of her for such a notion.

'No,' said my mother, 'it's probably more relevant to say it's a satirical commentary on the patriarchal trend from the vantage point of the future.'

The party chattered on about fiction, science fiction and so forth, and my mother particularly gave her thoughts on the flaws of civilization. I think she'd taken some kind of pill to bring out her creativity because she was talking most poetically, like Doris Lessing on the radio, or a crazy person in the park.

Tammy and JP sat closely together and Angelo had his head on Tammy's leg. And it really was like Sali Cortion's dinner, with the odd assortment getting on famously and everything just so, but just as I was thinking it Melody, who'd gone into my bedroom to adjust her eye make-up after tears of mirth, reappeared heaving a great square thing and saying, 'Oh my God, this is brilliant, who painted this?'

I leapt up, but too late, and she stood in the doorway, holding the painting out to face the party and, peering at the information on the back of the canvas, read, 'Tammy with Fawn – 1980'.

Tammy in the portrait now had blacked-out front teeth and heavy spectacles. She was pregnant (with the fawn). The fawn seemed to have an erect penis and to have been stabbed with a dagger. A pretty black lace-effect border ran all around.

No one spoke for a moment until Mrs Woodward said, 'Is it Dadaism?'

Tammy hid her face and rocked with laughter or weeping, or both, but probably laughter.

And Bill said, 'Thank goodness Jossy's not here to see that.'

'What is it?' various people asked and my mother explained.

'Husband –' pointing at JP – 'presents wife with a portrait he's commissioned, the result so deeply chauvinistic and patronizing it provokes an uncharacteristically violent response in previously docile spouse.'

'Spouse!' said Tammy, giggling.

'Hang on!' said Bill Turner. 'Jossy did a pretty good job considering JP knocked her down to twenty quid.'

'I wish I'd stuck to my original offer – a free scale and polish,' said JP.

'It's worth more than thirty quid now,' observed Melody.

Tammy and JP left together, which was a triumph and a huge relief, particularly considering the appearance of the defaced painting. JP didn't seem to care, just as long as he'd got Tammy back. On the way out he said, 'Thank you for a delightful evening, nurse,' and told me not to bin the portrait because he was going to salvage the frame.

The Woodwards went home next, saying how much they'd enjoyed the evening too, especially the reading. Soon there was only Priti and me left.

'You must be so proud – your mother is such a great writer,' she said.

'She is, actually.'

'I hope she gets the book published.'

'It's unlikely.'

'I can't wait to read the whole thing.'

'Yeah.'

'You don't sound very enthusiastic.'

'The thing is,' I told her, 'my mum is teaching Andy to drive at the moment, and he's living at her house, so it all feels a bit – odd.'

'Oh,' said Priti, and she looked up, like someone trying to imagine something.

The party had been a success in that Tammy had gone back to Blackberry Lane and it was just me in the flat. I still didn't know how things stood with Andy and me, and found myself pining for him one minute, and furious and suspicious of my mother the next, and then suffering great queasiness about it all.

Late one afternoon after the surgery had closed, when all this was going through my mind, Andy called in unexpectedly. He'd enjoyed the dinner party, he said; he'd liked meeting my father, he'd heard from JP we were having trouble with the aquarium, and he'd been quite stunned by the unveiling of Tammy's portrait, having seen it before it had been altered.

'What a party!' he said.

'Yes, but it was a success overall.'

Then, quite abruptly, he asked me what I thought was going on.

'What do you think is going on?' he said, looking very serious.

Assuming he meant in our relationship and, glad for the opportunity to thrash it all out, I said, 'Well, since you ask, I feel uncomfortable about the driving lessons, especially hearing that new chapter of my mother's novel.'

'Umm, I'm talking about the aquarium,' he said.

'Oh,' I said, 'I see.' And we switched subject immediately and discussed the shock-absorbing pads to go underneath the tank, the slam-proof door-closing mechanism that Mr Skidmore was about to fit, and the new *DO NOT TAP ON THE GLASS* sign, official looking and less likely to be ignored, so that Tammy's desk could come back into the surgery. And that was that.

Andy was reminded of the Babel fish from his favourite book and how it simultaneously proved the existence and the non-existence of God. And because he showed no inclination to return to the other subject, which I had now clearly flagged as 'troubling me', I told him I was busy and said goodbye without even going up into the flat or having so much as a peck on the cheek.

After he was gone, I thought about the Babel fish and how perfect it was for Reverend Woodward, and took the extraordinary step of phoning the vicarage. Mrs Woodward answered and I didn't dare say I wanted to speak to her husband in case she thought we were embroiled. So I pretended to want to check the time of our next lesson, and brought up the main point of my call as an afterthought.

'Oh, and by the way, please tell Reverend Woodward to remind me to tell him about the Babel fish,' I said. 'It simultaneously proves the existence and the non-existence of God.'

'Goodness gracious,' said Mrs Woodward, 'isn't it clever.'

'Yes.'

'Have you got one in your aquarium?'

21. The Prolapse and the Honeysuckle

A few weeks after the dinner party I received an unusual phone call from Mr Holt. Unusual because he never used the phone. His voice sounded a bit strangled when he explained that my mother had had a prolapse and the doctor had referred her to the infirmary for an operation. 'The Fothergill repair,' he told me.

We'd all had our times at Leicester Royal Infirmary. My mother for some of her babies, miscarriages, varicose veins, and a car crash so ridiculous it looked deliberate, though it definitely wasn't. There was my fractured pelvis, the strange psychosomatic paralysis that affected my sister's wrist and shoulder joints after a mental breakdown on a North Devon camping holiday, Little Jack's hearing test – after we suddenly realized he couldn't hear with his eyes shut – the birth of baby Danny, and the death of a patient called Miss Emma Mills which I'd accidentally caused during my time as an auxiliary nurse. There was also Mr Holt's broken foot, which he denied was broken so as not to make a fuss and because of the times before the NHS when he couldn't breathe due to asthma and his mother would beg him not to need the doctor when he was actually suffocating, because of the cost.

The word 'prolapse' sounded like water lapping at the edge of an old stone pool rather than the grim thing it actually was, and we bandied it around. We all enjoyed saying it. Its effect was better than cursing.

'My mother's had a prolapse,' one of us might say to the post lady for no reason other than to see her horrified face.

'Tell him I've had a fucking prolapse,' my mother might say when a neighbour called round to ask if we'd mind moving a vehicle from outside their house. And thinking she'd detected a sigh or a tut, she would invite him inside to have a look.

'My mother's had a prolapsed uterus,' I told Tammy, to explain why I needed a few days off work.

Tammy resented my mother having the prolapse because, A) it added another tiny cloud to the horizon of femaleness, and B) it meant she'd have to assist JP alone without me to chat to, because I'd need some time off work.

'Oh, my goodness, whatever caused it?' she asked.

The prolapsed uterus was a straightforward consequence of having so many children and pushing them out too quickly and not leaving gaps between pushes and, in addition, suffering with the Benson bowel, which meant straining on the toilet every few days.

'Straining on the toilet mostly,' I told Tammy, to keep it simple, not being quite sure of Tammy's baby/fertility situation, and not wanting to stray into the childbirth arena.

'Silver lining though,' she said. 'It'll put Andy off.'

'What do you mean?' I asked, horrified, but having already thought that exact thing.

'No, I just mean she won't seem such a superwoman now with her female organs hanging out.'

'Oh. I see,' I said.

There was a few days' wait for the surgical repair and my mother wasn't allowed to do much except drink orange juice and eat laxative powders. She concentrated on the novel and managed to crowbar a compromised uterus into the plot. And then she was admitted to the Leicester Royal Infirmary and operated on the next day. It was such a gloriously bright day that I felt sure she'd die under the anaesthetic, or die of blood loss or the surgeon sneezing at the wrong moment and severing an important vein that couldn't be fixed.

I imagined that, if the worst happened, I could bring Danny up as my own. I'd make him forget the past and call me Mother and that way I'd be accepted by society without having to go through with actual childbirth and risk having a child who was scared of water or dogs or didn't like music or stayed awake at night, or had long arms and could reach out from its pram. I'd seen a baby like this in Fenwick's, literally grabbing things off the shelves. 'He always does that,' said the mother. 'He's got extra-long arms.'

Then there were April Jickson's twins – I can't remember their real names, because she always called them Thing One and Thing Two – for whom I'd babysat a few times after her husband had suffered a life-changing accident in Rimini. Thing One was quite sweet and normal, but Thing Two, my God, he was a real fusspot, and yet they were biological twins. Thing One would tuck into his fish-finger igloo with nothing but praise and admiration ('Look, Lizzie made an igloo') whereas Thing Two would angrily want to know why I'd fooled around with his food and would dig at the mashed potato dome with his kiddy-fork looking for his fish fingers, and the only song he'd allow was 'Calling Occupants of Interplanetary Craft' by the Carpenters, and that's not a song you can take more than once or twice.

I once reported Thing Two to April. 'He's a bit fussy, isn't he?' I'd said.

'Tell me about it!' said April. 'He can be a right little cunt.'

I've never forgotten that moment, the terrifying realization that you have no control over what kind of baby you produce – you might get Danny, but then again, you might get Thing Two or that baby with the long arms.

Thing One and Thing Two were a good reminder to think jolly hard before having babies if you like your current life. April's life had been pretty much perfect, according to her, without them. She'd been on friendly terms with Lynsey de Paul, Alvin Stardust and Liza Goddard before the twins came along and put paid to her trips to London for gadding about.

Luckily, in spite of all the tiny signs that my mother would die – the honeysuckle coming out early, the radio playing 'Imagine' (*there's no heaven*) followed by 'Seasons in the Sun', a patient telling us his wife had died 'in theatre', and the sandwich of the week at the Lunch Box being '*vache morte et moutarde*' – the operation went well and she was ready to go home a couple of days later.

My sister drove her home in the Flying Pea which she'd borrowed until my mother would need it back, and I went over there that day, on the bus, straight from work with a small holdall. I'd taken the rest of the week off.

It had been agreed that I would sleep in my old room and Andy Nicolello would take the Zedbed in the lounge. I was very grateful, but also felt it was the least he could do.

I'd been very much looking forward to helping my mother convalesce; the weather was set fair and I imagined it as a kind of holiday, playing Scrabble or working on the novel together. Things weren't quite as I'd planned though; firstly my mother was much iller than I'd expected – in mental and physical discomfort. The warm weather did at least mean she could lie out on her three-position recliner, though, and rest under the shade of some spindly trees and an umbrella, which was something, and I lay near her on a beach towel. I dragged various bits of furniture outside including a coffee table and assorted seats. It looked rather like the Nicolellos' encampment.

I didn't see much of Mr Holt or Jack or Andy, who all had work and school to go to and were making themselves scarce. Mr Holt, particularly, was averse to getting involved with anything in the health department unless it entailed opening a stiff jar of ointment or digging a grave. My mother's tired-out uterus having come free of its moorings was to be avoided.

When she was a bit better, I pointed out that her hair had gone brittle because of the hormonal shock. I'd read about this in a magazine article called 'Do You Understand Your Hair?' and I offered her a fifteen-minute moisturizing treatment that had come in a free sachet with that same magazine. She'd seemed keen and I'd combed it through, but then, when it was time to wash it out, she'd flopped down on to the recliner with the treatment still on under a turban, too tired to come inside for a rinse. I read a book with Danny, who then fell asleep next to Sue the dog, who was also asleep, and I lay down and was just dropping off when my mother suddenly said, 'I've had my tubes tied at the same time as the repair – to kill two birds.'

After my littlest brother baby Danny was born in 1977 Mr Holt had told my mother, 'No more children.' And made it clear that if she snuck any more babies out, he'd run away, knowing all too well that she'd had Danny deliberately and without asking and against their 'no babies' agreement. The pregnancy had caused ructions until he arrived and was the best baby anyone ever had and as soon as he could smile he smiled and as soon as he could talk he said the nicest things, and lay on the carpet on his stomach, singing with his little legs stirring the air, drawing wax crayon pictures of teapots and dogs. And now he was nearly four and getting nicer by the day.

She was furious with Mr Holt about the tube-tying, almost as if he'd crept into the operating theatre with his bolt of green gardening twine and, while the real surgeon was distracted by the tulip tattoo on my mother's flank, begun tying up bits of her pink tubing the way he tied the wayward stems of the climbing rose and willowy beanstalks, with a secure but gentle knot.

But actually, it had been her choice.

Mr Holt had only said, 'Let's have no more.'

And she'd said, 'One more.'

And then he'd said, 'No more. We haven't any money, love, and we've got four.'

And so, because of the past and knowing she couldn't trust herself to put her thing in, and because she didn't fancy the inter-uterine device, and the pill made the blood in her veins dangerous, and because she knew that the painful urge to produce had got the better of her more than once, more than twice . . . she'd had Dr Mutts do it while he was in there, repairing the old equipment.

I squinted in the sun. I said I was sorry and that we'd all try to be the best we could be so that she wouldn't need any more babies, and that must have sounded ridiculous because she said that wasn't the point and she didn't know what she'd done to deserve such wonderful children, she really didn't. So I picked up her book and offered to read it to her so she could relax. She was still wearing the turban, with the treatment on her hair underneath. It wouldn't hurt to give it a bit longer, I thought.

I began reading aloud from a book my aunt Josephine had sent, *On Lies, Secrets and Silence*, which I'd expected to be poetry but wasn't and therefore not easy to read. I wasn't able to get any flow because it wasn't the easiest to understand and I'd have to pause every now and again to collect my thoughts – it was boring and devastating by turns. I felt sad and a little angry that my mother had wilfully poisoned herself with men, drink and pills, and starved herself of food and now lay here taunting herself, and me, with selected prose of Adrienne Rich. I closed it.

'I can't get going on this,' I said. 'I'll read you a magazine instead.'

She groaned.

'It's Britain's top-selling weekly for women,' I said, and she rolled slowly over and listened as I read her an article about Sylvester Stallone and reincarnation, and then a thing on regressive hypnosis, and then Marguerite Patten's teatime treat recipes. My skin prickled in the heat and I felt strangely afraid. I looked at my sleeping mother and couldn't help but wonder what was the point of everything – the teatime treats, the shampoo that knew your hair, the vials of sparkly green eyeshadow, the polka-dot sweater with collar and pocket, tiny chequered headscarves that made us look simple and adorable – if all it boiled down to was this.

Andy drifted into sight and offered to make some tea. I declined. I'd started to enjoy declining offers of food and drink from him. It was all I had. But to be fair he was keen to be helpful and at one point he threw a rug over the washing line and began banging it with a hard brush.

'You're throwing up dust,' I told him.

Later, he did some gardening, which bothered my mother no end. He reassured her that he'd been trained in gardening and had grown a whole hedge from seed but I doubted it and this proved right when he cut clean through the gnarly stem of the honeysuckle and began yanking it off the shed where it had been delightfully scrambling since the house was built in 1969. I was embarrassed for Andy and sad for my mother who loved well-established climbers with nests and fragrance. But actually, because she'd just had her tubes tied, the honeysuckle didn't seem such a tragedy.

Later Andy apologized. 'I'm sorry about the climber,' he said.

'Oh, it's nothing really. It's got a good old root – it'll spring up in no time.' And that must have made her sad because she pretended to yawn and turned away.

I knew she was expecting visitors. My grandmother was threatening to call in, and my sister and my mother's friend, the well-meaning idiot, Carrie Frost.

I pulled myself together and, inspired by Marguerite Patten, I made a pair of sponge cakes and put butter icing in between. Out of pure habit I made the icing in two shades of pink, and had been about to write *Get Well Soon* across the top in the darker pink but when I practised on a plate, the writing put me in mind of denture gums and women's tubes. So I daubed it all over the top and dusted it with icing sugar to disguise its fleshy tones.

My sister arrived and, to my mother's dismay, had JP Junior in tow. They sat on carver chairs in the garden and Junior had to listen while my mother told him about the time his father had been prejudiced against Abe. Junior seemed terribly unhappy about it all and said, 'Oh my God,' a few times, and eventually Tina said, 'Jesus, Mum, can you stop going on and on about his father.'

My mother ended by saying it was OK, Abe would have the last laugh because he was great pals with Bill Turner and Jacobs the accountant.

'What are you wearing on your head?' my sister asked.

'Lizzie has done me a beautifying hair treatment.'

Mr Holt appeared and joined us and then Jack, and my mother decided, at that moment, to remove the towelling turban. Her hair stood on end in stiff waves, like Elsa Lanchester in *The Bride of Frankenstein*. To be fair, no one laughed out loud, but snorts escaped and my mother, sensing something wrong, made a lurch to cover it up again and was in sudden, acute pain. My sister said, 'What the hell, Lizzie?'

It felt for a moment as though my life was caving in on itself. My sister, in a bikini top, arm slung across the shoulders of my boss's son who was pouring tea and cutting into the pink-iced cake. My boyfriend (ex-boyfriend) sitting next to my recumbant, towel-covered mother, as if protecting her from me. Mr Holt, awkward, looming over us but unwilling to sit among us, for fear of being trapped in the frightful tableau. Little Jack, who'd always been a boy, with moped grease under his fingernails, no longer little, and baby Danny, saying things like 'architectural' and 'kebab'.

Junior offered a plate of cake to my mother, and my sister said, 'Not for her, June, she's borderline anorexic.' And somehow that made everyone laugh again, but openly this time – though what we were laughing at, I do not know, and my own laughter very nearly turned to tears. And then, to cap it all, Granny Benson arrived. To her credit, she had brought my mother a tin of fruit drops for refreshment, and suggested she go inside now as it was getting chilly, which was quite right and motherly.

'Good grief!' she said. 'Who are all these enormous men?' and touched her hair, and then, for something else to say, turned to me. 'How's the driving going, Lizzie?'

'Slowly,' I said, and so, after a small whisky and soda, she let me take her for a spin around the block in her Volkswagen. She agreed that I was a bit clunky and offered to pick me up one day the following week – I could drive her to the hairdresser and the library and we could have tea at her house, she said. And though she was a bossy boots, and usually to be avoided, I was glad of the offer.

'Yes, please,' I said.

I left after five days, by which time my mother was quite back to normal, mentally if not physically. I told her that Andy and I were not going out, as such, any longer and she was surprised.

'Oh, why?' she asked.

'It's just not working – he's weird, I'm weird, I don't know.'

'That's a shame.'

'I was annoyed with him for having driving lessons from you when I couldn't,' I said, 'and then it went wrong from there.'

'Well, I can't just chuck him out, if that's what you're suggesting,' she said, 'like some sort of Rachman.'

'No, I wasn't suggesting that, but you could give him notice, say six months. That would be plenty long enough for him to fix up somewhere else.'

'But then what? We actually need his rent.'

'Get another lodger.'

'But we like him.'

And then we stopped discussing it because Andy was probably somewhere around and I felt confused and sad about the whole thing.

22. Immediate Restoration

I was at home in my flat the following Sunday when Andy appeared, unexpectedly, and acted as if nothing had happened, and I gave him a cup of coffee. And then Priti was at the door, also unexpectedly. Her tooth was hurting again, so I walked her round to the emergency dental clinic which was open at the weekends on Granville Road, near to my flat. The dentist on duty, by chance, was Bill Turner.

It was that same upper left two bothering her, of course.

Bill had a look around her mouth. She jumped when he touched her upper left incisors.

'This is all rather sensitive up here, is it?' he said.

Priti nodded. He tapped again. She jumped. He tapped and she cried out.

Bill told her the tooth could most likely not be saved and that the only option was to take it out. But that this would leave a gap, right at the front of her mouth. He asked her if she thought she'd be able to manage the pain with painkillers and antibiotics while her own dentist made her a denture to put into the socket.

'If I take this tooth out today,' he explained, 'you can't have a temporary denture put in the gap for some weeks, until the socket has healed. If I extract it today, you must find another dentist to make you a false tooth. This clinic is only for emergency procedures – we don't make dentures.' Bill spoke as though Priti were an idiot.

'OK,' she said, seeming bewildered. 'I don't want a missing front tooth.'

'Well, if you can hang on and see your own dentist and get a denture made, he can fit it straight into the socket, and later make you a bridge.'

'OK.'

'So you're going to try to hang on?' Bill Turner checked.

'Yes,' I answered for Priti, who looked ghastly.

'Yes,' she repeated.

Bill wrote her a prescription for some strong painkillers. He seemed to assume JP was Priti's dentist.

'The nurse can book you in,' he said.

'Could you take her on, Bill?' I asked, using his name to remind him how well we knew each other.

'I'm full to bursting,' he said. 'I could see her on my private list – but since she's a friend of yours, why not book her in with JP?'

'He's full too.'

Priti took her prescription and we left.

Priti came back to the flat with me. She was horrified at the thought of going to school with a gap at the front of her mouth.

'If that happens, I will leave school,' she said.

Andy ran down to the pharmacy at the infirmary to have Priti's prescription made up. And by the time he got back I had it all worked out.

'We could treat her,' I said quietly, at the kitchen sink.

'Who could?' said Andy.

'We could. You make the denture and I'll extract the tooth.'

'Can you do that?'

'I treat everyone else, why not her? She needs us.'

I had it all worked out. Andy would take the impressions, now, that day, and make the denture in his lunch hour over the following days – to fit immediately after I'd extracted the tooth, which I'd do as soon as possible. It was all entirely normal, except that I wasn't actually a dentist.

'We could have it done by Tuesday,' I said. 'She's never going to find a dentist to do this on the NHS – and you know it.'

'But then she'd have a denture,' Andy said. 'She won't want a denture.'

'She's got no choice,' I whispered. 'She's not registered anywhere.'

I appealed to Andy along political lines, knowing it was my best bet. 'Dentists aren't providing dentures on the NHS except for their long-standing patients, and people like Priti are falling into a gap.' I almost asked him to excuse the pun, but didn't. 'You know this. You see the work coming into the lab, and it's nearly all private, isn't it?'

Andy jabbed at the sugar with a teaspoon while he thought about this.

'You're right.'

'And then, once it's all settled down,' I said, 'you can make her a bridge, and it'll be perfect and free and justice will be served.'

'Oh my God,' said Andy.

We put the idea to Priti and she seemed quite relaxed about it. We planned it all out, including the idea of replacing the denture with a bridge in a few months' time. Andy made absolutely sure she knew that this was not the orthodox route, and illegal.

'But you're never going to find an NHS dentist to do this,' I said.

We went down to the surgery and within a few minutes Andy had made Priti's dental impressions and forty-eight hours later he was back again with a perfect little denture he'd made during two lunch hours. Priti came to look. She held it up to her mouth, and I think she was pleasantly surprised because she laughed. She'd been ringing around all day, she told us, trying to find a real NHS dentist, but with no luck, and the pain was still there in spite of the tablets – throbbing, building.

She had no qualms. 'Yes, please, please, do it.'

So then – God – that night, we broke the laws of the land in order to help our friend.

Injecting Priti was difficult. She was nervous and suddenly turned her head. Somehow the needle went through her lip – the local squirted out in an arc of tiny clear jewels across the surgery. Priti was unaware of it and I mention it now only because it was such an extraordinary sight. I told Andy he must assist, like a dental nurse. I started again with a new syringe and this time held her under the chin so she couldn't move, and Andy was there, ready.

'You have to keep still,' I said.

While we waited for the anaesthetic to take, Andy got Priti to write a note saying she was one hundred per cent aware of the treatment – just in case it ever got investigated and Priti changed her story. Years ago, he'd done a home-made tattoo for a boy who claimed afterwards not to have wanted it – a solicitor had been involved and Andy had been cautioned.

I extracted the tooth perfectly and discovered, as expected, an old abscess on the root, which I showed to Priti. Andy fitted the little denture. Priti felt slightly dizzy afterwards and had to sit with a kidney dish between her knees, taking steady breaths. The socket stopped bleeding quite quickly and she peered into the vanity mirror. The new tooth looked perfect, much better than the original which, as I said previously, had stood out at an unattractive angle.

'You like it?' I asked.

'Yes, I'm happy.'

She was happy. Was that all? It was an anticlimax.

Soon Priti wanted to go home. I unlocked the front door.

'Are you OK?'

'Yes.'

'You mustn't drink any alcohol. You mustn't fiddle with, or remove, the denture, and don't rinse your mouth out today. And only gently tomorrow, with salty water.'

'I know.'

'And come in tomorrow evening so we can have a look.'

It wasn't until she said, 'Thank you,' that I could then hear how affected her voice was by the thing in her mouth. And I felt a wave of panic. What had we done?

I couldn't relax the following day until Priti called in. And when she did, all was well, thank God. And a couple of weeks after that we had an official inspection of the socket and denture to see how it was doing.

I double-locked the front door. Andy made conversation while Priti rinsed her mouth. He asked her about the real Koh-i-Noor.

'You mean the diamond?' said Priti.

'Yes.'

'I don't know anything about it,' she shrugged.

Andy said he was sorry but he'd assumed that if your family ran a restaurant called after a famous stolen diamond you'd know the story of it.

'My family run the Raj Restaurant,' said Priti, 'not the Koh-i-Noor, and I was born in Uganda, not India.'

Andy apologized and then hooked his finger under her palate and pulled the denture out. He dipped it into the glass of mouthwash and inspected it and then dropped it into the glass and looked at the socket. He asked if I'd like to look at it. I nodded and Priti swallowed and tipped her head back on to the headrest.

I could have cried. It was healed, pink and healthy and I felt the most enormous surge of emotion. Priti looked at me, her eyeballs straining uncomfortably low to meet mine. I stood back and wiped my eyes with my sleeve.

'Is it OK?' she asked.

I tried to say yes but nothing came out.

'It's perfect,' said Andy.

Priti and I reached toward each other awkwardly and brushed hands. She gave me a nod and I bowed slightly, in respect of her perfectly healed gum. Nods and bows of acknowledgement and approval are an underrated gesture I think, between men and women, and even between a cowboy and his unruly but brave horse. Priti's nod was the best I'd had since my mother had nodded to me through a crowd when I was ten years old and we'd wordlessly communicated something secret and elaborate between us. I can't even remember what it was.

Priti's nod meant the world to me and I felt a little dizzy with the sense of achievement. Andy spoke about denture care and the future. How she must always be sure to clean it over a basin of deep water so that if it dropped, it would fall into the water and be safe, and not on to the hard porcelain and crack. And that she must keep the spare (he'd made her one) in a moist cloth or tissue.

And I'd stood there, beaming, happy, proud, looking at her, and she'd sat there beaming back.

'What about the bridge?' I said. 'She won't want to go to university with a denture.'

'No,' said Andy, 'we'll make you a bridge, a top-class porcelain bonded on gold. But you need to let that socket heal and settle for a bit longer.'

'How long?'

'A couple of months, maybe three.'

'OK,' she said, then got up from the chair and took off the bib.

'Come up to the flat,' I invited, meaning both of them.

Andy couldn't – he had a prior engagement – but Priti came and we ended up making animal biscuits again because she loved baking but never had the time, and anyway she was still too scared of the oven to put the baking tray in or take it out.

She asked me about Andy.

'Is he your boyfriend?'

'Yes,' I said, assertively just in case she got any ideas.

23. The Cheese Knife

A couple of days later I drove my granny Benson to the hairdresser. We talked about the future, my future. I said I'd quite like to move to London later, and do some writing.

'So what will you do?' she asked, and I muttered about working with children or horses and getting some accommodation before starting on a proper career. She'd seemed unconvinced and said what a shame it was I'd left school at such a young age. I hadn't expected this. Only days before I had extracted someone's tooth and made her life bearable, righted a wrong, etc. and I'd forgotten that to my grandmother I'd still just be me.

While my granny was in Steiner's having her hair done I wandered around the shops, but I was waiting in the car when she reappeared, with awful neat waves, and tapped on the window with her fingernail. I was supposed to get out, open the door for her to get in, close it, and get back in myself.

'Your hair looks nice,' I said.

'Don't be silly. It never looks nice on the first day,' she said. 'Drive on.'

'Oh, well, I think it looks lovely,' I lied, again.

'That reminds me,' she said, and then asked if I'd be good enough to return a little cheese knife she'd given me – completely unbidden – when I'd first moved into the flat.

'This is a jolly useful little knife,' she'd said. 'Here, you may as well have it since it can't go through the dishwasher and I never use it any more.'

And now, she was suddenly asking for it back. It seemed to occur to her when I'd said her hair looked nice, as if to punish me for the lie. She just came out with it, saying how jolly useful it was and that she hadn't realized how much she relied on it, for all sorts of funny little cutting jobs, until it was gone. And if I wouldn't mind, she'd like it back.

I told her that I found the cheese knife really useful and didn't know how I'd manage without it as I had no other handy little knife, and that I loved it.

'Well, what do you use it for?' she asked. 'Do you eat much cheese?'

'I use it to peel potatoes and parsnips,' I said. Another lie.

In fact, I mostly used a small Kitchen Devil from Priti's kitchenware stall in Leicester Market that came free with a spice rack.

'Really?' she said. 'Well, it's not meant for potatoes. You need a peeler for that. And why are you peeling potatoes, anyway? You should be baking them and eating them whole with all the goodness lying close to the skin, and dietary fibre. Not to mention the economics of the thing.'

I held my nerve as we parted after the practice outside my flat.

'Are you going to run up and get my little knife?'

'No, I'm used to it now and want to keep it,' I said. 'Bye.' And I jogged up the steps.

In truth I hardly used the knife at all. Its wooden handle never quite dried out after the washing-up and had a slimy, unhygienic feel. That's the thing with wood – however lovely, there's a sense of it harbouring germs.

I analysed the incident later. Why had she given me the knife in the first place and then asked for it back, and why at that precise moment – just after I'd complimented her hair? And then, why had I refused to return it when I didn't even like it? It struck me that life was going to be very complicated if I had no idea why people did things, and even more so if I didn't know why I did things back.

I felt a *Woman's Own* column coming on but decided it was too complex and stupid for the poor readers to have to put up with. It was more the kind of thing you'd see in the *Observer* explored by a psychologist from Edinburgh who had a book out, or Sue Arnold.

24.   Andy's Test

Andy's driving test was upon us. I was glad because it gave me an excuse to make contact. I sent him a good-luck card. It was basically an L-plate ripped in half, like the advert for the Fosse School of Motoring. Inside I wrote, *Good Luck! Hope you pass!!*

I couldn't decide whether or not I did want him to pass, though. It would seem unfair when he'd stolen the lessons I might have had from my mother, and it would certainly be more satisfying if I passed first.

Andy had arranged a couple of lessons with qualified instructor Mr Giddens of the Fosse School of Motoring for the morning of the test. He passed, of course, and according to my mother, who phoned with the news, Mr Giddens had patted him on the back and said, 'That's my boy.'

'As if he'd been the one who'd taught him,' she said to me. 'Bloody cheek.'

'Congratulations!' I said to her.

Later that day I had a lesson with Mrs Woodward and had to tell her the news.

'Well, that'll be you in a few weeks' time.'

'Yes.' And I imagined Mrs Woodward patting me on the back and saying, 'That's my girl.'

After our lesson she told me I needed to concentrate on vehicles around me and read the road ahead.

'Anticipate what Mr Bus over there is going to do,' she said, 'and make sure you're not in his way.' And then as we went to pull in to the tram stop outside the flat we couldn't because there was Andy parked up in the Flying Pea.

Mrs Woodward told me to mount the kerb just beyond and she clambered out to congratulate him.

'Well done!' she said.

And Andy said, 'Hopefully it'll be her next time,' meaning me. Then he told us about reversing around a corner and that kind of thing.

Mrs Woodward left and I jumped in beside Andy. He wanted to drive down into the centre of town to have something to eat.

'Let's go to the Swiss Cottage,' he said. 'They do a lovely steak pie.'

I found the invitation confusing. Was he just asking me because he longed to eat in cafés? Did he still not know that I would never *want* to go to the Swiss Cottage? And even if I did, I'd have the spring vegetable soup with a bread roll. But I said OK because it seemed as though romantic public dining was the only way our relationship was going to lead anywhere.

'Great,' said Andy, and he drove us to the Haymarket car park where he negotiated a very narrow, twisty ramp with great skill. I ran off on an errand and said I'd meet him at the café in a few minutes.

'Get us a nice table,' I said, which was one of the best things I've ever heard myself say to a man. And I walked briskly to Green's the Jewellers on Church Gate. This was my mother and sister's jeweller of choice, and my granny's too since the horrid man at the other, better, jeweller had made lewd comments about her wearing her pearls in the bath. In Green's the Jewellers I was approached by a helpful assistant whom I'd seen twice before. He'd helped my mother choose wedding rings and came from Galway. I remembered every detail about him that he'd shared with my mother, but was shocked to find that he also remembered me.

'How was your mother's wedding?' he asked.

'That was three years ago,' I said. 'It was fine and they're still married.'

He laughed at that, because I suppose it was funny.

'I'm looking for a cheap but lovely St Christopher on a chain,' I told him. 'For a man.'

'Lovely,' said the assistant. 'We have some beauties.'

I looked at the various depictions of St Christopher on the

different-sized pendants and medallions. I wasn't entirely taken with him. I asked if there were any other saints available. The assistant laughed and told me that St Christopher was a widely popular saint – good for farmers, ferrymen, gardeners, motorists, bachelors, athletes and all sorts of others.

'What does the lucky fellow do for a living?' he asked.

'He makes dentures, but he's just passed his driving test as well.'

'Oh, then St Christopher is perfect.'

I bought the nicest I could afford, a smallish one depicting the saint's top half, holding a tiny child on his shoulder and with the words *Saint Christopher Protect Us* running around the rim.

'He's sure to love it,' said the assistant.

In the Swiss Cottage I felt quite confident. It was a café that opened out on to the first-floor walkway of a shopping centre and Andy had chosen a table opposite the exit. Maybe the openness made it a less anxious situation, but whatever it was, I felt fine and suddenly turned to Andy and blurted out that I loved being with him. He was pleased and we hugged and he asked if that was just because he was a driver now and I said, yes, he'd shot up in my estimation.

My plan was to present the jewellery gift (boxed) there at the café and tell him that I would ignore Willie Bevan, and that since my mother's uterine problems, I felt less threatened by her, and that actually I might borrow a sexy camisole from Tammy's secret cupboard, and clamber on top of him in my old bedroom, and that I'd go on the pill or the Dutch cap, or whatever that thing was that caused a mini miscarriage every month, I didn't care, I was pining for him, I felt rampant. But, before I could even begin, Andy whipped out the Highway Code booklet and banged it down on the table.

'Right, miss,' he said, 'let's go through this.'

25. The Photograph

Mrs Woodward had become over-ambitious after Andy's pass, and she pushed me to take the first available driving test, which in my opinion was a bit too soon. On the day, she gave me an hour-long lesson in which everything went perfectly.

'You see,' she said, 'you didn't put a tyre wrong.'

She was right. I'd gone round the whole city, the underpass, past the old Vogel factory and negotiated Lee Circle like a professional driver. Mrs Woodward had been so relaxed she'd fallen asleep, and woke with a jolt when I tooted at Tammy whom I spotted walking in a daydream past Redmayne & Todd. The perfect hour's driving didn't cheer me though. I put it down, in part, to Andy's St Christopher, which I'd taken to wearing having never found the right moment to hand it to him, but I couldn't help thinking I'd used up all my driving energy and luck.

And I was right. During the actual test I got myself sandwiched between a bus and a lorry. Firstly, I told myself to 'buck up or fuck up' and Mr Blick, the examiner, coughed reprimandingly, and so I'd had to apologize and he'd had to say, 'Keep your eyes on the road,' and then I'd had to switch lanes, which I did safely albeit annoyingly to other drivers, who sounded their horns and gesticulated at me. I hated that about other drivers. They were like competitive siblings, all too keen to point out the tiniest mistake or indiscretion, knowing full well that it could easily be them having to switch lanes, and then they'd have their hands up, gesturing, 'Sorry, relax, for God's sake,' as I did on that day.

The worst bit, the incident that must have outright failed me, was just past Leicester prison. I'd noticed a tiny sandwich shop, a place I'd forgotten, from where I'd bought a cheese-salad cob one morning when Mr Holt had dropped me early and I'd been in need of breakfast. I'd thought it miraculous that this café was not only open at 7 a.m. but also serving freshly made sandwiches. Then, to my surprise, as I ate it walking across the green, I found that as well as cheese salad, it also contained egg slices. I remembered thinking it the height of happiness and good fortune to be walking in the early-morning sunshine, eating a cheese-salad cob with egg slices in it.

My mind had been meandering on this as I pootled along in the correct lane, in second gear just in case of the need to manoeuvre, and then, quite as though a spirit had seized the steering wheel, we veered across the lanes and if Mr Blick hadn't reached violently across, grabbed the wheel and righted our course, I would have ploughed us straight into the side of the bus which had stopped opposite the Granby Halls.

'Pull over in that lay-by ahead please,' Mr Blick said, slightly shaken.

'Sorry about that. I'm fine, though,' I said, glancing at him.

'Pull over.'

I pulled over.

'Have I failed?' I asked.

'Drive on when it's safe to do so, please, and continue straight ahead until I tell you otherwise.'

'Have I failed, though?' I said. 'I really want to know.'

'Well, yes, of course you have, you almost killed us.'

I was so cross with myself I told Mr Blick I was too shaken to continue driving and we swapped seats and he drove us in silence to the test centre on Saffron Lane.

Mr Blick did the paperwork and gave me the official chit-chat. And then he got out of the car and spoke to Mrs Woodward.

Mrs Woodward kept glancing over as they spoke. She looked crestfallen.

She wasn't the sort to lie or withhold information and so she'd given a full and frank report to my mother who'd shared it later at home. Andy was very kind about it for a while and then wanted to know what had happened.

'What happened?' he asked. 'Why did the examiner have to take over?'

'I lost control of the vehicle,' I said. 'That's the only way I can describe it.'

'You'll pass next time,' he said, giving me a hug, 'or the time after. What can I do to cheer you up?'

'Come for a day out with me.'

My mother joined in. She suggested London. There was no place outside of Italy better for art, the parks were divine, and if we ran out of things to do we could take the number 31 bus to Kilburn to see Aunt Josephine. I agreed.

'I think you'll love the zoo,' I told Andy, 'and it takes almost all day.'

We went by train. Andy wore a most attractive cream cable sweater with a turtle neck – the sort you might see in a free knitting pattern – and dark blue jeans. I won't tell you what I wore because it was awful but it didn't matter because I was able to bask in the glow of Andy who looked like a young Captain Birdseye, and so I was very pleased to be seen by a handful of people I knew.

I recognized a woman in our carriage – a friend of my mother's. I smiled at her, and then realized it was April Jickson from Best End Boutique who'd supplied my mother with pills, sexy underthings and whatnot over the years, and whose twins (Thing One and Thing Two) I'd babysat for a few times. She got up from her seat and came over to say hello. She asked how my mother was doing and when I said she was fine but had had a prolapse, April made a lot of facial expressions and said she was sorry to hear it and to send her best wishes for a speedy recovery. I asked after the twins, who must now be at least six years old and worse than ever, I imagined. April ignored that and told us she was going to look at a retail premises with a view to expanding her fashion business into London. We wished her good luck and she went back to her seat and opened her magazine (*Vogue*).

When the train pulled in at St Pancras I marched us expertly along to the taxi rank and we took one to Devonshire Place in the Marylebone area. This wasn't because I wanted Andy to see Devonshire Place or Marylebone but because that's where my previous London trips had always begun and I knew where I was there in relation to the places I did want to go, which were London Zoo and Regent's Park. When the taxi pulled up I paid and gave the driver a tip of approximately ten per cent which I'd learned to do after a previous driver had called my sister and me 'a pair of fucking bitches' for not tipping. We'd been nine and eleven years old at the time and, not knowing the rules, couldn't think what we'd done to deserve it. My sister asked the driver of our next taxi and he'd been appalled at our ignorance and was only too happy to put us right. I mentioned this to Andy so he'd never find himself in the same position.

Andy was slightly nonplussed by Devonshire Place – it being after all just a row of identical houses with no gardens or anything of any interest about them.

'Why are we looking at this street?' he asked.

'We used to come here as kids.'

'What for?'

'The dentist,' I lied.

It was actually the address of the doctor who used to turn a blind eye and supply my mother with pills for cash when she'd reached her limit at home. But I didn't tell Andy that.

London Zoo was only a short walk away and I paid the entrance fee with a cash gift from Mr Holt. Andy was mesmerized by various bears and birds, and all the African mammals. He dawdled and read every bit of information, about each animal, out loud, and told me extra things he knew from his pre-trip reading. Some bombs had hit the zoo in World War Two, he told me; one had damaged the rodent house and some zebras had escaped.

'Yikes,' I said.

'All the venomous snakes had to be destroyed at the outbreak of war,' he said, blinking.

'In case they got into enemy hands?' I asked.

'No, so they couldn't escape in the event of a bombing, and go round biting people.'

'As if the citizens of London hadn't got enough on their plates,' I tutted.

We didn't take taxis after that first one because Andy had brought the *A–Z* of London and felt we should walk. For me, zooming around in a taxi was the epitome of London. For Andy, it was walking as slowly as possible through the park, to avoid arriving at places where he might be in the way of bustling London people, and so we ambled, arm in arm, in the winter sun and though it was perfectly pleasant I was aware that Andy wasn't exactly enjoying London.

His map-reading took us along a canal and into Camden Town and then from there on to the Underground, which Andy was keen to use, to get us back to St Pancras station. We took the wrong branch and had to get off and return to Camden, or something like that; whatever it was we ended up on a Tube that stopped in between Mornington Crescent and Camden Town, and didn't move again for two minutes. I imagined the worst and kept glancing at Andy – opposite me – but he was deep in his book, *London Underground from Construction to Commuters*, which had people sleeping in Holborn Tube station, presumably during the Blitz, on the front cover. He didn't look up to grimace at me, which I thought unfriendly, and I told him later he shouldn't really read a book about the London Underground while on it – it made him look ridiculous, I said, like a tourist, a thing I'd avoid at any cost.

'But I am a tourist, and where better to read about it?'

We were back at St Pancras hours early for our train. I considered my aunt Josephine but felt Kilburn might be cutting it a bit fine for the return train, and instead suggested we get back into the Tube and go to Charing Cross – where my sister was born, but more importantly, to see Trafalgar Square. Andy agreed and so we set off again.

Trafalgar Square looked quite impressive – full of pigeons and people feeding pigeons and having their photograph taken with pigeons on their arms and heads. We gazed at the scene and I felt

I had triumphed, that this was London at its best: the stone lions, the buildings, the buses circling and Nelson up there in the sky.

A man nearby was photographing the scene and in so doing, became part of the scene himself. He was a professional, wearing a smart but baggy suit, using a good camera. He saw me looking at him and turned to us.

'You want me to take your photograph?' he asked. 'The two of you together.'

We smiled and shrugged.

'A proper portrait? I'll post you the picture.' He showed us an example of a handsome couple in black and white, in that very place.

'Yes,' I said, gripping Andy's arm, 'let's do it.'

It was expensive but the photographer made a big deal of getting us in the right position. He wanted key things in the background and the sun in front and that kind of thing, and not to have Nelson's Column coming out of one of our heads – amateurs made mistakes like that all the time, he said. We posed; arms around one another, looking straight to camera. I did the new smile I'd been perfecting in the mirror for just such an event – lower lip covering lower bottom half of upper teeth, as if I was about to say a word beginning with V (imagine Anita Harris) – and I believe Andy said, 'Cheeeese.'

Click! went the camera.

We laughed, and then we kissed and, click! – he'd taken another, of our kiss.

'Hey!' he said. 'I took another for free – I'll send both. That'll be a good one, I'm telling you, that's my trick to get the best shots!' He was thrilled.

We paid him. I seem to remember the cost was £10, which sounds outrageous but felt worth it. We'd spent very little money all day except for the taxi to Devonshire Place for me to get my bearings, and the zoo tickets had been a present. The photographer wrote down Andy's name and address in a little notebook. He flipped the pages and I saw the names of other people he'd snapped.

'How long until it comes?' I asked, impatient.

'Ah, a week, maybe two?' he said. 'It depends how busy I get. Maybe a big story blows up and I'm off, or things are quiet.'

I often think of that man. The photographer. You couldn't meet a nicer person.

'You here for sightseeing?' he'd said. 'Where have you been?'

'London Zoo.'

'Beautiful – such a gorgeous day, lovely light, winter light, good for photography.'

Andy asked him about his job and he described it as documenting the greatest city on earth and I felt it might be just what was needed to awaken Andy's love of London. It certainly awakened mine – because London Photographer wasn't a million miles away from Jobbing Writer, in terms of wandering around, engaging with people, noting the lovely light.

'You've got to be there,' he said, 'and click, click, and that's it.'

Having our photograph taken had been my highlight of the day. The being approached. The discussion. The pose, the self-conscious laughter, the embrace. And that kiss – although quick, and chaste – was our best kiss ever. It was public, in front of a London Photographer, surrounded by people and pigeons and sharply contrasting shadows and under the pale blue sky and Nelson. It was a statement of our togetherness.

On the train home I asked Andy – deep in his book – 'What's been your highlight of the day?'

I always like to ask people their highlight, to give them a chance to describe a thing. They might say the thing they most enjoyed, or a bun they've liked, or a funny moment, but they might say something surprising, something difficult or troubling, like Andy did then.

'Probably the one hundred and twenty-nine seconds in the Tube train, stationary, between Mornington Crescent and Camden Town.'

'What?' I said. 'That was my lowlight.'

'It was real,' said Andy, 'and unexpected.'

'Well, I hated it.'

'It happens a lot,' said Andy, 'on that bit of the Northern Line.'

He didn't have to ask me my highlight, he already knew it. Having that photograph taken has been one of the highlights of my whole life. Not that we ever saw it. After three weeks had passed I concluded the photographer must have lost his notebook.

26.   The Ossie Dress

The fail didn't put me off driving; on the contrary, I asked Mrs Woodward to book me in for the next possible test.

'Just get behind the wheel whenever you possibly can,' she advised.

And I did. I took any driving practice I could find, with anyone.

'Are you going anywhere in the car during the next couple of weeks?' I asked JP.

'Not that I can think of,' he said, 'unless you'd like to drive us home for lunch and back during the week?'

'OK, yes, I'll do it,' I said.

It was hard work, driving to Blackberry Lane every lunchtime with that pair. Tammy didn't like sitting in the back, but she had to since JP had to be in the driving-instructor role. We'd arrive at the house, and I'd have to feed him his cigarettes while Tammy cooked an omelette on sardines on toast or whatever they were having.

As I say, I found it difficult.

'I say,' said JP one lunchtime, 'how would you like a run out to the Swan Hotel in Loughborough next week?'

'Oh, yes!' said Tammy. 'Good thinking.'

'It's the BDA Annual Winter Dinner Dance,' said JP. 'You could drive us there, and then I can have a drink.'

'When is it?' I asked.

'A week on Monday,' said Tammy.

'A dance, on a Monday?' I asked.

'It's always on the second Monday of December,' said Tammy. 'It's officially the most Christmassy night of the year, bar Christmas Eve, and we get the Tuesday off.'

'OK,' I said, quite excited at the thought of attending a dinner dance, dressing up, maybe dancing with a lovely dentist who cared about the dentally needy, or would change. Or just dancing in the dark with people who didn't know me.

'Is it a dressy occasion?' I asked.

'Very,' said Tammy.

'I should say so,' agreed JP. 'It's the British Dental Association.'

'It's the one that Andy Nicolello protested at that time,' said Tammy.

The thought that Andy might also be outside the Swan Hotel, in a bobble hat and donkey jacket with a placard reading, *BDA = BLOODY DISGRACEFUL ATTITUDE*, added to the excitement. I'd enjoy breaking away from JP and Tammy as we approached the entrance of the hotel, greeting Andy with exaggerated pride and admiration, and further infuriate them by giving him a long, loving embrace and kiss (I'd be like Jane Fonda) – after which only the most progressive-thinking dentist would dream of approaching me on the dance floor.

And Andy, having watched me disappear inside, might have a passionate epiphany on the cold stone steps.

I was going to kill a few birds with one stone that night.

'You can't be over-dressed,' Tammy told me. 'Last year Jossy Turner arrived wrapped, literally, in a silver bandage underneath a fur coat with a matching muff and no one batted an eyelid.'

'What will you be wearing?' I asked.

'The Halston, of course.'

The Halston – Tammy's favourite outfit – was an original fake orange halterneck-and-pants jumpsuit. It was amazing.

Inspired to find something equally lovely, I walked over to Barbara Road, to Best End Boutique, whose proprietor was April Jickson, the woman I'd met on the London train, who knew my mother and had the twins. I knew I'd feel confident in April's empty shop, more comfortable than in the thronging teenage shops in town, such as Chelsea Girl and Rosie O's. The downside being the prices, but then April had a buy-back service where she'd let you display your dress on her pre-worn rail in return for twenty-five per cent of whatever she got for it.

The window was a fashion tableau for the older, better-off woman. Mrs Greenbottle popped unbidden into my head, not that I'd ever imagined her before. One mannequin, draped in a camel coat, had such fiercely projecting nipples that you could see the beige plastic through the fine-knit black vest. The other two wore different-coloured tartan kilts with white polo necks, and assorted winter bits and bobs. Ski equipment was dotted about, and snow-flakes dangled from on high.

'What's the occasion?' asked April Jickson.

'The British Dental Association Annual Winter Dinner Dance.'

'Oh, my,' said April and her eyes lit up. She told me about the silver bandage she'd sold to Jossy Turner last year. 'You should have seen it – oh my God, it was the sexiest dress ever made.'

'I've heard about it.'

'Jossy's wearing a mackerel fishtail this year,' she said. 'She's not long ago been in for it.'

'Sounds lovely.'

'It is, unless she ruins it with a knicker line.' April tutted at the thought.

I tutted too.

'OK, so how many weeks' salary are we spending here?' she drawled, sliding hangers along a rail.

'One,' I said, meaning about £20.

April looked me up and down for a while and said she knew the exact dress and dragged out a hard-boned kind of thing but held it up against me and declared me a tricky shape. I knew I was a pear. I'd assessed my body shape with help from *Woman's Own* and I knew not to wear a hard-boned tube.

'I'm a pear,' I said.

She snatched a Zandra Rhodes off the pre-worn rail, making it float through the air before she held it quivering against me.

'No,' she said, it needed more shoulder than I had. And she took another and another and another until I began feeling anxious that I was going to have to buy something whether I liked it or not, because of all of this displaying, effort and interest – like the obligation to kiss at the cinema if you'd been driven there or paid for. But worse, because of the expense. Finally, she pulled out a turquoise wraparound called the Ossie.

'Oh, turquoise,' I said.

'Never say turquoise,' said April. 'It's "sea-coloured" when you're talking about beautiful frocks.'

Whatever it is officially called, the colour was a certain kind of bluey-green. I'd never seen the sea that shade, except maybe a distant smear of water in a pastel seascape. But it is a colour so lovely it catches my eye if I see it, fleetingly, in a bunch of things, say at Patel's Homewares, or in a magazine. It's so nice to look at, so soothing and yet dazzling at the same time and – here's the big thing – it makes my pale, blotchy skin look creamy and my eyes look green on the green parts and white on the white parts, and all in all I look my best.

That's what colour the Ossie was and it was made from the thinnest, finest, slipperiest, silkiest material. A kind of high-quality nylon that clung to every protuberance. I saw this when I was trying it on. I saw that the skirt outlined each leg as I walked quizzically towards the mirror. I saw the shocking chest area, a thing that looks deliberate and sexual and provocative – of course I saw it – the unevenness, the veins and the boss-eyed nipples.

'Is it a bit clingy?' I said.

And April said, 'Oh, no – it's lovely, so sexy.'

'Sexy? But I don't . . .'

'Subtly, though, sexy in a modest way,' she corrected herself.

'But . . .' I gestured to the bra area and plucked at it a bit.

'Oh, you can sort that out with decent undies,' she said, waving the worry away. She pulled the fabric about with both hands, cigarette between her teeth. I remembered the Dorothy Perkins bra and the little cleavage I could create wearing it and how alluring it looked.

'Shave your legs, obviously – and never wear knickers, for Christ's sake, never wear knickers under a dress. And if you're on, wear two tampons at once and pray, or stay at home, but don't wear knickers.'

'OK.'

While I was trying various pre-worn handbags, beads and sandals to accessorize the Ossie, a woman burst in and greeted April like an old friend.

'Can I try something on, April?' she asked. 'Not that I can buy anything, I just need cheering up.'

'Yes, yes.' April flung her arms out. 'Have a play, then come and have a fag and a drink.'

The woman tried on a huge silky thing and a fake punk dress, but took them off again and then tried some boots. She wandered about in her underwear and the boots, had a cigarette, and complained about her horrible husband – who was a pig and whose name was Denis, same as April's, a discovery that made them both laugh. The customer wondered if they might be married to the same man, a bigamist, but April said she doubted it – her Denis being housebound. The customer stubbed her cigarette out.

'Thank you, darling, I feel much better,' she said as she left.

'All part of the service,' April called after her.

Another woman came in to buy 15-denier tights and a chain belt and had a glass of wine and soda, and borrowed a screwdriver. And then another who bought a ready-made pleated sari in gold and fuchsia, without even trying it on, and wrote down the number of April's chiropodist. I decided that April Jickson's shop was the manifestation of the spirit of *Woman's Own*. It was a refuge, a playroom, a dressing-up chest, a pub and a toy shop, all rolled into one.

I bought the Ossie reduced from £21.50 to £20 and – because April said I must not, under any circumstances, wear my Jesus sandals with it, or I'd be breaking a tacit agreement with the designer – I also bought a pair of pre-worn gladiator sandals (£4).

'When you wear someone's dress, it's your duty to accessorize properly, otherwise you have no right to wear it,' she said.

At home, I got the Ossie out of the bag and regretted it immediately. April had warned me that this might happen – 'Buying an expensive dress can feel like getting pregnant,' she'd said. 'You thought it was what you wanted but in the cold light of day, it's truly terrifying' – so I was prepared for the feeling and reminded myself that it was only a dress and would not, could not, ruin my life and I didn't let it upset me. I did realize, though, in the freedom of my own flat, that wraparound dresses only look nice when you're standing still, inside, and looking at yourself face on. In the real world, the dress opens and your leg slides out as you walk and therefore you have to lean slightly forward holding the flap closed with a finger and thumb around mid-thigh.

I rang my mother and she called in later, especially. She said 'holding a dress closed' was itself a 'look' and came from the 1960s when, suddenly, people were wearing sexy dresses in non-sexy places and had to hold them shut so as not to be in the papers with their backside on show.

She declared the Ossie 'gorgeous and erotic'. She'd had no doubts anyway, because April was a pro at dressing women of all shapes and ages. I begged her not to call it erotic, and begged her even more not to try it on because I knew it would look far, far nicer on her than on me – and then I wouldn't want to wear it.

She said of course she wouldn't try it on, partly because she was still a bit wobbly after the prolapse and because, yes, it probably would look nicer on her – forty-year-old women were bound to look nicer in dresses than eighteen-year-olds, they'd had twenty years of practice. The awfulness of eighteen-year-olds in lovely dresses being partly the beauty of them, she said, which was perfect of her and made me feel better. I told her about the dinner dance – reciting the menu and the name of the band, and listing the people I knew to be attending.

'I wonder if Andy will be there protesting outside with a placard this year?' I said.

'I doubt it,' said my mother. 'He's going to a talk at the village hall about a bird hide with that friend of his, Andy Lewis.'

'Andy Lewis?'

'Not Andy Lewis, Andy Harris,' she said. 'So many Andys.'

'Probably all named after Prince Andrew,' I said.

'Not our Andy.'

'How do you know?'

'Andy predates Prince Andrew,' she said, with much pleasure. 'He's named after Andrew Marvell. "Had we but world enough, and time, this coyness, lady, were no crime."'

On the night of the dinner dance I applied a lot of blue eyeshadow and three coats of mascara. I threw my herringbone coat over the Ossie dress and put the gladiator sandals in a carrier bag, and in the end, apart from the Jesus sandals (which I planned to change out of in the car park, after driving there), I looked very glamorous.

JP and Tammy called for me in the Stag and I got straight into the driver's seat. JP made a lot of fuss about my seat position and rear-view mirror because of it being such a long journey. Tammy looked lovely in the Halston jumpsuit and with eyelids so golden they looked heavy and the wet-look mouth of cartoon fish. Her earrings, delicate silver chains with intermittent beads of lapis lazuli, were so long they nestled in the hollows behind her clavicles and reminded me of the time I'd done Andy's filling, when his had filled with blue/black gravelly water.

'Oh, Tammy,' I said, 'you look lovely.'

Tammy said, 'Thank you,' without moving her lips.

Neither of them complimented me on the Ossie. To be fair, I was wearing socks and sandals for the driving part of the evening, but anyone with a flicker of interest would have noticed the sea-coloured sateen underneath my coat, or my clogged-up eyelashes.

I drove us perfectly safely albeit rather slowly over to Loughborough and reversed the Stag with ease into a spot behind the Swan Hotel even though it was pitch dark. I switched into my strappy gladiator sandals and Tammy applied even more lipgloss without looking in a mirror and then we chattered as we made our way into the bar. It was then that Tammy turned to ask me if I'd be all right on my own – and noticed the dress.

'Oh,' she said, 'you got dressed up.'

And I said, 'Well, of course.'

And JP said, 'You know you can't come into the dinner dance with us, don't you?'

And I said of course I'd known that, though naturally I hadn't known and felt the pain of embarrassment and devastation in my chest. 'I'll just wait here in the bar.'

Tammy said, 'But then why are you so dressed up in that funny dress and, oh, my goodness, you're wearing mascara?'

And JP butted in. 'Only dental surgeons and other halves allowed into the dance, I'm afraid.'

And I said, 'Yes, I know that. I'm meeting someone for a drink.'

'Non-alcoholic, I hope,' said JP, and then the pair of them swished into the ballroom and I was left there in my wraparound dress with three or four hours to wait.

I phoned my mother from the phone booth in the foyer. Andy Nicolello answered.

'Oh, it's you,' I said. 'Is my mother available?'

'She's taken Sue the dog for a walk,' he said. 'How are you?'

I told him I was at the Swan Hotel in Loughborough, all dressed up but not invited into the dinner dance, waiting to drive JP and Tammy home. I thought he might laugh but he was upset on my behalf.

'Only dental surgeons allowed,' he said. 'Fucking BDA.'

'I know, and I'm all dressed up,' I said, and my voice wobbled. 'I look lovely.'

'You always do.'

'No,' I said, 'you should see me, I have on the sexiest dress you've ever seen and no pants.'

'Oh,' he said, 'it sounds wonderful.'

'Why don't you come over here? We could have a meal. You could borrow the Flying Pea, and buy some Durex on the way.'

'Erm, I don't know, it's Monday night, and Loughborough's a long drive.'

'But I'm in this amazing dress that cost twenty pounds,' I said, 'and no one's going to see it because I'll never wear it again.'

'I don't know. I'll see what your mum says.'

'No, don't worry, I was only joking.' And the pips went and I shouted, 'Bye, bye.'

An hour later, Andy walked in. I hardly recognized him. He was dressed smartly in a white shirt.

'I hardly recognized you,' I said, and he smiled.

'I'm going to ask Wintergreen what he thinks he's playing at, getting you driving them all the way out here and then just leaving you here, sat like a twat on your own in the bar all night.'

'No,' I said, 'please don't say anything – I really couldn't stand the humiliation.'

'But the arrogance of the man.'

'I asked for the driving practice and I expect they assumed I'd go over the park and visit my father.'

We ordered chicken and chips and drank shandy and chatted about my old life. Somehow my worries about eating in public had disappeared.

'How is Sue the dog?' I asked. 'And Jack?'

We talked about my mother's sci-fi novel and Andy said it was coming along nicely. I told him about Tina and Junior and every other bit of gossip I could dredge up. I asked about the bird hide and he was genuinely excited.

'We need to raise two hundred pounds,' he said. While we chatted, I fiddled with the St Christopher pendant which was around my neck, and was reminded that I should present it to him.

Eventually he said I looked nice in all the mascara and the Ossie. And I asked if we were getting back together. And he asked if we ever had been together in the first place and I said, 'Very much so – in my mind.' And he said he couldn't read minds.

After the food Andy peeped through into the ballroom and beckoned me over. The banqueting tables had been moved, the lights were low and a band played gentle disco music. The dance floor was busy with couples moving together. I could see Tammy dancing with Bill Turner, both of them smiling, doing the kind of exaggerated dancing you'd see in a 1960s film, which looked ridiculous.

JP was smooching with Jossy – slowly and out of time with the music, her draped over him, drunk. April from Best End Boutique would have been dismayed at the distinct and horribly unsymmetrical outline of her pants.

'Jump to the Beat' faded and the band started again with a slower song.

'Come on,' I said, and pulled Andy in. We danced to 'The Sun Ain't Gonna Shine Any More', 'Cracklin' Rosie', and then 'Sunshine after the Rain', and after that 'Don't Give Up on Us, Baby', and it was truly the most romantic thing, and seemed to go on and on. Andy was such a dancer, not his steps but the way he felt in my arms and the way we swayed; it was so perfectly nice, like the beginning of a dance I knew so well but had never been taught, like suddenly swimming or flying. And the grand setting, although not quite a sunset beach, or a New York bar, the disco ball scattering light, the trumpets dipping, the sensual brushing on the drums, and the singer – a woman who reminded me of Shirley Bassey in looks, but Elkie Brooks in voice – and Andy smiling and confident, not watching television, and the Ossie shimmering, it was all glorious.

JP looked over and saw us, shocked. He opened his mouth as if to protest but Jossy whispered something into his ear and, whatever it was, he forgot about us.

I could feel something on my hip – it might have been the mini Gonk on my mother's car keys. Whatever it was, it felt sexual for the moment and I realized that Andy and I had never been together until now.

As the first of the dancers began to leave the ballroom Andy said, 'Let's go.' I reminded him I had to drive JP and Tammy home. He questioned me – in that male way. He couldn't understand why I was so obliging when they were such utter cunts. I reminded him that it had been my idea and, if I didn't take them, how were they going to get back home?

'OK,' he said. 'I'll pick you up where Blackberry Lane meets Half Moon Lane.' He'd be parked in the gateway opposite the Half Moon pub.

'Where Blackberry Lane meets Half Moon Lane – in the gateway opposite the Half Moon Pub,' I repeated. And we kissed and I've never felt so happy.

I'd driven JP and Tammy home, parked the Stag in the garage, said goodnight to JP and Tammy. They'd had a super night and JP had tried to call me a taxi but I'd told them Andy was picking me up outside the pub at the end of Blackberry Lane. JP frowned.

I went – as agreed – to where Blackberry Lane meets Half Moon Lane, in the gateway opposite the Half Moon pub, but Andy wasn't there. I sat on a bench and thought about him and us and it.

Why had it taken us so long? It was difficult in those days – post-permissiveness but pre-sexual equality – to be sexy or act sexually; and to have sex but also still be you (me) was impossible. I had erotic feelings towards Andy but couldn't act upon them because, A) I was female, and B) because we'd discussed the workings of the human jaw in a scientific way together and devised a strategy for putting the bins out without my having to go into a dark alleyway at night. We couldn't cross over into sex because I'd been too real and clever.

Maybe intellectuals like Adrienne Rich could be clever and sexual. But even my mother, who'd always liked sex, said she had to work herself up to it with Mr Holt now they'd dismantled and fixed a gas boiler together and he'd glimpsed her uterus.

Why had it been so sexy in the Swan Hotel? Not because I was in the Ossie with strappy gladiator sandals, but because no one knew me, and he'd come all that way to see me in that context, and we'd danced, we'd moved about together and faced each other, with a Four Tops song playing. And now that all that had happened, and here I was waiting for him in the dark, I felt electrified. My smoky breath swirled in the night air and I said out loud,

'Come on, Andy,' like a drunk. My elongated words bounced around and I said it again, and then, all of a sudden, I was cold.

I began walking. There was a shortcut through a housing estate, which I couldn't take in case Andy came along, which I assumed he would. This was what it was like to be my mother, I realized. Planning to have sex with a man, walking alone in a slinky dress at almost midnight, anxious, bewildered and other things, except I wasn't drunk. My feet started to hurt as the straps of the gladiator sandals began to rub. But never mind, I sat on a low wall and changed back into my Jesus sandals. The feel of the crisp cotton socks and the padded Clark's footbed were so soothing and reassuring, I took back all my anger at myself for being such a sensible Jenny and stick-in-the-mud. These socks and shoes could literally save my life and I should congratulate myself.

I walked along beside the golf course and then reached Allendale Road and London Road and Station Road and soon I was at the front door of the Wintergreen practice, expecting the Flying Pea to be sitting in the lay-by – but it wasn't. Andy hadn't arrived.

Had he rejected me? Run out of petrol? Got catastrophically lost? Crashed the car? I climbed the stairs and considered phoning my mother to see if Andy had gone home but Mr Holt would answer and ask me what I thought I was playing at ringing at almost bloody midnight. I was sure Andy would turn up. He'd driven home to get something: a change of clothes, clean underwear, a Durex, a bottle of Blue Nun.

I kept the Ossie dress on. I didn't want him arriving to find me in my Snoopy pyjamas or in the nude. I knew from *Woman's Own* that men didn't find nudity very attractive; partial clothing was much more alluring because they liked to move it aside or take it off and feel in control. I turned up the radio, hoping for some late-night love songs, and lay provocatively on the sofa. Then I fell asleep and dreamt I was knocking on a window and woke to hear the front door banging and the bell. Andy at last.

I checked my appearance in the mirror. I still looked alluring, more so in fact.

I trotted sleepily down the stairs, laughing, relieved, saying something like, 'I thought you'd had a better offer,' as I flung the door open and saw Mr Holt and my mother standing hunched, in the dark.

BBC Radio Leicester:

Latest news just in. A local man lost control of his vehicle at the notorious accident black spot on the corner of Melford Road, Leicester, at approximately 11 p.m. this evening. The man, aged twenty-four, was pronounced dead at the scene. Next of kin have been informed.

PART THREE

27. Reverend Woodward

I got up to turn the radio off. My mother and Mr Holt and I sat drinking tea. We ate the arrowroot biscuits that JP always had in for his sensitive tummy. It was four in the morning. Then five, then six and then, at seven, Mr Holt put the radio on to break the silence and we heard that John Lennon had been shot dead in New York. We listened to the report and switched it off. Mr Holt went to the window. John Lennon was my mother's preferred Beatle. Her preferred man, actually, and I seem to recall her saying, 'The waste, the waste.' And Mr Holt standing at the window just staring at the dark.

Eventually, after some involuntary calculations and conjecturing in my head, I felt quite certain that even if John *had* been shot dead in New York before Andy had crashed the Flying Pea, Andy could not have known – because of the time difference.

'Do you think Andy could have known?'

'Leave it, love,' said Mr Holt.

Later the same morning, my mother and I waited at the doctor's surgery. She had Danny on her knee, rocking him and chanting, 'All shall be well, and all shall be well and all manner of things shall be well.' It was me she was talking to, but of course I couldn't be rocked, not in Flatstone Village Surgery – Mrs Forsythe was there, and Pop Philips from the grocer's shop, for various ailments, and a woman with a grizzly, bunged-up baby – and not knowing if they knew anything, or whether they cared or not, about who we were and what had happened, and our involvement, and so forth.

Our involvement. The notion gave me a jolt. Not 'Andy's death' but 'our involvement'.

We'd been to this same doctor's together a few months previously, my mother and I, before the prolapse. Her being measured up for a new diaphragm and some spermicidal jelly, and me wanting to know if there was a contraceptive pill that didn't cause loss of libido, pimples or depression. We'd laughed, that time, my mother and I, wondering what Dr Gurley must think of us. Mother and daughter, sexually active but neurotic. Goers.

Dr Gurley knew what had happened.

'Are you Andy's doctor?' I asked.

'The Nicolellos are registered at the practice, yes,' she said.

She asked why I thought I might need Valium. I gave her my rehearsed speech. I knew she'd be reluctant – she'd spent years weaning my mother off double doses of the stuff.

'It's completely normal to be sad at a time like this,' she said. 'This isn't depression or anxiety – it's grief.'

'I'm not just sad,' I told her, 'I'm embarrassed.' And she looked at me, wrote me the prescription, and said, 'Come and talk to me any time.'

I woke in my old room, to what sounded like a trapped bird. An orangey glow came from a little light I now saw plugged into a socket by the door. There was no trapped bird, only a poster of Ian Dury that had come unstuck at one corner, flapping in the breeze from the open window. Andy had been dead three days.

I knew now why people feared outer space. It wasn't the going there, of course, it was the knowledge of it and the constant dwelling on it, the eternity, the void, the dark. I believed Mrs Woodward who'd been in the day before telling me, 'Give it time and your mind will leave it be.'

She should know – she'd had three deaths, a jilting, a divorce, most of her teeth out and was now married to a vicar. And my mother – whose losses had been profound and complex – told me the same. 'Give it time, all shall be well.'

My mother and I decided, tacitly, not to talk about Andy in the early days. Though she was usually very good in crises and tragedies, this one was too close and too awful. And I knew for certain that she must be blaming herself. Not that she'd done anything wrong but, we had to face it, she had lent him the car and she was in those days evangelical about seizing the day and being spontaneous.

I imagined Andy getting off the phone that evening – the evening I'd been alone at the Swan Hotel in the sea-coloured dress – and saying to my mother, 'Lizzie wants me to go all the way over to Loughborough just to have chicken in the basket with her because she's waiting in a pretty dress to drive those idiots home.' And sighing, as if to say, 'How absurd.'

And my mother probably saying, 'Oh, Andy, go, borrow the car – surprise her, it's so romantic.'

And giving one of her talks about life being short, and magical adventures being routinely smothered by the mundane things we have to do and Andy saying that driving over to Loughborough on a dark night was mundane in itself and my mother saying, 'Find the magic, Andy,' or something along those lines and sending him off.

And then because of that, directly because of that, him dying. In the Flying Pea. Her car. That she had taught him to drive in.

So we didn't discuss any of it. We asked each other if we were OK and my mother went to visit Angelo and Miss Smith. But on the whole we talked about Faber & Faber and Danny's development at Curious Minds – and how he was a marvellous reader already, and showing signs of becoming a great artist.

I lay in my old bed, in my clothes, under Andy's autumn leaves duvet, surrounded by his things. His Mickey Mouse alarm clock, his copy of *Down and Out in Paris and London*, a page marked with a tattered yellow ribbon, the framed photograph of a man who looked like Pablo Picasso in high-waisted swimming trunks, lighting a woman's cigarette with the end of his own, like a kiss – who I realized with a shock were his parents, the ones who'd ended up taking cyanide tablets to avoid hospital, or whatever actually happened.

The doorbell went and I heard voices. It was Reverend Woodward, of course. I fixed Ian Dury and went downstairs. I'd decided

I might as well let Reverend Woodward dish out his vicar balm. It seemed unfair to keep avoiding him.

My mother brought us coffee and then left us alone. The coffee wasn't frothy, which I thought a bit lazy – under the circumstances. I raised something with Reverend Woodward that had been troubling me for a while.

'I've always found the name "Woodward" tricky to say.'

This was nothing new, and he shrugged. 'The easiest thing is to just say Wood-wood – two woods!' he said.

'It's annoying,' I said, 'don't you think, having to say it a certain way and not being able to just say it as it looks?'

And he said, 'Yes, it really bugs me too.'

It really bugged him.

He suddenly looked earnest and said, 'I really am so sorry.' And I realized he thought our discussion about his name was really about Andy. It was one of the most irritating things I've ever experienced.

'I don't know why you're sorry – it's not your fault,' I said.

And then he started saying he didn't know why we always told each other we were 'sorry' and that being sorry implied blame somehow and that that was due to subtle changes in language usage over time. Vicars, even nice ones, seem to think the rest of us are idiots.

'If I'm supposed to just say "Wood-wood", why is it spelt Wood-ward?' I persisted.

He laughed nervously.

'Well, I suppose I could start pronouncing it "Wood-Ward",' he said.

'Or you could spell it "Woodwood".'

'Life is so darned difficult.'

My mother crept in at that point and asked if we'd like another drink. We didn't. I think she wanted to join in, but I didn't look at her so she went away again.

'It's not that I'm sad,' I said. 'I can live with the sadness. It's the . . .' I began, then paused, needing a little break, and Reverend Woodward waited. As he waited, my opinion of him soared.

'It's the mystery of it,' I said. 'Have you any thoughts on that?'

'You can think of the fun you had together,' he suggested. 'Think of the times you really laughed.'

I paused and thought of Scamp, the terrier that Clarence Beale had run over in the forklift truck, which wasn't funny at all but had made Andy fall about. And I remembered a video of a woman popping a ping-pong ball out of her vagina − and I snorted. This was what they must teach them in vicar school, I thought, I mean, the memories thing, not the ping-pong.

'I wondered if you might call in on Tony Nicolello?' he said. 'I think it would mean a lot to him.'

I rolled this over in my mind, imagining the owl-scarer fighting tears, as I eulogized Andy. My mother had already been; she'd rushed over there with an apple tree sapling from Glebe Gardens to plant in the garden in his memory − knowing they wouldn't want anything decorative − and had presumably told Tony what a great union leader Andy would have made and that, had he lived, he might successfully have campaigned for the release of political prisoners abroad. I could only imagine his brother's bemused response.

'My mother's already been,' I said. 'She took them a tree.'

'Yes, but I think he'd like to see you. You were Andy's girl-friend, after all.'

'I know,' I said, although I didn't.

'I'm going over there tomorrow and thought I could take Andy's things to Tony, if you agree − and you could come with me.'

I told him I'd think about it.

Reverend Woodward seemed happy to leave it there but I found myself asking, in a whisper, if he thought my mother was to blame for Andy's death. I knew this was putting a lot on his plate, espe-cially as she was just a room away and the walls in my mother's house were paper thin − but it was his job after all, as he often said.

'I can't help thinking it,' I whispered.

'No. Your mother is not responsible in any way,' he whispered back, emphatically.

'Really?'

'She's there in your mind like a hat stand,' he said, 'or a coat hook.'

'Yes, a coat hook, an already groaning coat hook,' I said, and in my mind I pictured Andy as a flimsy cagoule with old things in the pockets, no longer waterproof, no longer useful, hanging mournfully, uselessly, on a lovely curled brass hook by a greasy little loop in its collar.

'Do people blame her, do you think?' I asked.

'I think people sometimes let their imagination run away with them and arrive at a strange verdict, but it's not good for anyone, and it's deeply unkind.'

And with that, I reached into my mind, grabbed the back of the cagoule and pulled it sharply downwards, until the greasy little hoop in the collar broke away and it fell to the floor tiles. Reverend Woodward nodded, and my mother appeared with a tray of unrequested coffee.

Later that day my mother and I cleared Andy's room. She emptied the drawers and cupboard, 'in case there are things Andy wouldn't want you to see'. Meaning copies of *Razzle*, presumably, or letters from other lovers. Apart from his clothes, all she found was his ancient wind-up musical teddy bear, which chimed 'Teddy Bear's Picnic' and rotated its head.

My mother wondered if I'd like to hang on to it. 'Or would it be like being haunted?' she said. I put it into a bag and its muffled chimes continued intermittently.

Soon we had everything neatly packed and boxed up and ready in the porch for Reverend Woodward to take to Tony Nicolello and I remember clapping my hands, as if to brush away dust.

Reverend Woodward turned up the following afternoon.

'I've come for Andy's things,' he reminded me, 'to take to Tony.'

I pointed to the boxes in the porch, and between us we loaded them into his car. 'Bye then,' I said, and scurried inside.

'Hang on,' he called. 'Will you come with me? You were going to think about it, remember?'

My mother appeared. 'We'd be glad to.' She'd remembered and was ready and had put down a few glasses of wine. Her teeth and lips had a purplish tinge.

My mother told my brother Jack to look after Danny while we were gone, ran her fingers through her hair in the mirror, picked up her bag.

'Ready?' she said, but I hung back.

Reverend Woodward stretched out one arm, like Jesus on the shore.

'Come on, let's go,' he said, and we all piled into Mrs Woodward's car, the one I was learning in, and there, in the back, was my copy of *Hitchhiker's Guide* that I'd lent her.

The Reverend's terrible driving was comical – he twice hit the kerb so badly that I saw sparks fly up on the passenger side, and it broke the solemn mood. He never once looked in his mirror before manoeuvring, but just ploughed onwards, crunching gears, turning and braking suddenly with no consideration whatsoever for other road users. How ironic it would be, I thought, if we ended up dead and other vicars had to visit our grieving relatives.

My mother, an advanced driver, looked uncomfortable in the passenger seat. 'Are you driving this badly for comedy purposes?' she asked.

'Oh, sorry,' he said. 'Am I driving badly?'

'Yes, you're going to get us killed. Pull over, let me drive.'

'But you've been drinking,' he said, pulling in to a bus stop.

I drove.

'They seem like a very eccentric family,' my mother said, turning to Reverend Woodward who was now crouched in the back seat. 'The Nicolellos.'

'Yes, they live a fairly alternative lifestyle,' he said, 'but a lot of what they believe makes sense . . . worry about the planet, you know, the ozone layer and "Plant a Tree in '73" and all that, and the exploitation of the working man.'

'Were you here for the parents' suicide?' she asked, making it sound like a community event.

'Their deaths were almost immediately after we arrived.'

'Bad luck,' said my mother. 'I hope you didn't take it personally.'

'It got the rumour mill going, and that can be tricky to deal with in a parish, very unsettling. The bishop worried it might lead to a spate, you know. But fortunately it didn't.'

Tony Nicolello came out to the car and invited us in. The shack was surrounded by a privet hedge, my least favourite sort, and this one was a really bad specimen, being a patchwork of the usual flat, dead green and that awful lime-green variety, and the ground underneath hard, dry clay. This was the hedge Andy had grown from seed.

Things were slightly awkward to begin with. We stood around in a sort of kitchen area and then, after Tony's wife appeared, we were ushered through to the living room – a lean-to containing three sets of double bus seats arranged around a walnut coffee table, which I recognized as my grandmother's, and which had a cutting from the *Leicester Mercury* lying on it. I hadn't yet seen Andy's death written down and was momentarily taken aback, mostly by the words 'man' and 'dead'.

Man Dead in Accident Black Spot

Andrew Nicolello (24) lost control of his vehicle on the corner of Melford Road, Leicester at approximately 11:00 p.m. on Monday night and was pronounced dead at the scene.

Tony asked my mother, 'Which one of you was Andy's girlfriend? We could never quite work it out.'

Neither my mother nor I responded but Reverend Woodward handled it.

'Lizzie was Andy's girlfriend,' he said, flipping his hand in my direction, 'and Mrs umm . . . Vogel, Lizzie's mother, was just his landlady.'

My mother rambled about her relationship with Andy being

meaningful but platonic – almost like mother and son, until Reverend Woodward piped up again to put a stop to it. He was delighted, he said, honoured, that they'd asked him to do the funeral, he said, and was there anything particular they'd like? Hymns, readings and so forth.

Andy's brother was very quiet. 'I'll have a think about it,' he said.

'If there's anything I can do to help, with the funeral or anything,' my mother said, 'just say.'

'Actually, the funeral . . .' said Tony. 'If you could arrange it, plan it, or whatever, seeing as you're so close to the vicar, that would be . . .'

And she said, 'Of course.'

'Would you or your family like to do a reading, or speak about Andy, at all?' asked the Reverend.

'It's not really my sort of thing,' said Tony, looking anxious.

'Well, you don't have to decide that now.'

'No, really, I'd . . . we'd just prefer for you to arrange it, if you could just not delve into old history, you know.'

'As you wish, Tony. That's fine, but call me any time if something pops into your mind. Ring any time.'

Tony's wife, whose name I forget, rather shyly showed us some photographs. Andy in school uniform, Andy getting into a little rowing boat – you could see the water in the bottom, among the ribs – a school portrait that made him look like Charlie Chaplin, and a lovely one in which he had an owl perching on his fist.

I heard myself say, 'Oh, he loved owls.'

And Tony shot a look at me.

And then I remembered the London photograph. God, I thought, if ever a photograph was needed, it was that one – the one of us kissing.

And I suddenly knew, at that precise moment, there in Tony Nicolello's shack, four days after Andy had died, that the photographer hadn't lost his notebook. I laughed to myself – there was no photograph, there never had been. There'd been no film in his camera.

It was a huge and complex realization and I needed to ponder it.

I stopped listening to proceedings in the lean-to lounge. I sat back in the bus seat, closed my eyes and remembered it, all of it: arriving at Charing Cross station, walking to Trafalgar Square, the pigeons, the people, the photographer who looked like Frank Sinatra, the pose, click! The laugh, the kiss, click! I fantasized about going back there, tracking him down, asking where our photograph had got to and then opening his empty camera.

On the way home my mother said, 'We need to get things sorted as soon as possible,' and Reverend Woodward joined in.

'You're right,' he said. He'd taken the passenger seat this time. 'So, Lizzie, do let us know if there's anything you'd like to include.' And they started to plan the funeral right there in the car. 'Funerals should be celebratory, if at all possible,' said Reverend Woodward, 'but of course it's so hard.'

They admitted that Andy's would probably be a strange affair. They'd do their best but in truth, no quantity of pop songs would turn it into a celebration of his life. There'd be no poignant tear-stained laughter about funny things Andy had done.

'Our only hope is to get it off on the right note with a splendid sermon from you, vicar,' my mother said, and then added that it was a tall order because he hadn't really known Andy.

Various ideas for prayers, readings and music were chucked about. Reverend Woodward considered my suggestion for music – 'Bat Out of Hell' – potentially provocative. I said yes to Pam Ayres's poem about teeth, and to 'Blackbird' by the Beatles, but no to 'Bright Eyes'. I privately wondered whether we should bring Willie Bevan in on the planning but then thought not in case he tried anything with my mother.

'I always feel sorry for the congregation when the funeral is bleak,' said the Reverend.

'Yes, and the poor choir! God, death is so gloomy,' said my mother and then went on to describe her own funeral, which would include Nunc Dimittis (the Walmisley arrangement) and Psalm 67 because of its descant at the end. She couldn't quite decide between 'Rejoice in the Lord Alway' by Purcell and 'Thou

Knowest Lord the Secrets of Our Hearts', and the hymns would be 'All People that on Earth Do Dwell' (the Vaughan Williams Old Hundredth arrangement) and then 'Angel Voices Ever Singing' – in a high key, to brighten things up a bit, and finally the organ playing Widor's Toccata and Fugue to walk out to.

Reverend Woodward was ecstatic to hear this. 'Gosh, how lovely,' he said, humming one of the tunes in question.

My mother was very pleased with herself. 'I planned it while I was waiting for my Fothergill repair,' she said. 'You know, in case something went wrong.'

'Well, it's going to be magnificent,' said the Reverend. 'I look forward to it immensely.'

'Could we use it for Andy?' I asked. 'Seeing as you survived.'

'No, we bloody well couldn't,' said my mother.

And we chatted like that until we got back home. Visiting Tony Nicolello had been a good thing to do, I had to admit it.

The next day, for the third day running, Reverend Woodward appeared. He was struggling with the funeral words, apparently.

'I'd be very grateful if we could have a talk about Andy,' he said. 'I'm struggling rather.'

I agreed, though it occurred to me that he might not really need to talk about the funeral sermon at all, that he was trying to help me come to terms with everything. I told him interesting, sermon-worthy things about Andy – his eating my display fruit, his long baths, his love of electrical appliances, talcum powder, restaurants, the pride in his work, his fury at the dental profession, and the cleverly worded placards – while the Reverend pretended to take notes. I briefly imagined Andy there, in Mr Holt's chair, listening, chuckling. And actually, hats off to the Reverend again – it was very nice to talk about Andy, cathartic and satisfying.

Then, all of a sudden, the funeral was happening. The church was crammed with elderly people from the village and it felt cold and a bit Christmassy. The organ played, and people sang 'Morning Has Broken' but incredibly slowly and with none of the beauty of Cat Stevens. And then Reverend Woodward spoke.

28.   The Sermon

'We are gathered here today to remember Andrew Julius Nicolello.'
  Pause.
  'Andrew, or Andy as he was known to his friends and family, produced the best dentures in Leicester and, in so doing, he made people smile, literally. Andy Nicolello's dentures fitted like gloves – gloves for the mouth. Better than gloves, actually. His work was exceptional.
  'All the dentists who use the services of Mercurial Laboratories – and I've spoken with a number of them – had started to request Andy particularly, and many asked what his secret was, and none would believe him when he told them it was simply the slight closing of the bite that made them so comfortable. Andy's dentures, once fitted, needed no adjustment whatsoever. People left the surgery smiling, eating corn on the cob and apples, as they had in their pre-denture days – as my own wife can attest.
  'It wasn't just dentures, either. Andy's porcelain crowns fitted so well, they sometimes didn't even need cement. His inlay work, too, was invisible even to the most sensitive of tongues.
  'Andy was a conscientious, hard-working lad whose high and exacting standards in his professional life were mirrored in his personal life. After a bath, for instance, Andy would dry his whole body thoroughly with a hairdryer so as not to leave damp towels lying around. He ate fruit willingly and was kind to animals. A keen birdwatcher and lover of the countryside.
  'In fact, a birdwatching hide is to be built in his honour on the River Sense by the birdwatching club, who counted him as an active and knowledgeable member. Donations to this can be made at the end of the service.
  'Andy was also a champion of the allied dental professions and

demonstrated against the British Dental Association's bar to technicians and dental nurses from joining. To quote Andy, "People think it's dentists who make dentures but they're wrong. It's the technicians – people like me and Fred Burridge – who craft the teeth. We're precision engineers, dentists just fit them."

'Andy made people smile, literally.'

The congregation – apart from Tony Nicolello and Mr Burridge who looked sad, and my grandmother who looked bemused – seemed cheered by the thought of all these glorious, comfortable teeth, and Andy's fluffy, blow-dried body. My sister, my mother and I were crying and shaking with suppressed laughter at the same time. It hadn't been what we'd been expecting at all. It was a triumph.

As Reverend Woodward stepped down from the pulpit, he looked at me. I nodded and he nodded back and blinked.

Willie Bevan, the unknown friend of Andy's who'd warned him my mother was a goer, stood to read a poem about owls:

> 'Downhill I came, hungry, and yet not starved;
> Cold, yet had heat within me that was proof
> Against the North wind; tired, yet so that rest
> Had seemed the sweetest thing under a roof.

> 'Then at the inn I had food, fire, and rest,
> Knowing how hungry, cold, and tired was I.
> All of the night was quite barred out except
> An owl's cry, a most melancholy cry

> 'Shaken out long and clear upon the hill,
> No merry note, nor cause of merriment,
> But one telling me plain what I escaped
> And others could not, that night, as in I went.

> 'And salted was my food, and my repose,
> Salted and sobered, too, by the bird's voice
> Speaking for all who lay under the stars,
> Soldiers and poor, unable to rejoice.'

After which, I was quite startled to see Tony Nicolello, in an ill-fitting black suit, take to the pulpit to read. He stood for a while patting around in the unfamiliar pockets for his specs and then, finding them, struggled to open them up because his hands were shaking so. My mother clapped her hand to her mouth in sadness at the pitiful sight and tears filled her eyes. Tony continued to fiddle around up there for what seemed like an hour, arranging sheets of paper, adjusting the lectern, and moving a large Bible. He cleared his throat more than once and by the time he spoke, everyone was in a state of high anxiety. He looked across the congregation, and then, looking down at the quivering piece of paper in his hand, he read:

'Andy loved birds, all birds, but especially owls. This is a note he left for me last time he was in our house. It's a birdwatching tip that I'd like to share with you all.'

He coughed.

' "Go out at dusk, walk by the scrub field and you'll see them swooping, or wait till dark and you'll see them in the trees above the churchyard. Your eyes will get used to the dark. Keep still. Never shine a torch up into the trees. It'll scare them and can cause blind flight." '

After that, there was a family-only event, which I was allowed to miss but which Reverend Woodward attended, and then there was the bun fight in the village hall. My granny Benson stayed by my side throughout. We'd not seen eye to eye on a few things recently, especially after the cheese-knife incident. Now she was being subtle and supportive in the way formidable people sometimes are when it really matters. Towards the end of the afternoon, when people were no longer sad, but merrily chattering, she said she had a cheque for me.

'What for?' I asked.

'Driving lessons.'

'But, Mrs Woodward,' I said, looking across the room where she was busying herself with the clearing-up.

'I think it might be time to move along from the Woodwards,' said my granny.

The final thing was Tony Nicolello giving me an old John Collier bag containing Andy's gruesome wind-up teddy.

'If you don't want it, give it to charity,' he said.

The next day, Sunday, I wanted the world back to normal and it almost was. I phoned Tammy at home, apologized for disturbing them on the Sabbath, and said I'd be coming back to work. I would remain living at home though, for the time being, and travel in every day by bus.

'Thank heavens,' said Tammy, but quickly added, 'but take as long as you want.'

I took the bus in on Monday morning and dropped Danny at Curious Minds where Mrs Danube, the principal, was quite rude to me.

'Make sure to collect on time, please.' Which felt lovely.

JP was also very business-as-normal, which I admired, and Tammy was self-conscious and odd, of course, but that was Tammy and it didn't matter, especially after Mrs Danube.

29.   Claire Rayner

One lunchtime after the Christmas break, I was queuing for a sandwich at the Lunch Box when Priti tapped me on the shoulder.

'Hi,' I said, glancing at her upper left two.

Since doing Priti's dental treatment, I'd always stared at her new tooth. I knew it was rude and I'd catch myself and then look her in the eye, but nevertheless she started unconsciously shielding the tooth, either with a raised hand or sometimes with her tongue.

'Hi,' she said, 'happy New Year! How's everything going?'

'Yeah, fine,' I said. 'I'm just getting a sandwich.'

'Me too.'

And then there we were, with our sandwiches (me, salad on toasted granary, her, cheese and onion on Rearsby), sitting on a bench in the weak January sun, and I realized I'd got to tell her about Andy. I couldn't do it while she was eating, so I made small talk about her studies and told her that Tammy had left the salad spinner in the flat, knowing that would set her off grumbling about customers returning defunct spinners, denying empty-spinning and wanting their money back or a replacement.

I tutted at these people and Priti said, 'You just know they've been spinning them.'

'Idiots,' I said.

Priti shook her head, tutted too, and took a bite of her sandwich. I gazed down at mine, which sat on paper in my lap, and it struck me that I'd started to prefer the top half of a slice of bread to the bottom half. This hadn't been a whim; I'd always eaten the crusted top half of a slice of toast, to get it out of the way before enjoying the softer underneath half. And now it was the other way around. It was a shocking realization. What had made me change?

I don't know – perhaps I was eager to change as many things as possible. I'd known sadness before, I'd seen it, but I'd not experienced the sort of pain that makes a person switch sandwich preference.

Eventually, Priti finished eating, brushed her knees and began folding up the paper bag. I had to tell her now; she'd be terribly upset and our friendship would be changed.

'Priti,' I said, and she looked up. 'I'm afraid Andy died.'

'Andy died? Your Andy?'

'Yes.'

'When? How?' she said, almost in disbelief, her eyes imploring me to explain, her tongue hiding that tooth. And to my horror I felt emotion rising in my neck. I coughed and swallowed and breathed deeply through my nostrils and did all the things you're supposed to do when anxiety starts in public. Priti understood and put her hand on my arm.

'Come on,' she said, 'let's walk.' So we walked towards the park and I explained what had happened and Priti was shocked and saddened of course and asked if there was anything she could do.

She offered to come to the flat later, to make animal biscuits. So I had to tell her I was staying at home with my mother for a while.

And she said, 'Oh, your mother? How is she taking it?'

'She's taking it OK.'

'Good,' said Priti, 'good.'

'And, don't worry, I fully intend to sort out your dental work,' I said. 'Obviously Andy can't make the bridge now but I'll sort it out – you won't have to go to university with a denture.'

'Oh, no, you mustn't worry about that.'

'I *do* worry,' I said, 'and I will sort it.' And I realized I did worry and it was nice to have a worry of this kind. Difficult but possibly solvable, if 'solvable' was a word.

I was now the girlfriend of someone who had died and, to put it poetically, death was like a fine dust that covered my sandals, my sea-coloured dress, my tiny cleavage, my ex-bistro/taverna-style kitchenette, the surgery, my family, the dog, and just about everything else in my life. You could brush it off but it'd settle again. It was in the air.

As often as I had the energy, I'd walk up to the King's Head for a pint of weak shandy and a snack. I didn't care any more if people saw me red-necked from the alcohol, tucking into chips and ketchup, covered in metaphorical dust. I honestly didn't care whether they stared at me, avoided me, or came over to tell me they were sorry to hear about that bloke, etc. I'd just sit there, reading my book and licking my fingers – anything to not be at home.

In the end, the only person I felt I could talk to was Claire Rayner and so one day, when I hadn't taken a pill, I poured my heart out to her, but within the allotted word count which seemed to be one hundred:

> Dear Claire Rayner,
>
> I am 19 years old. My boyfriend recently died in an accident (nothing to do with me). I loved him and I'm sad about it but, if I'm honest, we didn't know one another all that well. My problem is that people are defining me by his death and my emotional proximity to it. My question is, can I move away to a new life, or do I have to stay in the area and mourn for a year?
> I know I must sound selfish but I think I'm going mad.
> Name and address supplied.

I wrote 'emotional proximity' so that Claire would clock that I wasn't as simple as some of the readers. And though I addressed it to the *Woman's Own* counselling team I really, truly hoped and believed it would find its way to Claire Rayner because she was the best at advising on real-life things.

Regarding my getting back to normal, when I wasn't at the surgery my mother's novel was a godsend – for both of us.

She started writing long, awful chapters for me to edit – just to give me something to do, and coming up with new working titles, some bad ('The Noble Bird') and some good ('Calipastra and Powdered Soup'). I fell for it and though I was disappointed at what a poor writer she'd turned out to be, and though her inability to work within the rules of her own sci-fi world actually quite worried me (re her cognitive ability), the occupation knocked the death dust off my life. I'd write copious notes about how she might fix things, and suggestions for the story.

> *Mum* [I'd write], *chapter 5 doesn't make sense because of something important in chapter 3. How can you have forgotten that it's illegal for an unaccompanied woman to drive a car in 2024?*
>
> *Mum, you write here that Calipastra's husband is benign. Have you forgotten he's twice tried to strangle her for not laughing at his joke?*

And then, to help us further, my mother received a most positive letter from an editor at the Heron Press regarding the actual novel. This was good because it boosted her confidence, and yet bad because she might be tempted to abandon Faber & Faber, just to get published, which wasn't the point.

The letter – addressed to my mother's nom de plume – from the Heron Press went like this:

> *Dear Mildred Quietly,*
>
> *Thank you very much for sending us the outline of your novel 'The Waiting Room'.*
>
> *We cannot offer you a contract on such a short synopsis but it is very promising and I should like to see more when it's ready. I like the science-fiction aspects and would very much like to see how the novel develops.*
>
> *In anticipation,*
>
> *S. J. Barmy*

'S. J. Barmy?' I said. 'God!'

'I know,' said my mother. 'I'm still hoping for Patience Tidy. But I'm going to use S. J. Barmy as a lure.'

She read me her letter to Patience:

Dear Patience,

I am writing to let you know that S. J. Barmy of the Heron Press has been in touch to say she is very interested in 'The Waiting Room'. Which is the new title for my book. Please could you explain why she is so keen, when you're not. What is it S. J. sees that you cannot?

I should hate for you to miss out on this book and, indeed, for me to miss out on Faber & Faber when I know in my heart that we are meant for each other.

Yours,
Mildred Quietly
(Elizabeth Benson-Holt)

PS If we two are not to be, perhaps you might know something about S. J. Barmy to help our acquaintance, should it come to that.

'What does that last line mean?' I asked.
'It means, "Spill the beans to me about S. J. Barmy,"' she said.
A letter from Patience came by return. She wrote:

Dear Mildred Quietly,

Thank you for your letter yesterday.
I too should be pleased to see more of 'The Waiting Room'.
S. J. Barmy is a well-regarded editor at the Heron Press.
Yours,
Patience Tidy

My mother thought this rather dull but supposed Patience was being professional.

I hadn't discussed the future with anyone, other than Claire Rayner c/o *Woman's Own*, or even given it much thought. I was deliberately keeping my mind focused on my mother's novel, the surgery, and baby Danny's reading progress. And beginning to think about how to get Priti's bridge made on the NHS.

One day I'd been in the middle of a long explanatory note to my mother about some of the basics of science-fiction writing, such as: whatever rules you invent for your world, you must be clear and you must abide by them throughout, and can't just go back in time to save a robot's life – and perhaps she might abandon time travel altogether – when Mrs Woodward appeared, tapping at the window. What was it with those bloody Woodwards? I supposed the clergy had to do this otherwise they might never see anyone. Anyway, she came in and said yes to a beverage. I made frothy coffee because she was one of the few adults I knew to take three sugars (the sugar in the mix being the frothing agent – the more sugar, the more froth).

She let me prattle on about time travel – how you can't just go forward (or back) in time and save someone's life and think the present will be OK because it doesn't work like that – before telling me that she'd been worrying about a thing she'd said to me some time before and wanted to say she was sorry.

'I'd like to apologize for a thing I said, a flippant thing about Jesus.'

'Oh?'

'About us not all meeting up again in heaven.'

'That's OK,' I said. 'I don't believe that either.'

'Well, I just wanted to say I was sorry.'

'But it's true,' I said. 'I'm not hoping to meet Andy again in a future life, if that's what you mean.'

'I know, but it was wrong of me.'

'It's fine.'

Mrs Woodward wanted me to resume my driving lessons. She knew I'd be reluctant, she said, but if there was one thing she knew about life, it was that you needed to get on with it.

Also, she told me, London was missing one of its journalists – and that was me. I'd forgotten I'd told her of my plan or had assumed her to be fast asleep as I'd rambled, and I laughed at the idea of London waiting for me.

'No, Lizzie, I'm not joking,' she said, and leaned across the table and took my hands in hers. And I began to cry. Not about Andy but about her and life and time travel and her lovely old hands.

'Come on, lovey,' she said, and I agreed to get back out on the road. We finished our coffee and I put my sandals on, and was suddenly back in her car, adjusting the seat and the rear-view mirror, with her arranging the travel blanket over her knees.

'Where shall we go?' she asked.

'Shall I just drive ahead until you give me directions?'

'Yes, you just drive,' she said, and within two minutes she was fast asleep with her hands in her lap and I was heading east and keeping to the speed limit. After we'd left the familiar villages behind, I took a turn which led us up a lane to a farm where you could have tea and scones, and look around at young animals.

I parked by a plough and Mrs Woodward woke.

'Very good,' she said. 'Oh, where are we?'

'Cambridgeshire, I think.'

We got out and had tea and stroked some calves and I bought a jar of honey, and to tell the truth it was very nice, chatting and laughing and gazing at the teeth on Mrs Woodward's upper denture that Andy had made so, so long ago. She told me I was a very good driver and that Reverend Woodward had found me 'easy to work with', and also that Mr Burridge had made a donation to the Nicolello family. And, a thing that had almost choked me, my grandmother had paid for Andy's funeral.

'That's hundreds of pounds when you add it all up,' said Mrs Woodward.

Later that evening I returned my granny's cheese knife and the cheque, and gave her the jar of farm honey. Also, I smoked a cigarette in front of her and stayed for dinner and watched a hard-hitting TV documentary.

Time went by and I did very little except work, watch TV, edit my mother's novel, and practise driving. I don't know if it was the weather warming up or the days getting longer, but I decided it was time to try living in the flat again. It seems strange, looking back, but being at home wasn't helping anyone. I hadn't stayed at the flat since the accident. (I'd started calling it 'the accident' because my sister told me that calling it 'Andy's death' was upsetting for people.)

Anyway, Mr Holt drove me back to the flat one Saturday morning. We stopped at the lights at the top of the hill, and they stayed on red so long I imagined for a moment they were out again and that we'd gone into a time-warp scenario reminiscent of the one in my mother's novel.

Mr Holt carried my bag upstairs for me and checked everything was OK. We had a cup of tea while he rewired the plug on my hairdryer, although he was disappointed that I'd forgotten how to do it myself and ran through it with me. And then because he didn't bring it up, nor did he seem to be peering at me for clues as to how I was coping, I found myself talking about Andy, and being honest about how I felt – as honest as I had been in my letter to Claire (Rayner) but more so, having no word limit.

'I'm just someone whose boyfriend has died,' I said, 'and now I want time to fly by and for people to stop seeing me like that.'

'It won't stop, love,' he said. 'The only way is to get away.'

'Get away? Where to?'

'London, Glasgow, Dublin, Norwich . . .' He listed big cities.

'But can I just go?' I asked him. 'Doesn't it seem callous to move on?'

'Why would it be?'

'Callous about Andy.'

'No, you get on and live,' he said. 'That's what he'd have wanted, without doubt.'

Mr Holt was shy of the subject, and wasn't the sort to blow his own trumpet, but there was a thing he was keen to share. He told me that Andy had been scared of the dark and had had to have the little light on all night; he'd asked for permission to do so, vis-à-vis the electricity bill. Mr Holt had found him a low-wattage plug-in one (7 watts, I believe) – enough light to ward off the fears but not so much as to stimulate his brain and keep him awake.

'That little bit of light worked a treat for him,' said Mr Holt, 'and I felt like a hero giving it to him.'

He got ready to leave and I admitted that I was worried about being lonely. He told me to ring any time and they'd come and get me. We hugged goodbye, he took my favourite spoon out of his pocket and then went. It felt horrible. I stood still for what seemed like an hour. And then the doorbell went and I glanced out of the window to see the Snowdrop van in the tram stop. I trotted down, pulled the door open and was about to say, 'Hurrah, take me home,' when I saw Angelo in Mr Holt's arms.

'Miss Smith says you can have him for the weekend – for company.'

God, I hugged that dog.

'What did you tell her?' I asked him.

'That your boyfriend died and you're trying to get back to normal.'

The weekend went OK and I delivered Angelo back on the Monday morning. And I decided Mr Holt was right. I needed to move on, and I should at least start thinking it through.

I approached my father about the Massachusetts job and he told me they had hired a mature woman – an American – to go with them, who'd double as a secretary for him and help them settle in and know the American ways of doing things and save them weeks, if not months, of doing slightly the wrong thing. They needed someone who'd say 'chips' and 'dairy' in the right place and not accidentally say 'vagina' when they meant 'envelope'. They wanted someone who could hit the sidewalk running and so forth; what they didn't want was my sister and me and our confusing blend of familiarity and resentment. So Massachusetts was off the list.

If I got a job in London I'd need accommodation.

Which do you organize first: job or accommodation? I had assumed job, but what if you couldn't find anywhere to live and you were working all day interviewing women for *Woman's Own* and then having to pretend to be waiting for a late train at Waterloo but really sleeping on a bench? We'd recently visited my mother's friends Aunt Josephine and Uncle Peter who lived in a sweet little flat in Kilburn, north London. Its garden was a whitewashed box, covered in vines that made it seem like a forest clearing, and it was so sheltered you could sit out under the moon, drink tea and smoke, even in winter. My mother had mentioned my ambition to move to London and Josephine immediately offered to put me up if I ever did. I didn't take it seriously because I felt her a bit beyond me, intellectually, and anyway, according to my mother – who'd sneakily read her diary that evening – Josephine's marriage was on the rocks. My mother had tried to get her to talk about it over our Spudulike supper but Josephine hadn't been drawn. The problem, according to the diary, was a difference of opinion on cultural issues and that Uncle Peter wasn't being offered enough protein at mealtimes (but this was according to the diary, which, of course, only gave Josephine's side).

So really, I needed a job which came with accommodation – nanny or au pair or housekeeper. I wasn't in a hurry so I could be quite fussy. I kept an eye on the *Lady* magazine but never saw anything that one hundred per cent agreed with me. Either there were too many children (three), or they flitted between A and B (I didn't want to flit), or the home was Knightsbridge (I didn't fancy it), or in Surrey (was that even London?), or they wanted a non-smoker (I might want to smoke).

I did make one application – to be au pair to a small baby whose parents worked for the Parker Pen Company; the situation seemed almost perfect. They flitted between London and Geneva (I hadn't yet ruled flitting out entirely), and I was invited to an interview. It didn't work out though because I over-prepared and talked too much about the company's trademark quick-drying ink, Quink, which I was all for and knew to be a favourite among writers. And in my admiration for the product, I failed to make enough of the baby (a boy called Zebedee or similar). It was good practice though, and my mother and I had a marvellous time in London, taking in the Wallace Collection and the Tate and, at one point, a distant view across the river of King's Reach Tower, where *Woman's Own* was published. And then we went over to Kilburn for the Spudu-like supper with Aunt Josephine.

30. The Wheels of Justice

Early one morning, some weeks after I'd moved back into the flat, Priti appeared at the surgery door with a middle-aged man.

'This is my uncle,' she said and the uncle nodded sternly at me.

'Pritiben needs to get her treatment finished before she goes to university,' he said. 'Her tooth keeps falling out – she's very worried.'

'OK,' I said, opening the door, 'come in. I think we can squeeze you in this morning, if you don't mind waiting.' I supposed the game was up, but I was too weary to care. I'd taken one of the little pills – my last one, actually – and so things seemed slightly unreal. I had every intention of sorting out Priti's bridge, but not like this, with the uncle looking all cross and accusatory.

Soon JP arrived. No Tammy, though; she was apparently visiting a fertility specialist with Jossy Turner.

'OK,' he said, 'let's have the first patient, nurse.'

I ushered Priti through. She sat in the chair and her uncle took the low office seat.

Priti told JP she needed a bridge – the denture was beginning to droop. She had important exams looming, she'd be starting university in September, and she wanted the treatment completed well in advance.

JP told Priti he didn't do that kind of work on the NHS and she'd be looking at upwards of £300 for a three-tooth bridge.

Her uncle explained that she had been promised – when she had her extraction and the denture was made – that the next step would be a bridge.

'The denture no longer fits,' he said.

JP agreed – a bridge would be an obvious next step – but he was sorry, he did not do bridge or crown work on the NHS.

'The best thing for you to do is go back to the practice that did the original work,' he said, looking at the uncle.

I held my breath.

'The original work was here, at this practice,' said Priti.

'I don't think so,' said JP with a slight and sarcastic laugh. 'I remember seeing you and telling you I couldn't treat you on the NHS.'

'Your colleague did it,' said the uncle.

'My colleague? Well, that's where you're completely out of line – I don't have a colleague.'

'Your daughter,' said the uncle.

'I don't have a daughter,' said JP, turning to Priti, 'and you're not a patient here, so I'm going to ask you to leave.'

'She's a friend of mine. Couldn't you make an exception?' I interrupted.

'What?' JP scowled at me. 'No, I can't do work like that on the NHS.'

'If you refuse to complete the treatment I shall report you to the Family Practitioners Association,' said the uncle.

'Fine by me,' said JP. 'Goodbye.'

And after mentioning legal proceedings and the Citizens' Advice, they were gone. A wave of panic so strong washed over me that I thought I might collapse. It was worse than the time I was left in charge of the donkey derby and a kid got dragged.

JP was shaken too. He needed a cigarette. So we went up to the staffroom where he lit one and passed it to me to feed him.

'Thank you for your intervention, nurse,' he said sarcastically, between puffs. 'What on earth were you thinking?'

'She can't afford the fees,' I said. 'She's my friend, and I just don't see why you can't treat her.'

'If she doesn't want to go back to the practice that started the treatment she must find the money to pay for private treatment. Couldn't she sell her hair – isn't that what they do?'

And that was when I accidentally turned the cigarette around and JP closed his lips on the red-hot end. He shrieked, ran to the sink and splashed his mouth with water.

'You lunatic,' he cried.

'I treated her,' I said. 'I drained the abscess months ago but the tooth flared up again – well, you saw it – and then she turned up at the emergency clinic.' I paused.

He stared at me, damp-haired, from the sink.

'And then you refused to see her because it was your golf afternoon, and then – I don't know – no one would treat her on the NHS and so I asked Andy to make her the denture and then I extracted the tooth and fitted the denture as an immediate restoration and it was perfect.'

I paused for emphasis, but JP still didn't say anything.

'And I would have done the bridge prep with Andy,' I continued breathlessly, 'except Andy died –' I was crying – 'and now Priti's uncle's threatening to get a solicitor from the Citizens' Advice Bureau and if you weren't such a xenophobe then none of this would have happened.'

JP blinked and wiped his face with a tea towel.

'Nice try, nurse,' he said, attempting to leave the room.

'Everything I just told you is true,' I said and I leaned on the door to prevent him opening it.

'Are you seriously trying to tell me you extracted that girl's tooth and fitted a denture?'

'Yes.'

'No, I don't believe you. Now please get out of my way.'

He yanked at the door and left the room.

Priti came to see me that evening. I was making animal biscuits again. This time I cut more rabbits because she disliked dogs, even shortbread ones (even Angelo), and I baked them for less time to keep them softer, and then iced them.

She told me her uncle was going to see a solicitor on Friday. And once that happened, she said, wheels would apparently begin turning that could not be stopped until justice had been served.

'You mustn't tell anyone that I did the treatment,' I said.

'But that's what I'm saying,' she replied. 'Once the solicitor gets involved, the truth is bound to come out.'

I couldn't tell whether Priti understood the trouble I'd be in if/when the truth did come out. If she did, she didn't care and actually, I admired her for it. We ate the biscuits and then I called my mother. I told her everything on the phone. She didn't say much but an hour later she had arrived, with Abe. They listened carefully and Abe said he'd speak to Bill Turner, and I begged him not to tell Bill the whole truth, and Abe said Bill would most likely help without needing to know the details – that was the great thing about the Freemasons.

Early the following day Rhona, Bill Turner's nurse, appeared and asked if we had any dental records or open forms for a Pritiben Mistry.

I found the dental record which, as I knew, contained no details other than her name and address.

'We have a blank card. JP wouldn't treat her,' I said. 'Do you need it?'

'Yes, please,' said Rhona.

'Why, what's going on?'

'Bill's just booked her in to do a bridge prep later this week and wondered if you had any paperwork.'

'NHS?' I asked.

'Yes,' said Rhona. 'As a favour for one of his Freemason pals, I should think.'

Later, Priti called in to thank me for fixing things, and to ask me if I'd go to the appointment with her. She was nervous. I told her that it was Abe who'd arranged everything and she looked puzzled.

'The one who ate your bread at the party,' I reminded her.

Exactly two weeks later Bill fitted Priti's bridge and it was perfect and smart.

Bill had done a first-class job for Priti. My mother came to see it. Priti thanked her and asked her to thank Abe. She said she would.

My mother had other news. She couldn't afford Curious Minds

any more so Danny would go to a local playgroup until he started at the infant school in the village after the summer holidays. My mother was concerned that I'd feel lonely but I'd been ready for it. It seemed right and I was pleased for Danny to have classmates he could play with close to home.

Also, my mother had sent Patience Tidy more chapters of 'The Waiting Room', featuring Calipastra and Jim. Patience had responded immediately, thanking my mother but saying that she felt the book was too episodic and lacking texture. And that because Faber & Faber had lots of authors who could do story and texture and humour, they would not be able to offer her a contract.

My mother was terribly upset and surprised. She wrote straight back to Patience with what was basically a begging letter:

> Dear Patience,
>
> Please agree to a short meeting so that I can explain the aims and scope of my book. It is imperative that I get a chance to discuss this with you. Face to face.
> Yours, etc.
> Mildred Quietly
> (Elizabeth Benson-Holt)

'So we'll see,' she said.

And finally a letter had come for me from King's Reach Tower – from the *Woman's Own* counselling team:

> Dear Miss Vogel,
>
> Thank you for your letter. I am so sorry to hear about the death of your boyfriend. What a terribly tragic thing to happen and especially to someone so young. Of course it is only natural that you will feel sad for a while. However, you are not being selfish in not wanting to be defined by this event, and you most certainly shouldn't mourn for a year.
>
> My advice to you is to be ambitious for yourself, follow your dreams and become whoever you want to be. I know this is what your boyfriend would have wanted for you.
> Yours sincerely,

It was signed with two squiggles on behalf of the team but I felt sure it was Claire Rayner – I could just about make out the word 'Rayner' in the second squiggle, and I smiled at how similar her response was to that of Mr Holt.

I read it over and over, and felt bolstered by it. I started looking for new jobs and applying, in earnest.

Suddenly it was August and Priti was getting ready to leave for university. She'd done well in her A levels, as had my brother Jack, who'd taken them a year early, much to my mother's delight. Priti had narrowly avoided having to live with a second cousin in Bethnal Green; there'd been much drama on this subject, but finally she'd arranged a flat share with three other students, and her uncle had unhappily accepted it. Jack was going into halls of residence in Camden Town and I warned him that the Tube often stopped in between Camden and Mornington Crescent stations, and not to be afraid.

My mother had offered Priti a lift up to London, since she'd be taking Jack, and this worked out well as it meant that Priti's uncle could keep the restaurant open. I offered to go along too, to keep my mother company on the journey home, but she'd planned to collect her friend Josephine and bring her back for a visit so there was no need. I'd be more help at home, looking after Danny.

When the day came – a gloomy Saturday – my mother came in to town to collect Priti and her belongings and me. We went back for Jack, who was looking after Danny until I arrived. Priti had a whole boxful of books for her course already and masses of discounted kitchen equipment from Patel's. She'd had a haircut at La Croix and a medical check-up at the Regent's Road clinic and was in tip-top form. My brother only had an Anglepoise lamp and the proceeds of the sale of his moped. I'd made them each a tin of biscuits and told them they could keep the tin. I also gave Priti an oven glove, and Jack the St Christopher pendant.

'I'll make biscuits every week and that way I'll remember you,' said Priti.

'But I'll be in London myself soon. We can meet up.'

'Yes,' said Priti, 'we can.'

It was horribly emotional seeing them go. My mouth quivered so much I could barely speak, so I just clung on to my littlest brother. Priti and Jack were happy and excited, though, and I felt briefly like their mother. I watched as they drove away and stared into the distance for a while as if they might come back.

Finally Danny took his thumb out of his mouth to ask, 'Where have they gone?'

'London.'

'For ever?'

'Yes.'

Less than a week later, it was a golf afternoon and Bill Turner arrived to have a quick scale and polish. JP's name had been up for nomination at the Masonic Lodge the night before. Once he'd got Bill in the chair he asked how the vote had gone. He'd been ringing him all morning and was by now impatient to know the result. Bill tried to put him off until they'd got away from the surgery, but JP mithered him like a child.

Bill said he was sorry but JP had been blackballed again.

'Damn them,' said JP. '*Damn* them.'

'Sorry to be the bearer of bad news.'

'What is their ruddy problem?'

'They don't consider you a worthy candidate, for some reason.'

'What reason?' asked Tammy.

'Could it be because of JP's prejudice against coloured people?' I asked. 'His xenophobia.'

The three of them looked at me.

'That is utter nonsense,' said JP. 'How do you explain Miss Ojoko?'

'Miss Ojoko is his only coloured patient,' I explained, looking at Bill. 'He is sexually attracted to her.'

'Lizzie!' said Tammy. 'Don't say things like that.'

'You know it's true.'

'Could it be something to do with his wife?' asked Tammy. 'I mean, the way she was treated.'

'I didn't treat her badly,' said JP. 'I left her – that's allowed, isn't it, for God's sake?'

'You left her eventually,' said Tammy, 'but you lied to her for years.'

'So did you.'

Bill butted in. 'No, no, no. It won't have been anything like that – no one would judge you on that score.'

'So, what could it be, Bill?' said JP, his voice despairing. 'If it's about that bloody violin, I didn't steal it, I smashed it up.'

'I don't think it's about a musical instrument,' said Bill.

'So you *do* know?' said JP.

'People feel you haven't behaved in a compassionate manner befitting your profession. You haven't always helped people in need.'

'Who's said that?'

'Well,' I blurted, 'Abe from Abraham's Motors for one, I bet.'

'Don't bloody tell me he's a Mason,' said JP.

'Oh, yes,' said Bill. 'Abe's a Steward, and his father's a Senior Warden.'

'Right,' said JP, 'I see.'

'And I'm afraid, in all conscience, I couldn't back you either,' said Bill, 'under the circumstances.'

'So, is it a no – or a never?' asked JP.

'I think it's a never.'

The day after JP's blackballing, Tammy invited me for a drink.

'I need to speak to you about something,' she said.

'Do you want to come up to the flat?'

'I'd rather go round to the Belmont,' she said, and I assumed she was about to tell me she was pregnant.

When we got there, I saw she had a box containing her best cactus. I recognized its hexagonal pot and gangly limbs.

'I'd like you to have this,' she told me, and though it was the last thing in the world I wanted, I took it, thanked her profusely, and asked what was going on.

She told me she was leaving.

'Leaving JP?' I said.

'Leaving JP and the practice.'

'Where are you going?' I felt strangely sad.

'Massachusetts,' she said. 'I'm going with your father and his family, to be secretary and mother's help.'

'Oh, I see – you're the mature American lady.'

'Mature?' she said.

She hoped I didn't feel she'd betrayed me, and after a minute or two, I didn't. But I did remind her of my plan to write for *Woman's Own* about the tricks and tips of our American counterparts, and that she'd promised to do her best to get me an interview with Erma Bombeck.

'I know,' she cringed. 'I'm sorry.'

'He won't leave his wife for you, though,' I said. 'He's gay.'

Tammy laughed as if I were joking. I congratulated her again, more for leaving JP than for getting the job with my father, and I wished her well.

'Does JP know?' I asked as we left the bar.

'Not yet.'

Epilogue

A year had passed since I'd bought the Ossie dress from Best End Boutique and driven JP and Tammy to the BDA Winter Dinner Dance, and since Andy Nicolello and John Lennon had died. A whole year.

And I'd changed in so many ways – I'd passed my driving test on the third attempt, I'd gone on to John Player Special low tar, and my athlete's foot had completely cleared up.

I did not stay on at the Wintergreen practice after the showdown in front of Bill Turner. I managed to get a month's salary out of JP and went home to my old room, where I was unemployed except for faking my mother's call sheets, editing her novel, writing articles for women's magazines, and applying for jobs. Tammy was staying with Ann-Sofie and helping at the Lunch Box until the Massachusetts job started. She rang occasionally to ask something about my father's family in preparation for her new job. I was able to tip her off about their love of Laurel and Hardy, and Frank Cooper's diabetic marmalade.

One morning, early in the New Year, as I sat at the kitchen table looking at the situations vacant, my mother appeared with a letter from Patience Tidy of Faber & Faber.

'Patience has asked to have a meeting,' she said. 'Wouldn't it be nice if we went to London together?'

She passed me the letter, which read:

Dear Miss Quietly-Benson-Holt,

Thank you for suggesting a meeting. This is unusual but since you'll be nearby anyway, I would be happy to have a chat with you. I can't promise to be much help but I can certainly give you a cup of tea.

Yours sincerely,
Patience Tidy
Faber & Faber

Although it didn't sound like an offer so much as resigned compliance, I was excited and wondered if I might grill Patience Tidy on how to get a foot in the door at King's Reach Tower. I mentioned this to my mother and she put me straight.

'That won't be possible,' she said and told me I'd be going along A) for the trip and B) to mind Danny while she had her meeting because, while she fully expected Patience to be a fellow feminist, she didn't think Danny's presence would be conducive to a full and frank literary discussion. Patience might get tense and nervous if Danny drove one of his lorries repeatedly over Ted Hughes's latest poem, even though that would probably be just what Ted Hughes would want. I was to entertain Danny in the British Museum and buy him lunch in a café in order to give my mother the freedom she needed.

'Won't Danny be at school?' I asked.

'We shan't get back in time to collect him,' said my mother. 'He'll have an educational day in London instead.'

When the day arrived, in spite of it being a chilly winter morning my mother chose to wear a cream-coloured safari skirt suit with flaps and epaulettes. I hadn't taken much notice of this at home but seeing her pace about on the platform at Leicester station I referred to it in what I thought was a humorous comment:

'Dr Livingstone, I presume,' I said.

My mother took great offence.

'What do you mean, Dr Livingstone?'

'You know, you're in a safari suit,' I said. 'You look like an explorer on the Zambezi or something – it's nice, you look very nice.'

My mother had lost a bit of her confidence since Andy's death, on top of giving up drinking, and was a reduced version of her old (new) self. It was now her habit to look at her reflection whenever possible in a shop window, or to glance down at what she could see of herself, turning her leg out to the side, smoothing her midriff, and checking her fingernails, whereas previously she'd been carefree and relaxed. I regretted making the quip. That's the thing with ex-drunks, I thought, they're sensitive. She might now perform less well in her meeting at Faber & Faber and it would be down to my quip. I did my best to build her up again on the train, with much literary talk and bolstering reminders of her brilliance as a mother and a writer. I reminded her that she'd called JP a xenophobe and stood up for Abe and Priti when I hadn't, even though I was young and had nothing to lose, and so forth.

In spite of all this, I couldn't help but question the safari suit and wished she'd worn something warmer and more suitable. I myself was wearing a tartan kilt, frilly white blouse and high-heeled maroon boots, and looked very Christmassy even though it was January. There's a photograph of me in the outfit. I have Danny on my lap on a bench in a garden square in Bloomsbury, and I look very much like a brunette Lady Di. It would be rather a nice shot except I'm taking a puff on my cigarette and one eye is screwed up.

Soon it was time for my mother to go off for her meeting at Faber & Faber and I wished her luck and squeezed her hand. Danny and I went to the museum but he became bored after five minutes, not being quite old enough to appreciate the statues or the building itself, in spite of his Montessori education. So we went to a little café nearby – as agreed with my mother – and he had some spaghetti and did some drawings while I had coffee and toast. The waiters kept asking if I'd like to order something else.

'No, thank you,' I said, over and over. 'We're waiting for our mother.'

She was gone for almost two hours. I thought of Patience listening to her ideas and plots, and possibly marvelling at her safari suit. I hoped to God Patience wasn't the jokey type and hadn't said, 'Dr Livingstone, I presume,' to break the ice – though maybe editors were allowed to say that kind of thing.

Danny and I read *Not Now, Bernard* so many times that I started to question the logic of the story and to criticize the decor in Bernard's house, and then at last we saw our mother come swinging across the square in a whole new set of clothes – a trouser suit in mauve brushed denim with the hugest belt buckle you ever saw.

I could tell by her demeanour that the meeting had gone well. She ordered a black coffee and lit a cigarette.

'Did you win her over?' I asked.

'Yes,' she said triumphantly. 'I'm to send her a reworking, and this time I'm to *really* get inside Calipastra's head – I'm switching to a first-person narrative. She's very excited.'

But there was more. 'And I've got you a job interview,' she said, waving her fists in the air.

'At Faber and Faber?' I asked, terrified, thrilled.

'No, no, it's at Lulu's Boutique around the corner, where I got this.' She indicated the trouser suit. 'It's full of lovely clothes and trinkets and they have Radio Three going all day and you'll get a huge staff discount. I actually got a discount,' she said, indicating the new outfit again, 'as if you already worked there.' She was breathless with excitement.

'Lulu's,' I said.

'And we'd be able to meet for lunch whenever I come up for editorial meetings with Patience.'

'But I might not get the job. And where will I live?'

'You will definitely get the job, I promise, and you can lodge with Josephine in Kilburn.'

'I thought Aunt Josephine's marriage was on the rocks.'

'Oh, yes . . .' said my mother. 'But how do you know that?'

'You read her diary, remember?'

'God, yes, Uncle Peter was taking his meals in the pub,' she mused, 'and all that kind of thing, wasn't it – well remembered, Lizzie.'

'Won't I be in the way,' I asked, 'if the marriage is on the rocks?'

'No, it's lovely to have someone to complain to and eat with at times like that,' said my mother. 'You can spy on Uncle Peter for her. It'll be perfect, and you might even give her the confidence to sling him out.'

Danny, who was drifting off in my mother's lap, murmured, 'Don't spy on Uncle Peter.'

I imagined living with my aunt and her long-term partner – who was apparently clever but for some reason couldn't get a good job – in their lovely little garden flat. I certainly wasn't going to offer to spy on Uncle Peter, nor would I be responsible for his being slung out. On the contrary, I'd bring them back together. For a start, I'd help him improve his CV and I'd shorten her name to Jo, because who wouldn't want to be called Jo if they could be? And wouldn't that put her in a whole new light?

'I might be able to help them navigate the marriage off the rocks,' I said.

I'd already planned an article in my head and quickly described it:

Eleven Warning Signs that Your Husband is Bored with his Food.

Not asking for seconds.
Saying the food is dry.
Saying the food is bland.
Claiming not to be hungry.
Pushing his plate aside.
Playing with his food.
Asking, 'What's in it?'
Making suggestions.
Looking in the fridge.
Being late for meals.
Saying, 'Where's the protein?'

'I could pass on my recipe for eggs mornay, which is the most proteinous meal you can get without meat,' I said. And we spent the next few minutes thinking up high-protein dishes.

My mother suddenly thought of an omelette which consisted of eggs and water and involved getting the pan very hot and dragging the cooked edges to the centre and throwing in a lot of pepper, cheese and chilli powder – and apparently came from Jacqueline du Pré. And I remembered cheesy bean bake and all manner of lentil-based dishes.

Then she finished her coffee, paid the bill and gathered our things. I got Danny up for a piggyback, and we wandered out to find Lulu's Boutique.

'There it is,' my mother said, and pointed across the street to a quaint little shop with an awning and yellow spotlights illuminating a sumptuous window display. Three mannequins in excitable poses were togged out in at least two whole winter outfits each. Plaid shirts over cotton vests, under woollen waistcoats with toggles, fluffy cardigans, tweedy capes, silky shawls, and scarves slung around their shoulders, and floppy knitted hats and opened umbrellas. One green, one mustard, one dark red.

'It looks just like Best End Boutique,' I said.

My mother laughed, 'It *is* Best End Boutique,' and through the window I could see April Jickson speaking to a customer as she wrapped an item in white tissue paper. We waited for the transaction to come to an end before going in and, to my mother's delight, when the customer came out into the street it was none other than Elizabeth Jane Howard, and though my mother knew it must get tiresome, she couldn't help but stop her to say how much she admired her writing. Elizabeth Jane seemed pleased and thanked her for the kind words and we watched her stride away, the lead of her little spaniel in one hand and a Lulu's carrier bag in the other – containing, I guessed, a loose mohair jumper in different shades of red.

I turned to my mother and gave her a subtle little hug before nuzzling my face into her shoulder. The trouser-suit jacket gave off a musty, new-clothes smell.

'What happened to your safari suit?' I asked.

'I gave it to Patience Tidy,' she said. 'It was very her.'

Author's Note

The Wintergreen Dental Practice is fictional but the background
issues described – the non-availability of certain treatments on the
NHS, especially for underprivileged people – are not. They seem
to be an even greater problem today.

Acknowledgements

I would like to thank my friend Pam Baker-Clare, a brilliant and compassionate dental surgeon, who practised in Leicester from 1954 until 1996 – from a surgery at her family home for many of these forty-two years, meaning she was seldom off duty. Pam's memories, ideas and lunches have been an invaluable part of my research, as was the meeting with David Turner, dental technician of Leicester, which she arranged. Happy ninetieth birthday, Pam!

Thanks also go to Jacqui Eavis and Fergus Brown at Cathedral Practice, Truro; to Sharon Cole and Colin Storry at the Granville Clinic, Leicester; and to the staff at London's BDA museum – all of whom helped me get to grips with dentistry and the NHS in the 1980s.

At Penguin Books, first and foremost I'd like to acknowledge my editor, Mary Mount, and to thank her, yet again, for excellent editorial guidance, for her wit and wisdom and patience and for being a complete joy to work with.

I'd also like to thank the whole team behind this book. **Editorial:** Rosanna Forte, Natalie Wall. **Copy-editing and proofreading:** Mary Chamberlain, Sarah-Jane Forder, Sally Sargeant. **Contracts:** Matthew Blackett, Ruth Richardson. **Design:** Richard Bravery, David Ettridge. **UK Sales:** Samantha Fanaken, Ruth Johnstone, Tineke Mollemans, Richard Clesham, Rachel Myers, Ben Hughes, Katie Corcoran, El Beckford, Kate Gunning, Andy Taylor, Carl Rolfe, John Faiers. **International Sales:** Linda Viberg, Guy Lloyd. **Production:** Sara Granger, Hetty Kendall, Michael Perera, Ruppa Patel, Anya Wallace-Cook. **Publicity:** Poppy North, Anna Ridley. **Marketing:** Rose Poole, Georgia

Taylor, Amelia Fairney. **Rights:** Chantal Noel, Sarah Scarlett, Lucy Beresford-Knox, Alex Elam, Catherine Wood, Elizabeth Brandon, Celia Long, Harriet Peel, Ines Cortesao. **Audio:** Roy McMillan, Tom McWhirter, Samantha Halstead.

Thanks to trusted friends, Stella Heath, Julia Mount and Jon Reed, for invaluable help in reading drafts and advising as the book has progressed.

At Jo Unwin Literary Agency (JULA), I'd like to thank my wonderful minder, Jo Unwin, and colleagues Milly Reilly and Donna Greaves, for their marvellous support.

I'd like to thank family and friends, especially Meena Ackbarally, A. J. Allison, Elspeth Allison, John Allison, Paul Beaumont, Nigel Biggs, Elik Eddy, Divya Ghelani, Margrit Goldberg, Victoria Goldberg, Fiona Holman, Alfred Nunney, Eva Nunney, Cathy Rentzenbrink, Jeremy Stibbe, Tom Stibbe.

And finally, I'd like to thank my beloved Mark Nunney, for general brilliance, endless support and not minding another puppy.